THE WATER BABIES

SELECTED POEMS

CHARLES KINGSLEY

1819-1875

THE WATER BABIES
and
SELECTED POEMS

CHARLES KINGSLEY

With an Introduction by
DAVID DAVIS

Illustrated by
JEAN CRUICKSHANKS

COLLINS
LONDON AND GLASGOW

First published, 1863
This edition, 1954
Latest reprint, 1961

CHARLES KINGSLEY

CHARLES KINGSLEY was born on June 12th 1819 at Holne Vicarage in Devonshire. He was the second son of the Reverend Charles Kingsley. His mother was the daughter of Nathan Lucas, an Englishman resident in Barbados (West Indies). Of the other four sons of the Reverend and Mrs. Charles Kingsley, Gerald, the eldest, became a lieutenant in the Navy and died of an epidemic fever on board his ship; George Henry became a doctor and great traveller, and Henry, the youngest, a novelist of great repute. Another son, Herbert, died very young.

As a child Charles Kingsley (junior) lived successively at Holne, at Clifton (Nottinghamshire), at Barnack in the Fen country and at Clovelly, North Devon of which his father held the living from 1830–36. Charles was a precocious, sensitive child. He was twice attacked by brain fever accompanied by hallucinations. In 1831 he was sent to a preparatory school at Clifton (Bristol) where he soon proved himself a good Latin scholar and a great lover of natural history. While at Clifton he witnessed the Bristol riots of August 1831 and saw some scenes of horror which made an indelible impression on his mind. In 1832 he went to the Grammar School at Helston, Cornwall, where he did well but was not popular with his schoolmates. When in 1836 his father became rector of St. Luke's Chelsea, Charles accompanied his parents to London and for the next two years continued his schooling at King's College. In 1838 he entered Magdalen College Cambridge and a year later obtained a scholarship. He read classics and mathematics and practised every kind of sport including boxing.

During his years at the University (1838–42) he was much troubled by religious doubts and by moral-psychological conflicts springing from a somewhat over-severe conscience. These he confided in many letters to his

7

future wife, **Fanny Grenfell**, whom he had met during the summer vacation of 1839.

He was ordained in July 1842 and appointed curate at Eversley, a village situated in Hampshire on the borders of Windsor Forest. In 1844 he married Fanny Grenfell and the same year was given the living of Eversley which he was to retain for the rest of his life.

His first literary work, *The Saint's Tragedy*, a verse drama on the life of St. Elisabeth of Hungary, was published in 1848. *Yeast*, a novel dealing with the conditions of the agricultural labourer appeared in serial form in *Fraser's Magazine* the same year; it was followed by *Alton Locke, Tailor & Poet*, an indictment of the sweat-shop practice in the tailoring trade. These two works gave expression to Kingsley's deep sympathy for the suffering of the working classes and to his passionate interest in the movements of social reform which coincided with the industrial unrest and the revolutionary upheavals of the late eighteen-forties. In 1848 he became actively associated with Christian Socialism (under its leader J. D. Maurice), and under the pseudonym " Parson Lot " wrote tracts and pamphlets on topical social problems, as well as articles for the journals *Politics for the People* and the *Christian Socialist*. Over-exertion in his parish work coupled with over-excitement and controversy arising from his apparent championship of socialism led to several breakdowns in his health and, as a result, to periods of enforced idleness.

1849 saw the publication of his first volume of collected sermons *Twenty-five Village Sermons* which attracted widespread attention. In 1853 appeared his novel *Hypatia*, the theme of which—the conflict between early Christianity and Greek philosophy—is set in Alexandria in the fourth century A.D. It was followed, in 1855, by *Westward Ho!* (written during the winter of 1854–55 at Bideford, North Devon), his most popular work, and, in 1857, by *Two Years Ago*. In between the two last-named novels he wrote *The Heroes* (1855) a Christmas book of Greek Fairy Tales dedicated to his children Rose, Maurice and Mary.

In 1859 Kingsley was presented to the Queen and the

Prince Consort and shortly afterwards became one of the Queen's chaplains. A year later he was appointed Regius Professor of Modern History at Cambridge, an appointment which he held until 1869, though from 1863 onwards he went up to Cambridge only twice a year to deliver his lectures.

In 1863 he published *The Water Babies*, a fairy-tale dedicated to his youngest child Grenville. It became, next to *Westward Ho!* his most widely read work. In 1866 came his last novel, *Hereward the Wake*, an attempt at a historical romance in the manner of Scott. In 1864 Kingsley's impulsiveness and anti-Roman bias led to the famous public dispute with John Henry (later Cardinal) Newman, which resulted in the publication by Newman of his *Apologia* and did much damage to Kingsley's reputation.

Declining health in the years that followed forced him to seek frequent changes of climate and environment and to delegate part of his parish duties to a curate, the Reverend William Harrison, who later married Kingsley's youngest daughter Mary. In 1869, having resigned his professorship, Kingsley sailed to the West Indies at the invitation of Sir Arthur Gordon, Governor of Trinidad. He recorded the impressions of his journey in *At Last*, (1870). Later in the year 1869 he was appointed canon of Chester, an appointment he held until 1873 when he became canon of Westminster. Early in 1874 he went on a visit and lecture tour to America. At San Francisco he fell gravely ill with pleurisy. Though barely recovered and severely weakened, he returned to England in August to resume his many duties. Towards the end of the year he caught another cold which soon developed into pneumonia. He died at Eversley on January 23rd 1875 and was buried in Eversley churchyard.

His wife, who at the time of his final illness had been so ill herself that her life had been despaired of, survived him for sixteen years and became his first biographer.

H. d. R.

CONTENTS

INTRODUCTION

The Water Babies, and, curiously enough, *The Swiss Family Robinson*, were two of the very earliest books I can remember reading, and it is hard to put on one side those early impressions. Like your first theatre, your first concert, your first visit abroad, almost anything you do or meet or experience for the first time takes on a strange, unreal magic of its own. *The Water Babies* held that magic for me, and to my joy it holds it still. Reading it again the other day—a hot, still day of June, with the peonies spilling their crimson on the lawn, and all the scents and sounds of summer in the air—I was back at once in another summer morning, many years ago now, when I sat up in my little bed and opened a book which a favourite aunt had just given me and of which I knew nothing: *The Water Babies: A fairy tale for a Land Baby*. My copy was that strange contradiction in terms, a " Child's Edition." In those days, children's intelligence was not treated with quite so much respect as it is to-day, and many of the world's great books were chopped about and watered down so that the little ones might absorb the story without, shall we say, too much hard work. I am not sure, though, that that is always such a bad thing. Grown-up writers often have queer ideas as to what a child will like and understand, and a certain amount of intelligent pruning and cutting out of dead wood frequently does no harm at all. Certainly it did no harm to my appreciation of *The Water Babies*. If you have ever tried reading it aloud to a child, you will know what I mean. Those endless lists of adjectives, those meaningless references to old worn-out controversy, those sly pieces of propaganda, those outpourings of personal prejudice, are barnacles which slow and hinder the great ship's progress, and they ought to go.

That, though, is surely a matter for the reader. Does it really need the hard hand of an editor? The child learns early enough to do his own editing . . . " This is a boring bit: let's go on from here," and the wise parent obeys meekly. But I would rather have it all there, wouldn't you? And make my own choice as to what I would leave out. So I am glad the publishers of this edition have put away the scissors they must have itched to use, and have left us the original text, the pure milk of the word.

What a word it is! Can you think of any book which gives us such a picture of this countryside of ours? Yes, perhaps I can think of two: *Tafka the Otter* and *Salar the Salmon*. I dare say there are others. You may have your own preferences, and your parents may have theirs. But I think my little town-bred mind first woke to a perception of the English country, with *The Water Babies*. It is all so brilliantly done. The colours grow out of the story; they are never there for mere effect. It is the story that counts, right from the beginning, but the story is still only the bare bones; it is the colours which clothe it, and clothe it in words and phrases which, years after, linger in one's memory. " A mile off and a thousand feet down "; " Clear and cool, clear and cool "; " Those that wish to be clean, clean they will be; and those that wish to be foul, foul they will be "; " Down to the sea! Down to the sea! " And the names, too: what music there is in the very sound of them: " Peacepool "; " Shiny Wall "; " Mother Carey's Haven," where the good whales go when they die; " The Other-end-of-Nowhere "; " St. Brandan's Isle "; " Harthover Fell "; " Vendale." I wonder if they are as lovely in themselves as they seem to me now, or whether it is still that old " remembrance of things past " getting in the way again. I wonder.

But of one thing I am certain. There has never been such a picture of an English river. Not even that greatest of all river men, Kenneth Grahame, has caught the true, unforgettable river smell as Kingsley has caught it. Each of us has his river. Yours may be the upper reaches of the Thames: the quiet waters below Lechlade, the gentle murmuring shallows by Kelmscott. Or the cool green tree-shade of that busier Thames below Oxford. Or it may be the rivers of the south, the streams of Devon and Cornwall. Or the little meandering rivers of the Cotswolds, Evenlode and Windrush. Or the great rivers of the North. Or the Titans, Wye and Severn. I think I have two rivers, which have meant more to me than any others; the Cherwell, from Magdalen Bridge to the strange sunlit remoteness of its upper waters as far as Islip. And the brown tawny tumbling of the Dee, as it sings down the Vale of Llangollen. In, and on, and by the banks of these two rivers, I have looked and listened and dreamed. So perhaps will all of us. " Messing about in boats " is good, but messing about in boats in and by a river is better.

Tom's river may have been a Yorkshire river. Does it matter? Not a little bit, one way or the other. Tom's river is all rivers rolled into one. Above all it is the river of summer; the cool gentle refuge from the heat; the hot afternoon river of the water meadows and the dragon flies; the soft moonlit river of a summer night; the dark brooding river of thunder and storm. (I am not sure that Chapter 3 of *The Water Babies*, the " Down to the Sea " chapter, is not the finest thing that Kingsley ever wrote.)

Everyone will have his own favourite passage in this enchanting book. You who may be reading it now for the first time (you lucky persons!), I wonder which parts you will remember in the years to come? The excitement of the chase from Harthover? The bitter weary ordeal of the climb over Harthover Fell and down Lewthwaite Crag? The little old schoolmistress of Bendale, with her " Bless thy little heart! " and her " Water's bad for thee; I'll give thee milk"? The chiming and clashing of the church bells, that led Tom " down to the clear, clear limestone water, with every pebble at the bottom bright and clean . . . and he dipped his hand in and found it so cool, cool, cool; and he said, ' I will be a fish; I will swim in the water; I must be clean, I must be clean.' "?

Sometimes I think this great opening movement of Kingsley's splendid pastoral symphony is the finest thing in it. But then I remember the exquisite slow movement of the river in high summer "when all the world is young, lad, and all the trees are green "; the " Cool, clear water-world, where the sun is never too hot, and the frost is never too cold "; the river of the smooth gravel waterways; the river of the caddis, and the dragon-fly, and the trout, and the otter, and all the myriad water insects.

And what about the scherzo? The wild hurrying progress of the river and the river creatures " down to the sea "; the exultant tumult of the thunderstorm, when " the thunder roared, and the lightning flashed, and leaped across Vendale and back again, from cloud to cloud, and cliff to cliff, till the very rocks in the stream seemed to shake; and Tom looked up at it through the water, and thought it the finest thing he ever saw in his life."

Then the exquisite interludes of the water-baby world: Mrs. Doasyouwouldbedoneby, Mrs. Bedonebyasyoudid; Ellie; the poor silly lobster; the salmon. Sentimental stuff, perhaps, some of it, but written, if anything was, from the heart, and one can easily enough forgive the platitudes and the dogmas for the sake of a song like " I once had a sweet little doll, dears . . ."; or the picture of the babies coming home from their day's work of mending the broken seaweed and putting the rock pools in order, and planting all the shells again in the sand, so that no one may see " where the ugly storm swept in last week."

Last of all, the great, unequal, but magnificent finale. Tom's pilgrimage to the Other-End-of-Nowhere, to win his Manhood and redeem his soul; the great onward sweep of the journey to Shiny Wall, through the white gate that never was opened, and so to Peacepool, and Mother Carey's Haven, and Mother Carey herself. In some ways, though not in all, I find this the most moving part of the whole book. Such delightful characters appear and disappear; the mollys, those spirits of the old Greenland skippers long dead; the storm petrels, and all the thousands of sea-birds; the little dog, swept overboard from the wreck, who followed Tom faithfully to his journey's end; the good whales, the happy sleepy beasts upon the still oily sea; Mother Carey, " the grandest old lady Tom had ever seen ": " a white marble lady sitting on a white marble throne." And, last of all, the blunderbuss and the strange automatic truncheon in that terrible prison where, in Chimney No. 345, is confined, for his sins, which were many, Tom's old master and tyrant, Mr. Grimes; no longer the proud tyrant, but sad and sorry, pulling for ever at a pipe which will not draw. There is much in the writing of these closing chapters which we must all regret: the endless digressions, in which the author works off his spleen against politicians, educationists, Catholics, school inspectors, anything and anybody who offend his principles or his prejudices. This is Kingsley at his worst. The propagandist in him has run away with the story-teller, and the result is a confused, interminable mess, which may conceivably hold some interest for the social historian, but has none at all for the child or ordinary reader of to-day. It is this part of the book, more than any other, which needs the editorial scissors, or the brisk skipping of the reader. It almost succeeds in spoiling the beauty of this great finale. Almost, but not quite. For, aside from the journey, two things are left: the revelation to Grimes, by Mrs. Bedonebyasyoudid, of the death of his old mother, the little schoolmistress of Vendale; and Tom's meeting with Ellie. The first is one of those strange pieces of writing which, balanced on the razor edge of emotion, may so easily topple over into mawkish sentimentality. Some may think it does. Perhaps; we wear our rue to-day with a difference. I still find it deeply moving, because it is simple, because it is sincere, because remorse, when it comes too late, must always be something too terrible to contemplate. Grimes is freed from his chimney; he is given another chance, and goes off to expiate his sins by sweeping out the crater of Etna. But the little schoolmistress lies in the churchyard in Vendale, and there will be no more tears to be turned into hail by the cold heart of a forgetful son.

And the meeting with Ellie? It follows one of the loveliest passages in all this lovely book: the description of St. Brandan's Isle, with its black cedars, " high and sharp against the rosy dawn." Let me quote it in full; it is not long. ". . . St. Brandan's Isle reflected double in the still broad silver sea. The wind sang softly in the cedars, and the water sang among the caves; the sea-birds sang as they streamed out into the ocean, and the land-birds as they built among the boughs; and the air was so full of song that it stirred St. Brandan and his hermits, as they slumbered in the shade, and they moved their good old lips, and sang their morning hymn amid their dreams."

And so Tom meets at last his Ellie, " the most graceful creature that ever was seen, looking down, with her chin upon her hand, and paddling with her feet in the water. . . . ' Oh, Miss Ellie,' said he, ' how you are grown! ' 'Oh, Tom,' said she, ' how you are grown too! ' And no wonder: they were both quite grown up."

I wish Kingsley had ended the Water Babies there. Even the passage which follows, when the Irishwoman, and Mrs. Doasyouwouldbedoneby, and Mrs. Bedonebyasyoudid, and Mother Carey all stand revealed at last, beautiful as it is, is almost an anticlimax. About the " Moral," which ends the whole book, the less said the better. Even Kingsley did not always know when to stop.

Lastly, the poems. The publishers have included in this edition a selection of some of Charles Kingsley's verse. To my mind, there is nothing here to touch the beauty and simplicity of the two Water babies' songs, " Clear and Cool," and " I once had a sweet little doll, dears." But there are several poems that are familiar, and were much loved by our grandfathers and grandmothers, who set them to music, and sang them in the lamp-light of Victorian evenings. They are almost all pathetic; I can still be moved by " The Three Fishers," or " The Sands of Dee," even by " Lorraine, Lorraine, Loree "; and there is a genuine, haunting quality about the refrain of " The Last Buccaneer ": " the pleasant Isle of Avès, beside the Spanish main." But I prefer St. Brandan's Isle, with its black cedars, high and sharp against the rosy dawn.

DAVID DAVIS

THE WATER BABIES

A FAIRY TALE FOR A LAND BABY

CHAPTER ONE

I heard a thousand blended notes,
  While in a grove I sat reclined;
In that sweet mood when pleasant thoughts
  Bring sad thoughts to the mind.

To her fair works did Nature link
  The human soul that through me ran;
And much it grieved my heart to think,
  What man has made of man.

WORDSWORTH.

ONCE upon a time there was a little chimney-sweep, and his name was Tom. That is a short name, and you have heard it before, so you will not have much trouble in remembering it. He lived in a great town in the North country, where there were plenty of chimneys to sweep, and plenty of money for Tom to earn and his master to spend. He could not read nor write, and did not care to do either; and he never washed himself, for there was no water up the court where he lived. He had never been taught to say his prayers. He never had heard of God, or of Christ, except in words which you never have heard, and which it would have been well if he had never heard. He cried half his time, and laughed the other half. He cried when he had to climb the dark flues, rubbing his poor knees and elbows raw; and when the soot got into his eyes, which it did every day in the week; and when his master beat him, which he did every day in the week; and when he had not enough to eat, which happened every day in the week likewise. And he laughed the other half of the day, when he was tossing halfpennies with the other boys, or playing leap-frog over the posts, or bowling stones at the horses' legs as they trotted by, which last was excellent fun, when there was a wall at hand behind which to hide. As for chimney-sweeping, and being hungry, and being beaten, he took all that for the way of the world, like the rain and snow and thunder, and stood manfully with his back to it till it was over, as his old donkey did to a hailstorm; and then shook his ears and was as jolly as ever; and thought of the fine times coming, when he would be a man, and a master-sweep, and sit in the public-house with a quart of beer and a long pipe, and play cards for silver money, and wear velveteens and ankle jacks, and keep a white bulldog with one grey ear, and carry her puppies in his pocket, just like a man. And he would have apprentices, one, two, three, if he could. How he would bully them, and knock them about, just as his master did to him; and make them carry home the soot sacks, while he rode before them on his donkey, with a pipe in his mouth and a flower in his button-hole, like a king at the head of his army. Yes, there were good times coming; and, when his master let him have a pull at the leavings of his beer, Tom was the jolliest boy in the whole town.

One day a smart little groom rode into the court where Tom lived. Tom was just hiding behind a wall, to heave half a brick at his horse's legs, as is the custom of that country when they welcome strangers; but the groom saw him, and hallooed to him to know where Mr. Grimes, the chimney-sweep, lived. Now, Mr. Grimes was Tom's own master, and Tom was a good man of business, and always civil to customers, so he put the half-brick down quietly behind the wall, and proceeded to take orders.

Mr. Grimes was to come up next morning to Sir John Harthover's, at the Place, for his old chimney-sweep was gone to prison, and the chimneys wanted sweeping. And so he rode away, not giving Tom time to ask what the sweep had gone to prison for, which was a matter of interest to Tom, as he had been in prison once or twice himself. Moreover, the groom looked so very neat and clean, with his drab gaiters, drab breeches, drab jacket, snow-white tie with a smart pin in it, and clean round ruddy face, that Tom was offended and disgusted at his appearance, and considered him a stuck-up fellow, who gave himself airs because he wore smart clothes, and other people paid for them; and went behind the wall to fetch the half-brick after all: but did not, remembering that he had come in the way of business, and was, as it were, under a flag of truce.

His master was so delighted at his new customer that he knocked Tom down out of hand, and drank more beer that night than he usually did in two, in order to be sure of getting up in time next morning; for the more a man's head aches when he wakes, the more glad he is to turn out, and have a breath of fresh air. And, when he did get up at four the next morning, he knocked Tom down again, in order to teach him (as young gentlemen used to be taught at public schools) that he must be an extra good boy that day, as they were going to a very great house, and might make a very good thing of it, if they could but give satisfaction.

And Tom thought so likewise, and, indeed, would have done and behaved his best, even without being knocked down. For, of all places upon earth, Harthover Place (which he had never seen) was the most wonderful; and, of all men on earth, Sir John (whom he had seen, having been sent to gaol by him twice) was the most awful.

Harthover Place was really a grand place, even for the rich North country; with a house so large that in the frame-breaking riots, which Tom could just remember, the Duke of Wellington, with ten thousand soldiers and cannon to match, were easily housed therein; at least, so Tom believed; with a park full of deer, which Tom believed to be monsters who were in the habit of eating children; with miles of game preserves, in which Mr. Grimes and the collier-lads poached at times, on which occasions Tom saw pheasants, and wondered what they tasted like; with a noble salmon-river, in which Mr. Grimes and his friends would have liked to poach, but then they must have got into cold water, and that they did not like at all. In short, Harthover was a grand place, and Sir John a grand old man, whom even Mr. Grimes respected, for not only could he send Mr. Grimes to prison when he deserved it, as he did once or twice a week; not only did he own all the land about for miles; not only was he a jolly, honest, sensible squire as ever kept a pack of hounds, who would do what he thought right by his neighbours, as well as get what he thought right for himself, but, what was more, he weighed full fifteen stone, was nobody knew how many inches round the chest, and could have thrashed Mr. Grimes himself in fair fight, which very few folk round there could do, and which, my dear little boy, would not have been right for him to do, as a great many things are not which one both can do, and would like very much to do. So Mr. Grimes touched his hat to him when he rode through the town, and called him a " buirdly awd chap," and his young ladies " gradely lasses," which are two high compliments in the North country; and thought that that made up for his poaching Sir John's pheasants; whereby you may perceive that Mr. Grimes had not been to a properly inspected Government National School.

Now, I dare say, you never got up at three o'clock on a midsummer morning. Some people get up then because they want to catch salmon; and some, because they want to climb Alps; and a great many more, because they must, like Tom. But, I assure you, that three o'clock on a midsummer morning is the pleasantest time of all the twenty-four hours, and all the three hundred and sixty-five days; and why every one does not get up then, I never could tell, save that they are all determined to spoil their nerves and their complexions, by doing all night what they might just as well do all day. But Tom, instead of going out to dinner at half-past eight at night, and to a ball at ten, and finishing off somewhere between twelve and four, went to bed at seven, when his master went to the public-house, and slept like a dead pig: for which reason he was as piert* as a game-cock (who always gets up early to wake the maids), and just ready to get up when the fine gentlemen and ladies were just ready to go to bed.

So he and his master set out; Grimes rode the donkey in front, and Tom and the brushes walked behind; out of the court, and up the street, past the closed window

* Lively.

shutters, and the winking weary policemen, and the roofs all shining grey in the grey dawn.

They passed through the pitmen's village, all shut up and silent now; and through the turnpike; and then they were out in the real country, and plodding along the black dusty road, between black slag walls, with no sound but the groaning and thumping of the pit-engine in the next field. But soon the road grew white, and the walls likewise; and at the wall's foot grew long grass and gay flowers, all drenched with dew; and instead of the groaning of the pit-engine, they heard the skylark saying his matins high up in the air, and the pit-bird warbling in the sedges, as he had warbled all night long.

All else was silent. For old Mrs. Earth was still fast asleep; and, like many pretty people, she looked still prettier asleep than awake. The great elm-trees in the gold-green meadows were fast asleep above, and the cows fast asleep beneath them; nay, the few clouds which were about were fast asleep likewise, and so tired that they had lain down on the earth to rest, in long white flakes and bars, among the stems of the elm-trees, and along the tops of the alders by the stream, waiting for the sun to bid them rise and go about their day's business in the clear blue overhead.

On they went; and Tom looked, and looked, for he never had been so far into the country before; and longed to get over a gate, and pick buttercups, and look for birds' nests in the hedge; but Mr. Grimes was a man of business, and would not have heard of that.

Soon they came up with a poor Irishwoman, trudging along with a bundle at her back. She had a grey shawl over her head, and a crimson madder petticoat; so you may be sure she came from Galway. She had neither shoes nor stockings, and limped along as if she were tired and footsore: but she was a very tall handsome woman, with bright grey eyes, and heavy black hair hanging about her cheeks. And she took Mr. Grimes's fancy so much, that when he came alongside he called out to her:

" This is a hard road for a gradely foot like that. Will ye up, lass, and ride behind me? "

But, perhaps, she did not admire Mr. Grimes's look and voice; for she answered quietly:

"No, thank you; I'd sooner walk with your little lad here."

"You may please yourself," growled Grimes, and went on smoking.

So she walked beside Tom, and talked to him, and asked him where he lived, and what he knew, and all about himself, till Tom thought he had never met such a pleasant-spoken woman. And she asked him, at last, whether he said his prayers; and seemed sad when he told her that he knew no prayers to say.

Then he asked her where she lived; and she said far away by the sea. And Tom asked her about the sea; and she told him how it rolled and roared over the rocks in winter nights, and lay still in the bright summer days, for the children to bathe and play in it; and many a story more, till Tom longed to go and see the sea, and bathe in it likewise.

At last, at the bottom of a hill, they came to a spring: not such a spring as you see here, which soaks up out of a white gravel in the bog, among red fly-catchers, and pink bottle-heath, and sweet white orchis; nor such a one as you may see, too, here, which bubbles up under the warm sandbank in the hollow lane, by the great tuft of lady ferns, and makes the sand dance reels at the bottom, day and night, all the year round: not such a spring as either of those: but a real North country limestone fountain, like one of those in Sicily or Greece, where the old heathen fancied the nymphs sat cooling themselves the hot summer's day, while the shepherds peeped at them from behind the bushes. Out of a low cave of rock, at the foot of a lime-stone crag, the great fountain rose, quelling and bubbling, and gurgling, so clear that you could not tell where the water ended and the air began; and ran away under the road, a stream large enough to turn a mill; among blue geranium, and golden globe-flower, and wild raspberry, and the bird-cherry with its tassels of snow.

And there Grimes stopped, and looked; and Tom looked
26

too. Tom was wondering whether anything lived in that dark cave, and came out at night to fly in the meadows. But Grimes was not wondering at all. Without a word, he got off his donkey, and clambered over the low road wall, and knelt down, and began dipping his ugly head into the spring—and very dirty he made it.

Tom was picking the flowers as fast as he could. The Irishwoman helped him, and showed him how to tie them up; and a very pretty nosegay they had made between them. But when he saw Grimes actually wash, he stopped, quite astonished; and when Grimes had finished, and began shaking his ears to dry them, he said:

" Why, master, I never saw you do that before."

" Nor will again, most likely. 'Twasn't for cleanliness I did it, but for coolness. I'd be ashamed to want washing every week or so, like any smutty collier-lad."

" I wish I might go and dip my head in," said poor little Tom. " It must be as good as putting it under the town-pump; and there is no beadle here to drive a chap away."

" Thou come along," said Grimes, " what dost want with washing thyself? Thou did not drink half a gallon of beer last night, like me."

" I don't care for you," said naughty Tom, and ran down to the stream, and began washing his face.

Grimes was very sulky, because the woman preferred Tom's company to his; so he dashed at him with horrid words, and tore him up from his knees, and began beating him. But Tom was accustomed to that, and got his head safe between Mr. Grimes's legs, and kicked his shins with all his might.

" Are you not ashamed of yourself, Thomas Grimes?" cried the Irishwoman over the wall.

Grimes looked up, startled at her knowing his name; but all he answered was, " No: nor never was yet "; and went on beating Tom.

" True for you. If you ever had been ashamed of yourself, you would have gone over into Vendale long ago."

"What do you know about Vendale?" shouted Grimes; but he left off beating Tom.

"I know about Vendale, and about you, too. I know, for instance, what happened in Aldermire Copse, by night, two years ago come Martinmas."

"You do?" shouted Grimes; and leaving Tom, climbed up over the wall, and faced the woman. Tom thought he was going to strike her; but she looked him too full and fierce in the face for that.

"Yes; I was there," said the Irishwoman quietly.

"You are no Irishwoman, by your speech," said Grimes, after many bad words.

"Never mind who I am. I saw what I saw; and if you strike that boy again, I can tell what I know."

Grimes seemed quite cowed, and got on his donkey without another word.

"Stop!" said the Irishwoman. "I have one more word for you both; for you will both see me again, before all is over. Those that wish to be clean, clean they will be; and those that wish to be foul, foul they will be. Remember."

And she turned away, and through a gate into the meadow. Grimes stood still a moment, like a man who had been stunned. Then he rushed after her, shouting "You come back." But when he got into the meadow the woman was not there.

Had she hidden away? There was no place to hide in. But Grimes looked about, and Tom also, for he was as puzzled as Grimes himself, at her disappearing so suddenly; but look where they would, she was not there.

Grimes came back again, as silent as a post, for he was a little frightened; and getting on his donkey, filled a fresh pipe, and smoked away, leaving Tom in peace.

And now they had gone three miles and more, and came to Sir John's lodge-gates.

Very grand lodges they were, with very grand iron gates, and stone gate-posts, and on the top of each a most dreadful bogy, all teeth, horns, and tail, which was the crest which Sir John's ancestors wore in the Wars of the Roses; and very prudent men they were to wear it, for all their enemies must have run for their lives at the very first sight of them.

Grimes rang at the gate, and out came a keeper on the spot, and opened.

" I was told to expect thee," he said. " Now, thou'lt be so good as to keep to the main avenue, and not let me find a hare or a rabbit on thee when thou comest back. I shall look sharp for one, I tell thee."

" Not if it's in the bottom of the soot-bag," quoth Grimes, and at that he laughed; and the keeper laughed and said:

" If that's thy sort, I may as well walk up with thee to the hall."

" I think thou best had. It's thy business to see after thy game, man, and not mine."

So the keeper went with them; and to Tom's surprise, he and Grimes chatted together all the way quite pleasantly. He did not know that a keeper is only a poacher turned outside in, and a poacher a keeper turned inside out.

They walked up a great lime avenue, a full mile long, and between their stems Tom peeped trembling at the horns of the sleeping deer, which stood up among the ferns. Tom had never seen such enormous trees, and as he looked up he fancied that the blue sky rested on their heads. But he was puzzled very much by a strange murmuring noise, which followed them all the way. So much puzzled, that at last he took courage to ask the keeper what it was.

He spoke very civilly, and called him Sir, for he was horribly afraid of him, which pleased the keeper, and he told him that they were the bees about the lime-flowers.

" What are bees? " asked Tom.

" What make honey."

" What is honey? " asked Tom.

" Thou hold thy noise," said Grimes.

" Let the boy be," said the keeper. " He's a civil young chap now, and that's more than he'll be long, if he bides with thee."

Grimes laughed, for he took that for a compliment.

" I wish I were a keeper," said Tom, " to live in such a beautiful place, and wear green velveteens, and have a real dog-whistle at my button, like you."

The keeper laughed; he was a kind-hearted fellow enough.

" Let well alone, lad, and ill too, at times. Thy life's safer than mine at all events, eh, Mr. Grimes? "

And Grimes laughed again, and then the two men began talking quite low. Tom could hear, though, that it was about some poaching fight—and at last Grimes said surlily:

" Hast thou anything against me? "

" Not now."

" Then don't ask me any questions till thou hast, for I am a man of honour."

And at that they both laughed again, and thought it a very good joke.

And by this time they were come up to the great iron gates in front of the house; and Tom stared through them at the rhododendrons and azaleas, which were all in flower; and then at the house itself, and wondered how many chimneys there were in it, and how long ago it was built, and what was the man's name that built it, and whether he got much money for his job?

These last were very difficult questions to answer. For Harthover had been built at ninety different times, and in nineteen different styles, and looked as if somebody had built a whole street of houses of every imaginable shape, and then stirred them together with a spoon.

For the attics were Anglo-Saxon.

The third floor Norman.

The second Cinque-cento.

The first floor Elizabethan.

The right wing Pure Doric.

The centre Early English, with a huge portico, copied from the Parthenon.

The left wing Pure Boeotian, which the country folk admired most of all, because it was just like the new barracks in the town, only three times as big.

The grand staircase was copied from the Catacombs at Rome.

The back staircase from the Tajmahal at Agra. This was built by Sir John's great-great-great-uncle, who won, in Lord Clive's Indian wars, plenty of money, plenty of wounds, and no more taste than his betters.

The cellars were copied from the caves of Elephanta.

The offices from the Pavilion at Brighton.

And the rest from nothing in heaven, or earth, or under the earth.

So that Harthover House was a great puzzle to antiquarians, and a thorough Naboth's vineyard to critics, and architects, and all persons who like meddling with other men's business, and spending other men's money. So they all were setting upon poor Sir John, year after year, and trying to talk him into spending a hundred thousand pounds or so, in building to please them and not himself. But he always put them off, like a canny North-countryman as he was. One wanted him to build a Gothic house, but he said he was no Goth; and another to build an Elizabethan, but he said he lived under good Queen Victoria, and not good Queen Bess; and another was bold enough to tell him that his house was ugly, but he said he lived inside it, and not outside; and another, that there was no unity in it; but he said that that was just why he liked the old place. For he liked to see how each Sir John, and Sir Hugh, and Sir Ralph, and Sir Randal, had left his mark upon the place, each after his own taste; and he had no more notion of disturbing his ancestors' work than of disturbing their graves. For now the house looked like a real live house, that had a history, and had grown and grown as the world grew; and that it was only an upstart fellow who did not know who his own grandfather was, who would change it for some spick and span new Gothic or Elizabethan thing which looked as if it had been all spawned in a night, as mushrooms are. From which you may collect (if you have wit enough), that Sir John was a very sound-headed, sound-hearted squire, and just the

31

man to keep the countryside in order, and show good sport with his hounds.

But Tom and his master did not go in through the great iron gates, as if they had been Dukes or Bishops, but round the back way, and a very long way round it was; and into a little back door, where the ash-boy let them in, yawning horribly; and then in a passage the housekeeper met them, in such a flowered chintz dressing-gown, that Tom mistook her for My Lady herself, and she gave Grimes solemn orders about " You will take care of this, and take care of that," as if he was going up the chimneys, and not Tom. And Grimes listened, and said every now and then, under his voice, " You'll mind that, you little beggar? " and Tom did mind, all at least that he could. And then the housekeeper turned them into a grand room, all covered up in sheets of brown paper, and bade them begin, in a lofty and tremendous voice; and so after a whimper or two, and a kick from his master, into the grate Tom went, and up the chimney, while a housemaid stayed in the room to watch the furniture; to whom Mr. Grimes paid many playful and chivalrous compliments, but met with very slight encouragement in return.

How many chimneys he swept I cannot say: but he swept so many that he got quite tired, and puzzled too, for they were not like the town flues to which he was accustomed, but such as you would find—if you would only get up them and look, which perhaps you would not like to do—in old country houses, large and crooked chimneys, which had been altered again and again, till they ran into one another, anastomosing (as Professor Owen would say) considerably. So Tom fairly lost his way in them; not that he cared much for that, though he was in pitchy darkness, for he was as much at home in a chimney as a mole is underground; but at last, coming down as he thought the right chimney, he came down the wrong one, and found himself standing on the hearthrug in a room the like of which he had never seen before.

Tom had never seen the like. He had never been in

gentlefolks' rooms but when the carpets were all up, and the curtains down, and the furniture huddled together under a cloth, and the pictures covered with aprons and dusters; and he had often enough wondered what the rooms were like when they were all ready for the quality to sit in. And now he saw, and he thought the sight very pretty.

The room was all dressed in white; white window curtains, white bed curtains, white furniture, and white walls, with just a few lines of pink here and there. The carpet was all over gay little flowers; and the walls were hung with pictures in gilt frames, which amused Tom very much. There were pictures of ladies and gentlemen, and pictures of horses and dogs. The horses he liked; but the dogs he did not care for much, for there were no bulldogs among them, not even a terrier. But the two pictures which took his fancy most were, one a man in long garments, with little children and their mothers round him, who was laying his hand upon the children's heads. That was a very pretty picture, Tom thought, to hang in a lady's room. For he could see that it was a lady's room by the dresses which lay about.

The other picture was that of a man nailed to a cross, which surprised Tom much. He fancied that he had seen something like it in a shop window. But why was it there? " Poor man," thought Tom, " and he looks so kind and quiet. But why should the lady have such a sad picture as that in her room? Perhaps it was some kinsman of hers, who had been murdered by the savages in foreign parts, and she kept it there for a remembrance." And Tom felt sad, and awed, and turned to look at something else.

The next thing he saw, and that too puzzled him, was a washing-stand, with ewers and basins, and soap and brushes, and towels; and a large bath, full of clean water—what a heap of things all for washing! " She must be a very dirty lady," thought Tom, " by my master's rule, to want as much scrubbing as all that. But she must be very cunning to put the dirt out of the way so well afterwards, for I don't see a speck about the room, not even on the very towels."

And then, looking toward the bed, he saw that dirty lady, and held his breath with astonishment.

Under the snow-white coverlet, upon the snow-white pillow, lay the most beautiful little girl that Tom had ever seen. Her cheeks were almost as white as the pillow, and her hair was like threads of gold spread all about over the bed. She might have been as old as Tom, or maybe a year or two older; but Tom did not think of that. He thought only of her delicate skin and golden hair, and wondered whether she were a real live person, or one of the wax dolls he had seen in the shops. But when he saw her breathe, he made up his mind that she was alive, and stood staring at her, as if she had been an angel out of heaven.

No. She cannot be dirty. She never could have been dirty, thought Tom to himself. And then he thought, " And are all people like that when they are washed? " And he looked at his own wrist, and tried to rub the soot off, and wondered whether it ever would come off. " Certainly I should look much prettier then, if I grew at all like her."

And looking round, he suddenly saw, standing close to him, a little ugly, black, ragged figure, with bleared eyes and grinning white teeth. He turned on it angrily. What did such a little black ape want in that sweet young lady's room? And behold, it was himself, reflected in a great mirror, the like of which Tom had never seen before.

And Tom, for the first time in his life, found out that he was dirty; and burst into tears with shame and anger; and turned to sneak up the chimney again and hide, and upset the fender, and threw the fire-irons down, with a noise as of ten thousand tin kettles tied to ten thousand mad dogs' tails.

Up jumped the little white lady in her bed, and, seeing Tom, screamed as shrill as any peacock. In rushed a stout old nurse from the next room, and seeing Tom likewise, made up her mind that he had come to rob, plunder,

destroy, and burn; and dashed at him, as he lay over the fender, so fast that she caught him by the jacket.

But she did not hold him. Tom had been in a policeman's hands many a time, and out of them too, what is more; and he would have been ashamed to face his friends for ever if he had been stupid enough to be caught by an old woman: so he doubled under the good lady's arm, across the room, and out of the window in a moment.

He did not need to drop out, though he would have done so bravely enough. Nor even to let himself down a spout, which would have been an old game to him; for once he got up by a spout to the church roof, he said to take jackdaws' eggs, but the policemen said to steal lead; and when he was seen on high, sat there till the sun got too hot, and came down by another spout, leaving the policemen to go back to the station-house and eat their dinners.

But all under the window spread a tree, with great leaves, and sweet white flowers, almost as big as his head. It was a magnolia, I suppose; but Tom knew nothing about that, and cared less; for down the tree he went, like a cat, and across the garden lawn, and over the iron railings, and up the park towards the wood, leaving the old nurse to scream murder and fire at the window.

The under gardener, mowing, saw Tom, and threw down his scythe; caught his leg in it, and cut his shin open, whereby he kept his bed for a week: but in his hurry he never knew it, and gave chase to poor Tom. The dairymaid heard the noise, got the churn between her knees, and tumbled over it, spilling all the cream; and yet she jumped up, and gave chase to Tom. A groom cleaning Sir John's hack at the stables let him go loose, whereby he kicked himself lame in five minutes; but he ran out, and gave chase to Tom. Grimes upset the soot-sack in the newgravelled yard, and spoilt it all utterly; but, he ran out and gave chase to Tom. The old steward opened the park gate in such a hurry, that he hung up his pony's chin upon the spikes, and for aught I know it hangs there still; but he jumped off, and gave chase to Tom. The ploughman left his horses at the headland, and one jumped over the fence, and pulled the other into the ditch, plough and all; but he ran on, and gave chase to Tom. The keeper, who was taking a stoat out of a trap, let the stoat go, and caught his own finger; but he jumped up and ran after Tom, and considering what he said, and how he looked, I should have been sorry for Tom if he had caught him. Sir John looked out of his study window (for he was an early old gentleman), and up at the nurse, and a marten dropt mud in his eye, so that he had at last to send for the doctor; and yet he ran out and gave chase to Tom. The Irishwoman, too, was walking up to the house to beg—she must have got round by some byway: but she threw away her bundle, and gave chase to Tom likewise. Only My Lady did not give chase; for when she had put her head out of the window, her night-wig fell into the garden, and she had to ring up her lady's-maid, and send her down for it privately; which quite put her out of the running, so that she came in nowhere, and is consequently not placed.

In a word, never was there heard at Hall Place, not even when the fox was killed in the conservatory, among acres of broken glass, and tons of smashed flower-pots, such a noise, row, hubbub, babel, shindy, hullabaloo, stramash, charivari, and total contempt of dignity, repose, and order, as that day, when Grimes, the gardener, the groom, the dairymaid, Sir John, the steward, the ploughman, the keeper, and the Irishwoman, all ran up the park, shouting " Stop thief," in the belief that Tom had at least a thousand pounds' worth of jewels in his empty pockets; and the very magpies and jays followed Tom up, screaking and screaming, as if he were a hunted fox, beginning to droop his brush.

And all the while poor Tom paddled up the park with his little bare feet, like a small black gorilla fleeing to the forest. Alas for him! there was no big father gorilla therein to take his part; to scratch out the gardener's inside with one paw, toss the dairymaid into a tree with another, and wrench off Sir John's head with a third, while he cracked the keeper's skull with his teeth, as easily as if it had been a coco-nut or a paving-stone.

However, Tom did not remember ever having had a father; so he did not look for one, and expected to have to take care of himself; while as for running, he could keep up for a couple of miles with any stage-coach, if there was the chance of a copper or a cigar-end, and turn coach wheels on his hands and feet ten times following, which is more than you can do. Wherefore his pursuers found it very difficult to catch him; and we will hope that they did not catch him at all.

Tom, of course, made for the woods. He had never been in a wood in his life: but he was sharp enough to know that he might hide in a bush, or swarm up a tree, and, altogether, had more chance there than in the open. If he had not known that, he would have been foolisher than a mouse or a minnow.

But when he got into the wood, he found it a very different sort of place from what he had fancied. He pushed into a thick cover of rhododendrons, and found himself at once caught in a trap. The boughs laid hold of his legs and arms, poked him in his face and his stomach, made him shut his eyes tight (though that was no great loss, for he could not see at best a yard before his nose); and when he got through the rhododendrons, the hassock-grass and sedges tumbled him over, and cut his poor little fingers afterwards most spitefully; the birches birched him as soundly as if he had been a nobleman at Eton, and over the face too (which is not fair swishing, as all brave boys will agree); and the lawyers tripped him up, and tore his shins as if they had sharks' teeth—which lawyers are likely enough to have.

" I must get out of this," thought Tom, "or I shall stay here till somebody comes to help me—which is just what I don't want."

But how to get out was the difficult matter. And indeed I don't think he would ever have got out at all, but have stayed there till the cock robins covered him with leaves, if he had not suddenly run his head against a wall.

Now running your head against a wall is not pleasant, especially if it is a loose wall, with the stones all set on edge, and a sharp-cornered one hits you between the eyes, and makes you see all manner of beautiful stars. The stars are very beautiful, certainly: but unfortunately they go in the twenty-thousandth part of a split second, and the pain which comes after them does not. And so Tom hurt his head; but he was a brave boy, and did not mind that a penny. He guessed that over the wall the cover would end; and up it he went, and over like a squirrel.

And there he was, out on the great grouse-moors, which the country folk called Harthover Fell—heather and bog and rock, stretching away and up, up to the very sky.

Now, Tom was a cunning little fellow—as cunning as an old Exmoor stag. Why not? Though he was but ten years old, he had lived longer than most stags, and had more wits to start with into the bargain.

He knew as well as a stag, that if he backed he might throw the hounds out. So the first thing he did when he was over the wall, was to make the neatest double sharp to his right, and run along under the wall for nearly half a mile.

Whereby Sir John, and the keeper, and the steward, and the gardener, and the ploughman, and the dairymaid, and all the hue and cry together, went on ahead half a mile in the very opposite direction, and inside the wall, leaving him a mile off on the outside, while Tom heard their shouts die away in the wood, and chuckled to himself merrily.

At last he came to a dip in the land, and went to the bottom of it, and then he turned bravely away from the wall, and up the moor; for he knew that he had put a hill between him and his enemies, and could go on without their seeing him.

But the Irishwoman, alone of them all, had seen which way Tom went. She had kept ahead of every one the whole time: and yet she neither walked nor ran. She went along quite smoothly and gracefully, while her feet twinkled past each other so fast, that you could not see which was foremost; till every one asked the other who the strange woman was? and all agreed, for want of anything better to say, that she must be in league with Tom.

But when she came to the plantation they lost sight of her; and they could do no less. For she went quietly over the wall after Tom, and followed him wherever he went. Sir John and the rest saw no more of her; and out of sight was out of mind.

And now Tom was right away into the heather, over just such a moor as those in which you have been bred, except that there were rocks and stones lying about everywhere; and that instead of the moor growing flat as he went upwards, it grew more and more broken and hilly: but not so rough but that little Tom could jog along well enough, and find time, too, to stare about at the strange place, which was like a new world to him.

He saw great spiders there, with crowns and crosses marked on their backs, who sat in the middle of their webs, and when they saw Tom coming, shook them so fast that they became invisible. Then he saw lizards, brown, and grey, and green, and thought they were snakes, and would sting him: but they were as much frightened as he, and shot away into the heath. And then, under a rock, he saw a pretty sight—a great brown sharp-nosed creature, with a white tag to her brush, and round her, four or five smutty little cubs, the funniest fellows Tom ever saw. She lay on her back, rolling about, and stretching out her legs, and head, and tail in the bright sunshine; and the cubs jumped over her, and ran round her, and nibbled her paws, and lugged her about by the tail; and she seemed to enjoy it mightily. But one selfish little fellow stole away from the rest to a dead crow close by, and dragged it off to hide it, though it was nearly as big as he was. Whereat all his little brothers set off after him in full cry, and saw Tom; and then all ran back, and up jumped Mrs. Vixen, and caught one up in her mouth, and the rest toddled after her, and into a dark crack in the rocks; and there was an end of the show.

And next he had a fright; for as he scrambled up a sandy

brow—whir-poof-poof-cock-cock-kick—something went off in his face, with a most horrid noise. He thought the ground had blown up, and the end of the world come.

And when he opened his eyes (for he shut them very tight), it was only an old cock grouse, who had been washing himself in sand, like an Arab, for want of water; and who, when Tom had all but trodden on him, jumped up, with a noise like the express train, leaving his wife and children to shift for themselves, like an old coward, and went off, screaming " Cur-ru-u-uck, cur-ru-u-uck—murder, thieves, fire—cur-u-uck-cock-kick—the end of the world is come—kick-kick-cock-kick." He was always fancying that the end of the world was come, when anything happened which was farther off than the end of his own nose. But the end of the world was not come, any more than the twelfth of August was; though the old grouse-cock was quite certain of it.

So the old grouse came back to his wife and family an hour afterwards, and said solemnly, " Cock-cock-kick; my dears, the end of the world is not quite come; but I assure you it is coming the day after to-morrow—cock." But his wife had heard that so often, that she knew all about it, and a little more. And, beside, she was the mother of a family, and had seven little poults to wash and feed every day; and that made her very practical, and a little sharp-tempered; so all she answered was: " Kick-kick-kick—go and catch spiders, go and catch spiders—kick."

So Tom went on, and on, he hardly knew why: but he liked the great, wide, strange place, and the cool, fresh, bracing air. But he went more and more slowly as he got higher up the hill; for now the ground grew very bad indeed. Instead of soft turf and springy heather, he met great patches of flat limestone rock, just like ill-made pavements, with deep cracks between the stones and ledges filled with ferns; so he had to hop from stone to stone, and now and then he slipped in between, and hurt his little bare toes, though they were tolerably tough ones: but still he would go on and up, he could not tell why.

What would Tom have said, if he had seen, walking over

the moor behind him, the very same Irishwoman who had taken his part upon the road? But whether it was that he looked too little behind him, or whether it was that she kept out of sight behind the rocks and knolls, he never saw her, though she saw him.

And now he began to get a little hungry, and very thirsty; for he had run a long way, and the sun had risen high in heaven, and the rock was as hot as an oven, and the air danced reels over it, as it does over a limekiln, till everything round seemed quivering and melting in the glare.

But he could see nothing to eat anywhere, and still less to drink.

The heath was full of bilberries and whinberries: but they were only in flower yet, for it was June. And as for water, who can find that on the top of a limestone rock? Now and then he passed by a deep dark swallow-hole, going down into the earth, as if it was the chimney of some dwarf's house underground; and more than once, as he passed, he could hear water falling, trickling, tinkling, many many feet below. How he longed to get down to it, and cool his poor baked lips! But, brave little chimney-sweep as he was, he dared not climb down such chimneys as those.

So he went on, and on, till his head spun round with the heat, and he thought he heard church bells ringing, a long way off.

" Ah! " he thought, " where there is a church, there will be houses and people; and, perhaps, someone will give me a bite and a sup." So he set off again, to look for the church; for he was sure that he heard the bells quite plain.

And in a minute more, when he looked round, he stopped again, and said, " Why, what a big place the world is! "

And so it was; for, from the top of the mountain, he could see—what could he not see?

Behind him, far below, was Harthover, and the dark woods, and the shining salmon river; and on his left, far

below, was the town, and the smoking chimneys of the
collieries; and far, far away, the river widened to the
shining sea; and little white specks, which were ships, lay
on its bosom. Before him lay, spread out like a map, great
plains, and farms, and villages, amid dark knots of trees.
They all seemed at his very feet; but he had sense to see
that they were long miles away.

And to his right rose moor after moor, hill after hill, till
they faded away, blue into blue sky. But between him and
those moors, and really at his very feet, lay something, to
which, as soon as Tom saw it, he determined to go, for that
was the place for him.

A deep, deep green and rocky valley, very narrow, and
filled with wood: but through the wood, hundreds of feet
below him, he could see a clear stream glance. Oh, if he
could but get down to that stream! Then, by the stream,
he saw the roof of a little cottage, and a little garden, set
out in squares and beds. And there was a tiny little red
thing moving in the garden, no bigger than a fly. As Tom
looked down, he saw that it was a woman in a red petticoat!
Ah! perhaps she would give him something to eat. And
there were the church bells ringing again. Surely there
must be a village down there. Well, nobody would know
him, or what had happened at the Place. The news could
not have got there yet, even if Sir John had set all the
policemen in the county after him; and he could get down
there in five minutes.

Tom was quite right about the hue and cry not having
got thither; for he had come, without knowing it, the best
part of ten miles from Harthover: but he was wrong about
getting down in five minutes, for the cottage was more
than a mile off, and a good thousand feet below.

However, down he went, like a brave little man as he
was, though he was very footsore, and tired, and hungry,
and thirsty; while the church bells rang so loud, he began
to think that they must be inside his own head, and the
river chimed and tinkled far below; and this was the song
which it sang:

43

Clear and cool, clear and cool,
By laughing shallow, and dreaming pool,
Cool and clear, cool and clear,
By shining shingle, and foaming wear;
Under the crag where the ouzel sings,
And the ivied wall where the church bell rings,
Undefiled, for the undefiled;
Play by me, bathe in me, mother and child.

Dank and foul, dank and foul,
By the smoky town in its murky cowl;
Foul and dank, foul and dank,
By wharf and sewer and slimy bank;
Darker and darker the further I go,
Baser and baser the richer I grow;
Who dare sport with the sin-defiled?
Shrink from me, turn from me, mother and child.

Strong and free, strong and free,
The floodgates are open, away to the sea,
Free and strong, free and strong,
Cleansing my streams as I hurry along,
To the golden sands, and the leaping bar,
And the taintless tide that awaits me afar,
As I lose myself in the infinite main.
Like a soul that has sinned and is pardoned again.
Undefiled, for the undefiled,
Play by me, bathe in me, mother and child.

So Tom went down; and all the while he never saw the
Irishwoman going down behind him.

CHAPTER TWO

And is there care in heaven? and is there love
In heavenly spirits to these creatures base
That may compassion of their evils move?
There is:—else much more wretched were the case
Of men than beasts: But oh! the exceeding grace
Of Highest God that loves His creatures so,
And all His works with mercy doth embrace,
That blessed Angels He sends to and fro,
To serve to wicked man, to serve His wicked foe!

SPENSER.

A MILE off, and a thousand feet down. So Tom found it; though it seemed as if he could have chucked a pebble on to the back of the woman in the red petticoat who was weeding in the garden, or even across the dale to the rocks beyond.

For the bottom of the valley was just one field broad, and on the other side ran the stream; and above it, grey crag, grey down, grey stair, grey moor, walled up to heaven.

A quiet, silent, rich, happy place; a narrow crack cut deep into the earth; so deep, and so out of the way, that the bad bogies can hardly find it out. The name of the place is Vendale; and if you want to see it for yourself, you must go up into the High Craven, and search from Bolland Forest north by Ingleborough, to the Nine Standards and Cross Fell; and if you have not found it, you must turn south, and search the Lake Mountains, down to Scawl Fell and the sea; and then if you have not found it, you must go northward again by merry Carlisle, and search the Cheviots all across, from Annan Water to Berwick Law; and then, whether you have found Vendale or not, you will have found such a country, and such a people, as ought to make you proud of being a British boy.

So Tom went to go down; and first he went down three hundred feet of steep heather, mixed up with loose brown gritstone, as rough as a file; which was not pleasant to his poor little heels, as he came bump, stump, jump, down the steep. And still he thought he could throw a stone into the garden.

Then he went down three hundred feet of limestone terraces, one below the other, as straight as if Mr. George White had ruled them with his ruler and then cut them out with his chisel. There was no heath there, but——

First, a little grass slope, covered with the prettiest flowers, rock-rose and saxifrage, and thyme and basil, and all sort of sweet herbs.

Then bump down a two-foot step of limestone.

Then another bit of grass and flowers.

Then bump down a one-foot step.

Then another bit of grass and flowers for fifty yards, as steep as the house-roof, where he had to slide down on his dear little tail.

Then another step of stone, ten feet high; and there he had to stop himself, and crawl along the edge to find a crack; for if he had rolled over, he would have rolled right into the old woman's garden, and frightened her out of her wits.

Then, when he had found a dark narrow crack, full of green-stalked fern, such as hangs in the basket in the drawing-room, and had crawled down through it, with knees and elbows, as he would down a chimney, there was another grass slope, and another step, and so on, till—oh, dear me! I wish it was all over; and so did he. And yet he thought he could throw a stone into the old woman's garden.

At last he came to a bank of beautiful shrubs; whitebeam with its great silver-backed leaves, and mountain-ash, and oak; and below them cliff and crag, cliff and crag, with great beds of crown-ferns and wood-sedge; while through the shrubs he could see the stream sparkling, and hear it murmur on the white pebbles. He did not know that it was three hundred feet below.

You would have been giddy, perhaps, at looking down: but Tom was not. He was a brave little chimney-sweep;

Jean Cruickshanks.

and when he found himself on the top of a high cliff, instead of sitting down and crying for his baba (though he never had had any baba to cry for), he said, " Ah, this will just suit me! " though he was very tired; and down he went, by stock and stone, sedge and ledge, bush and rush, as if he had been born a jolly little black ape, with four hands instead of two.

And all the while, he never saw the Irishwoman coming down behind him.

But he was getting terribly tired now. The burning sun on the fells had sucked him up; but the damp heat of the woody crag sucked him up still more; and the perspiration ran out of the ends of his fingers and toes, and washed him cleaner than he had been for a whole year. But, of course, he dirtied everything terribly as he went. There has been a great black smudge all down the crag ever since. And there have been more black beetles in Vendale since than ever were known before; all, of course, owing to Tom's having blacked the original papa of them all, just as he was setting off to be married, with a sky-blue coat and scarlet leggings, as smart as a gardener's dog with a polyanthus in his mouth.

At last he got to the bottom. But, behold, it was not the bottom—as people usually find when they are coming down a mountain. For at the foot of the crag were heaps and heaps of fallen limestone of every size from that of your head to that of a stage-wagon, with holes between them full of sweet heath-fern; and before Tom got through them, he was out in the bright sunshine again; and then he felt, once for all and suddenly, as people generally do, that he was b-e-a-t, beat.

You must expect to be beat a few times in your life, little man, if you live such a life as a man ought to live, let you be as strong and healthy as you may: and when you are, you will find it a very ugly feeling. I hope that that day you may have a stout staunch friend by you who is not beat; for it you have not, you had best lie where you are, and wait for better times, as poor Tom did.

He could not get on. The sun was burning, and yet

he felt chill all over. He was quite empty, and yet he felt quite sick. There was but two hundred yards of smooth pasture between him and the cottage, and yet he could not walk down it. He could hear the stream murmuring only one field beyond it, and yet it seemed to him as if it was a hundred miles off.

He lay down on the grass till the beetles ran over him, and the flies settled on his nose. I don't know when he would have got up again, if the gnats and the midges had not taken compassion on him. But the gnats blew their trumpets so loud in his ear, and the midges nibbled so at his hands and face wherever they could find a place free from soot, that at last he woke up, and stumbled away, down over a low wall, and into a narrow road, and up to the cottage door.

And a neat pretty cottage it was, with clipt yew hedges all round the garden, and yews inside too, cut into peacocks and trumpets and teapots and all kinds of queer shapes. And out of the open door came a noise like that of the frogs on the Great-A, when they know that it is going to be scorching hot to-morrow—and how they know that I don't know, and you don't know, and nobody knows.

He came slowly up to the open door, which was all hung round with clematis and roses; and then peeped in, half afraid.

And there sat by the empty fire-place, which was filled with a pot of sweet herbs, the nicest old woman that ever was seen, in her red petticoat, and short dimity bedgown, and clean white cap, with a black silk handkerchief over it, tied under her chin. At her feet sat the grandfather of all the cats; and opposite her sat, on two benches, twelve or fourteen neat rosy chubby little children, learning their Chris-cross-row; and gabble enough they made about it.

Such a pleasant cottage it was, with a shiny clean stone floor, and curious old prints on the walls, and an old black oak sideboard full of bright pewter and brass dishes, and a cuckoo clock in the corner, which began shouting as soon as Tom appeared: not that it was frightened at Tom, but that it was just eleven o'clock.

All the children started at Tom's dirty black figure; the girls began to cry, and the boys began to laugh, and all pointed at him rudely enough: but Tom was too tired to care for that.

"What art thou, and what dost want?" cried the old dame. "A chimney-sweep! Away with thee. I'll have no sweeps here."

"Water," said poor little Tom, quite faint.

"Water? There's plenty i' the beck," she said, quite sharply.

"But I can't get there; I'm most clemmed with hunger and drought." And Tom sank down upon the door-step, and laid his head against the post.

And the old dame looked at him through her spectacles one minute, and two, and three; and then she said, "He's sick; and a bairn's a bairn, sweep or none."

"Water," said Tom.

"God forgive me!" and she put by her spectacles, and rose, and came to Tom. "Water's bad for thee; I'll give thee milk." And she toddled off into the next room, and brought a cup of milk and a bit of bread.

Tom drank the milk off at one draught, and then looked up, revived.

"Where didst come from?" said the dame.

"Over Fell, there," said Tom, and pointed up into the sky.

"Over Harthover? and down Lewthwaite Crag? Art sure thou are not lying?"

"Why should I?" said Tom, and leant his head against the post.

"And how got ye up there?"

"I came over from the Place," and Tom was so tired and desperate he had no heart or time to think of a story, so he told all the truth in a few words.

"Bless thy little heart! And thou hast not been stealing, then?"

"No."

"Bless thy little heart! and I'll warrant not. Why God's guided the bairn, because he was innocent! Away from the Place, and over Harthover Fell, and down Lewth-waite Crag! Who ever heard the like, if God hadn't led him? Why dost not eat thy bread?"

"I can't."

"It's good enough, for I made it myself."

"I can't," said Tom, and he laid his head on his knees, and then asked:

"Is it Sunday?"

"No, then; why should it be?"

"Because I hear the church bells ringing so."

"Bless thy pretty heart! The bairn's sick. Come wi' me, and I'll hap thee up somewhere. If thou wert a bit cleaner I'd put thee in my own bed, for the Lord's sake. But come along here."

But when Tom tried to get up, he was so tired and giddy that she had to help him and lead him.

She put him in an outhouse upon soft sweet hay and an old rug, and bade him sleep off his walk, and she would come to him when school was over, in an hour's time.

And so she went in again, expecting Tom to fall fast asleep at once.

But Tom did not fall asleep.

Instead of it he turned and tossed and kicked about in the strangest way, and felt so hot all over that he longed to get into the river and cool himself; and then he fell half asleep, and dreamt that he heard the little white lady crying to him, "Oh, you're so dirty; go and be washed"; and then that he heard the Irishwoman saying, "Those that wish to be clean, clean they will be." And then he heard the church bells ring so loud, close to him, too, that he was sure it must be Sunday, in spite of what the old dame had said; and he would go to church, and see what a church was like inside, for he had never been in one, poor little fellow, in all his life. But the people would never let him come in, all over soot and dirt like that. He must go to the river and wash first. And he said out aloud again and again, though being half asleep he did not know it, "I must be clean, I must be clean."

And all of a sudden he found himself, not in the outhouse

on the hay, but in the middle of a meadow, over the road, with a stream just before him, saying continually, "I must be clean, I must be clean." He had got there on his own legs, between sleep and awake, as children will often get out of bed, and go about the room, when they are not quite well. But he was not a bit surprised, and went on to the bank of the brook, and lay down on the grass, and looked into the clear, clear limestone water, with every pebble at the bottom bright and clean, while the little silver trout dashed about in fright at the sight of his black face; and he dipped his hand in and found it so cool, cool, cool; and he said, "I will be a fish; I will swim in the water; I must be clean, I must be clean."

So he pulled off all his clothes in such haste that he tore some of them, which was easy enough with such ragged old things. And he put his poor hot sore feet into the water; and then his legs; and the further he went in, the more the church bells rang in his head.

"Ah," said Tom, "I must be quick and wash myself; the bells are ringing quite loud now: and they will stop soon, and then the door will be shut, and I shall never be able to get in at all."

Tom was mistaken: for in England the church doors are left open all service time, for everybody who likes to come in, Churchman or Dissenter; ay, even if he were a Turk or a Heathen; and if any man dared to turn him out, as long as he behaved quietly, the good old English law would punish that man, as he deserved, for ordering any peaceable person out of God's house, which belongs to all alike. But Tom did not know that, any more than he knew a great deal more which people ought to know.

And all the while he never saw the Irishwoman: not behind him this time, but before.

For just before he came to the river side, she had stept down into the cool clear water; and her shawl and her petticoat floated off her, and the green water-weeds floated round her sides, and the white water-lilies floated round her head, and the fairies of the stream came up from the bottom, and bore her away and down upon their arms;

for she was the Queen of them all; and perhaps of more besides.

" Where have you been? " they asked her.

" I have been smoothing sick folks' pillows, and whispering sweet dreams into their ears; opening cottage casements, to let out the stifling air; coaxing little children away from gutters, and foul pools where fever breeds; turning women from the gin-shop door, and staying men's hands as they were going to strike their wives; doing all I can to help those who will not help themselves: and little enough that is, and weary work for me. But I have brought you a new little brother, and watched him safe all the way here."

Then all the fairies laughed for joy at the thought that they had a little brother coming.

" But mind, maidens, he must not see you, or know that you are here. He is but a savage now, and like the beasts which perish; and from the beasts which perish he must learn. So you must not play with him, or speak to him, or let him see you: but only keep him from being harmed."

Then the fairies were sad, because they could not play with their new brother, but they always did what they were told.

And their Queen floated away down the river; and whither she went, thither she came. But all this Tom, of course, never saw or heard: and perhaps if he had, it would have made little difference in the story; for he was so hot and thirsty, and longed so to be clean for once, that he tumbled himself as quick as he could into the clear cool stream.

And he had not been in it two minutes before he fell fast asleep, into the quietest, sunniest, cosiest sleep that ever he had in his life; and he dreamt about the green meadows by which he had walked that morning, and the tall elm trees, and the sleeping cows; and after that he dreamt of nothing at all.

The reason of his falling into such a delightful sleep is very simple; and yet hardly any one has found it out. It was merely that the fairies took him.

Some people think that there are no fairies. Cousin Cramchild tells little folks so in his Conversations. Well, perhaps there are none—in Boston, U.S., where he was raised. There are only a clumsy lot of spirits there, who can't make people hear without thumping on the table: but they get their living thereby, and I suppose that is all they want. And Aunt Agitate, in her Arguments on political economy, says there are none. Well, perhaps there are none—in her political economy. But it is a wide world, my little man—and thank heaven for it, for else, between crinolines and theories, some of us would get squashed—and plenty of room in it for fairies, without people seeing them; unless, of course, they look in the right place. The most wonderful and the strongest things in the world, you know, are just the things which no one can see. There is life in you; and it is the life in you which makes you grow, and move, and think: and yet you can't see it. And there is steam in a steam-engine; and that is what makes it move: and yet you can't see it; and so there may be fairies in the world, and they may be just what makes the world go round to the old tune of

C'est l'amour, l'amour, l'amour
Qui fait la monde à la ronde:

and yet no one may be able to see them except those whose hearts are going round to that same tune. At all events, we will make believe that there are fairies in the world. It will not be the last time by many a one that we shall have to make believe. And yet, after all, there is no need for that. There must be fairies; for this is a fairy tale: and how can one have a fairy tale if there are no fairies?

You don't see the logic of that? Perhaps not. Then please not to see the logic of a great many arguments exactly like it, which you will hear before your beard is grey.

The kind old dame came back at twelve, when school was over, to look at Tom: but there was no Tom there. She looked about for his footprints; but the ground was so hard that there was no slot, as they say in dear old North

Devon. And if you grow up to be a brave healthy man, you may know some day what no slot means, and know, too, I hope, what a slot does mean—a broad slot, with blunt claws, which makes a man put out his cigar, and set his teeth, and tighten his girths, when he sees it; and what his rights mean, if he has them, brow, bay, tray, and points; and see something worth seeing between Haddon Wood and Countisbury Cliff, with good Mr. Palk Collyns to show you the way, and mend your bones as fast as you smash them. Only when that jolly day comes, please don't break your neck: stogged in a mire you never will be, I trust; for you are a heath-cropper bred and born.

So the old dame went in again quite sulky, thinking that little Tom had tricked her with a false story, and shammed ill, and then run away again.

But she altered her mind the next day. For, when Sir John and the rest of them had run themselves out of breath, and lost Tom, they went back again, looking very foolish.

And they looked more foolish still when Sir John heard more of the story from the nurse; and more foolish still, again, when they heard the whole story from Miss Ellie, the little lady in white. All she had seen was a poor little black chimney-sweep, crying and sobbing, and going to get up the chimney again. Of course, she was very much frightened: and no wonder. But that was all. The boy had taken nothing in the room; by the mark of his little sooty feet, they could see that he had never been off the hearth-rug till the nurse caught hold of him. It was all a mistake.

So Sir John told Grimes to go home, and promised him five shillings if he would bring the boy quietly up to him, without beating him, that he might be sure of the truth. For he took for granted, and Grimes, too, that Tom had made his way home.

But no Tom came back to Mr. Grimes that evening; and he went to the police-office, to tell them to look out for the boy. But no Tom was heard of. As for his having gone over those great fells to Vendale, they no more dreamed of that than of his having gone to the moon.

So Mr. Grimes came up to Harthover next day with a very sour face; but when he got there, Sir John was over the hills and far away; and Mr. Grimes had to sit in the outer servants' hall all day, and drink strong ale to wash away his sorrows; and they were washed away, long before Sir John came back.

For good Sir John had slept very badly that night; and he said to his lady, " My dear, the boy must have got over into the grouse-moors, and lost himself; and he lies very heavily on my conscience, poor little lad. But I know what I will do."

So, at five the next morning up he got, and into his bath, and into his shooting-jacket and gaiters, and into the stable-yard, like a fine old English gentleman, with a face as red as a rose, and a hand as hard as a table, and a back as broad as a bullock's; and bade them bring his shooting pony, and the keeper to come on his pony, and the huntsman, and the first whip, and the second whip, and the under-keeper with the bloodhound in a leash—a great dog as tall as a calf, of the colour of a gravel walk, with mahogany ears and nose, and a throat like a church bell. They took him up to the place where Tom had gone into the wood; and there the hound lifted up his mighty voice, and told them all he knew.

Then he took them to the place where Tom had climbed the wall; and they shoved it down, and all got through.

And then the wise dog took them over the moor, and over the fells, step by step, very slowly: for the scent was a day old, you know, and very light from the heat and drought. But that was why cunning old Sir John started at five in the morning.

And at last he came to the top of Lewthwaite Crag, and there he bayed, and looked up in their faces, as much as to say, " I tell you he is gone down here! "

They could hardly believe that Tom would have gone so far; and when they looked at that awful cliff, they could never believe that he would have dared to face it. But if the dog said so, it must be true.

" Heaven forgive us! " said Sir John. " If we find him

at all, we shall find him lying at the bottom." And he slapped his great hand upon his great thigh, and said:

"Who will go down over Lewthwaite Crag, and see if that boy is alive? Oh that I were twenty years younger, and I would go down myself!" And so he would have done, as well as any sweep in the county. Then he said:

"Twenty pounds to the man who brings me that boy alive!" and as was his way, what he said he meant.

Now among the lot was a little groom-boy, a very little groom indeed; and he was the same who had ridden up the court, and told Tom to come to the Hall; and he said:

"Twenty pounds or none, I will go down over Lewthwait Crag, if it's only for the poor boy's sake. For he was as civil a spoken little chap as ever climbed a flue."

So down over Lewthwaite Crag he went: a very smart groom he was at the top, and a very shabby one at the bottom; for he tore his gaiters, and he tore his breeches, and he tore his jacket, and he burst his braces, and he burst his boots, and he lost his hat, and what was worst of all, he lost his shirt pin, which he prized very much, for it was gold, and he had won it in a raffle at Malton, and there was a figure at the top of it of t'ould mare, noble old Beeswing herself, as natural as life; so it was a really severe loss: but he never saw anything of Tom.

And all the while Sir John and the rest were riding round, full three miles to the right, and back again, to get into Vendale, and to the foot of the crag.

When they came to the old dame's school, all the children came out to see. And the old dame came out too; and when she saw Sir John she curtsied very low, for she was a tenant of his.

"Well, dame, and how are you?" said Sir John.

"Blessings on you as broad as your back, Harthover," says she—she didn't call him Sir John, but only Harthover, for that is the fashion in the North country—"and welcome into Vendale: but you're no' hunting the fox this time of year?"

"I am hunting, and strange game too," said he.

" Blessings on your heart, and what makes you look so sad the morn? "

" I'm looking for a lost child, a chimney-sweep, that is run away."

" Oh Harthover, Harthover," says she, " ye were always a just man and a merciful; and ye'll no harm the poor little lad if I give you tidings of him? "

" Not I, not I, dame. I'm afraid we hunted him out of the house all on a miserable mistake, and the hound has brought him to the top of Lewthwaite Craig, and——"

Whereat the old dame broke out crying, without letting him finish his story.

" So he told me the truth after all, poor little dear! Ah, first thoughts are best, and a body's heart'll guide them right, if they will but hearken to it." And then she told Sir John all.

" Bring the dog here, and lay him on," said Sir John, without another word, and he set his teeth very hard.

And the dog opened at once; and went away at the back of the cottage, over the road, and over the meadow, and through a bit of alder copse; and there, upon an alder stump, they saw Tom's clothes lying. And then they knew as much about it all as there was any need to know.

And Tom?

Ah, now comes the most wonderful part of this wonderful story. Tom, when he woke, for of course he woke—children always wake after they have slept exactly as long as is good for them—found himself swimming about in the stream, being about four inches, or—that I may be accurate —3.87902 inches long, and having round the parotid region of his fauces a set of external gills (I hope you understand all the big words) just like those of a sucking eft, which he mistook for a lace frill, till he pulled at them, found he hurt himself, and made up his mind that they were part of himself, and best left alone.

In fact, the fairies had turned him into a water baby.

A water baby? You never heard of a water baby. Perhaps not. That is the very reason why this story was written. There are a great many things in the world

which you never heard of; and a great many more which nobody ever heard of; and a great many things, too, which nobody will ever hear of, at least until the coming of the Cocqcigrues, when man shall be the measure of all things.

"But there are no such things as water babies."

How do you know that? Have you been there to see? And if you had been there to see, and had seen none, that would not prove that there were none. If Mr. Garth does not find a fox in Eversley Wood—as folks sometimes fear he never will—that does not prove that there are no such things as foxes. And as is Eversley Wood to all the woods in England, so are the waters we know to all the waters in the world. And no one has a right to say that no water babies exist, till they have seen no water babies existing; which is quite a different thing, mind, from not seeing water babies; and a thing which nobody ever did, or perhaps ever will do.

"But surely if there were water babies, somebody would have caught one at least?"

Well. How do you know that somebody has not?

"But they would have put it into spirits, or into the *Illustrated News*, or perhaps cut it into two halves, poor dear little thing, and sent one to Professor Owen, and one to Professor Huxley, to see what they would each say about it."

Ah, my dear little man! that does not follow at all, as you will see before the end of the story.

"But a water baby is contrary to nature."

Well, but, my dear little man, you must learn to talk about such things, when you grow older, in a very different way from that. You must not talk about "ain't" and "can't" when you speak of this great wonderful world round you, of which the wisest man knows only the very smallest corner, and is, as the great Sir Isaac Newton said, only a child picking up pebbles on the shore of a boundless ocean.

You must not say that this cannot be, or that that is contrary to nature. You do not know what nature is, or what she can do; and nobody knows; not even Sir Roderick Murchison, or Professor Owen, or Professor Sedgwick, or Professor Huxley, or Mr. Darwin, or Professor Faraday, or Mr. Grove, or any other of the great men whom good boys are taught to respect. They are very wise men; and you must listen respectfully to all they say: but even if they should say, which I am sure they never would, " That cannot exist. That is contrary to nature," you must wait a little and see; for perhaps even they may be wrong. It is only children who read Aunt Agitate's Arguments, or Cousin Cramchild's Conversations, or lads who go to popular lectures, and see a man pointing at a few big ugly pictures on the wall, or making nasty smells with bottles and squirts, for an hour or two, and calling that anatomy or chemistry—who talk about " cannot exist," and " contrary to nature." Wise men are afraid to say that there is anything contrary to nature, except what is contrary to mathematical truth; for two and two cannot make five, and two straight lines cannot join twice, and a part cannot be as great as the whole, and so on (at least, so it seems at present): but the wiser men are, the less they talk about " cannot." That is a very rash, dangerous word, that " cannot "; and if people use it too often, the Queen of all the Fairies, who makes the clouds thunder and the fleas bite, and takes just as much trouble about one as about the other, is apt to astonish them suddenly by showing them, that though they say she cannot, yet she can, and what is more, will, whether they approve or not.

And therefore it is, that there are dozens and hundreds of things in the world which we should certainly have said were contrary to nature, if we did not see them going on under our eyes all day long. If people had never seen little seeds grow into great plants and trees, of quite different shape from themselves, and these trees again produce fresh seeds, to grow into fresh trees, they would have said, " The thing cannot be; it is contrary to nature." And they would have been quite as right in saying so, as in saying that most other things cannot be.

Or suppose again, that you had come, like M. du Chaillu,

a traveller from unknown parts; and that no human being had ever seen or heard of an elephant. And suppose that you described him to people, and said, " This is the shape, and plan, and anatomy of the beast, and of his feet, and of his trunk, and of his grinders, and of his tusks, though they are not tusks at all, but two fore teeth run mad; and this is the section of his skull, more like a mushroom than a reasonable skull of a reasonable or unreasonable beast; and so forth, and so forth; and though the beast (which I assure you I have seen and shot) is first cousin to the little hairy coney of Scripture, second cousin to a pig, and (I suspect) thirteenth or fourteenth cousin to a rabbit, yet he is the wisest of all beasts, and can do everything save read, write, and cast accounts." People would surely have said, " Nonsense; your elephant is contrary to nature "; and have thought you were telling stories—as the French thought of Le Vaillant when he came back to Paris and said that he had shot a giraffe; and as the king of the Cannibal Islands thought of the English sailor, when he said that in his country water turned to marble, and rain fell as feathers. They would tell you, the more they knew of science, " Your elephant is an impossible monster, contrary to the laws of comparative anatomy, as far as yet known." To which you would answer the less, the more you thought.

Did not learned men, too, hold, till within the last twenty-five years, that a flying dragon was an impossible monster? And do we not know now that there are hundreds of them found fossil up and down the world? People call them Pterodactyles: but that is only because they are ashamed to call them flying dragons, after denying so long that flying dragons could exist. And has not a German only lately discovered, what is most monstrous of all, that some of these flying dragons, lizards though they seem, had feathers? And if that last is not contrary to what people mean by nature nowadays, one hardly knows what is.

The truth is, that folks' fancy that such and such things cannot be, simply because they have not seen them, is worth no more than a savage's fancy that there cannot be such a thing as a locomotive, because he never saw one running wild in the forest. Wise men know that their business is to examine what is, and not to settle what is not. They know that there are elephants; they know that there have been flying dragons; and the wiser they are, the less inclined they will be to say positively that there are no water babies.

No water babies, indeed? Why, wise men of old said that everything on earth had its double in the water; and you may see that that is, if not quite true, still quite as true as most other theories which you are likely to hear for many a day. There are land babies—then why not water babies? Are there not water-rats, water-flies, water-crickets, water-crabs, water-tortoises, water-scorpions, water-tigers and water-hogs, water-cats and water-dogs, sea-lions and sea-bears, sea-horses and sea-elephants, sea-mice and sea-urchins, sea-razors and sea-pens, sea-combs and sea-fans; and of plants, are there not water-grass, and water-crowfoot, water-milfoil, and so on, without end?

"But all these things are only nicknames; the water things are not really akin to the land things."

That's not always true. They are, in millions of cases, not only of the same family, but actually the same individual creatures. Do not even you know that a green drake, and an alder-fly, and a dragon-fly, live under water till they change their skins, just as Tom changed his? And if a water animal can continually change into a land animal, why should not a land animal sometimes change into a water animal? Don't be put down by any of Cousin Cramchild's arguments, but stand up to him like a man, and answer him (quite respectfully, of course) thus:

If Cousin Cramchild says, that if there are water babies, they must grow into water men, ask him how he knows that they do not? and then, how he knows that they must, any more than the Proteus of the Adelsberg caverns grows into a perfect newt?

If he says that it is too strange a transformation for a land baby to turn into a water baby, ask him if he ever heard of the transformation of Syllis, or the Distomas, or the common jelly-fish, of which M. Quatrefages says excellently well—" who would not exclaim that a miracle had come to pass, if he saw a reptile come out of the egg dropped by the hen in his poultry yard, and the reptile give birth at once to an indefinite number of fishes and birds? Yet the history of the jelly-fish is quite as wonderful as that would be." Ask him if he knows about all this; and if he does not, tell him to go and look for himself; and advise him (very respectfully, of course) to settle no more what strange things cannot happen, till he has seen what strange things do happen every day.

If he says that things cannot degrade, that is, change downwards into lower forms, ask him, who told him that water babies were lower than land babies? But even if they were, does he know about the strange degradation of the common goose-barnacles, which one finds sticking on ships' bottoms; or the still stranger degradation of some cousins of theirs, of which one hardly likes to talk, so shocking and ugly it is?

And, lastly, if he says (as he most certainly will) that these transformations only take place in the lower animals, and not in the higher, say that that seems to little boys, and to some grown people, a very strange fancy. For if the changes of the lower animals are so wonderful, and so difficult to discover, why should not there be changes in the higher animals far more wonderful, and far more difficult to discover? And may not man, the crown and flower of all things, undergo some change as much more wonderful than all the rest, as the Great Exhibition is more wonderful than a rabbit burrow? Let him answer that. And if he says (as he will) that not having seen such a change in his experience, he is not bound to believe it, ask him respectfully where his microscope has been? Does not each of us, in coming into this world, go through a transformation just as wonderful as that of a sea-egg, or a butterfly? and does not reason and analogy, as well as Scripture, tell us that that transformation is not the last? and that, though what we shall be, we know not, yet we are here but as the crawling caterpillar, and shall be hereafter as the perfect fly. The old Greeks, heathens as they were, saw as much as that two thousand years ago; and I care very little for Cousin Cramchild, if he sees even less than they. And so forth, and so forth, till he is quite cross. And then tell him that if there are no water babies, at least, there ought to be; and that, at least, he cannot answer.

And meanwhile, my dear little man, till you know a great deal more about nature than Professor Owen and Professor Huxley, put together, don't tell me about what cannot be, or fancy that anything is too wonderful to be true. "We are fearfully and wonderfully made," said old David; and so we are; and so is everything around us, down to the very deal table. Yes; much more fearfully and wonderfully made, already, is the table, as it stands now, nothing but a piece of dead deal wood, than if, as foxes say, and geese believe, spirits could make it dance, or talk to you by rapping on it.

Am I in earnest? Oh dear no. Don't you know that this is a fairy tale, and all fun and pretence; and that you are not to believe one word of it, even if it is true?

But at all events, so it happened to Tom. And, therefore, the keeper, and the groom, and Sir John, made a great mistake, and were very unhappy (Sir John, at least) without any reason, when they found a black thing in the water, and said it was Tom's body, and that he had been drowned. They were utterly mistaken. Tom was quite alive; and cleaner, and merrier, than he ever had been. The fairies had washed him, you see, in the swift river, so thoroughly that not only his dirt, but his whole husk and shell had been washed quite off him, and the pretty little real Tom was washed out of the inside of it, and swam away, as a caddis does when its case of stones and silk is bored through, and away it goes on its back, paddling to the shore, there to split its skin, and fly away as a caperer, on four fawn-coloured wings, with long legs and horns. They are foolish fellows, the caperers, and fly into the candle at night, if you leave the door open. We will hope Tom will be wiser, now he has got safe out of his sooty old shell.

But good Sir John did not understand all this, not being

a fellow of the Linnaean Society; and he took it into his head that Tom was drowned. When they looked into the empty pockets of his shell, and found no jewels there, nor money—nothing but three marbles, and a brass button with a string to it—then Sir John did something as like crying as ever he did in his life, and blamed himself more bitterly than he need have done. So he cried, and the groom-boy cried, and the huntsman cried, and the dame cried, and the little girl cried, and the dairymaid cried, and the old nurse cried (for it was somewhat her fault), and my lady cried, for though people have wigs, that is no reason why they should not have hearts: but the keeper did not cry, though he had been so good-natured to Tom the morning before; for he was so dried up with running after poachers, that you could no more get tears out of him than milk out of leather: and Grimes did not cry, for Sir John gave him ten pounds, and he drank it all in a week. Sir John sent, far and wide, to find Tom's father and mother: but he might have looked till Doomsday for them, for one was dead, and the other was in Botany Bay. And the little girl would not play with her dolls for a whole week, and never forgot poor little Tom. And soon my lady put a pretty little tombstone over Tom's shell in the little churchyard in Vendale, where the old dalesmen all sleep side by side between the limestone crags. And the dame decked it with garlands every Sunday, till she grew so old that she could not stir abroad; then the little children decked it for her. And always she sung an old old song, as she sat spinning what she called her wedding-dress. The children could not understand it, but they liked it none the less for that; for it was very sweet, and very sad; and that was enough for them. And these are the words of it:

When all the world is young, lad,
　And all the trees are green;
And every goose a swan, lad,
　And every lass a queen;
Then hey for boot and horse, lad,

And round the world away:
Young blood must have its course, lad,
    And every dog his day.

When all the world is old, lad,
    And all the trees are brown;
And all the sport is stale, lad,
    And all the wheels run down;
Creep home, and take your place there,
    The spent and maimed among:
God grant you find one face there
    You loved when all was young.

Those are the words: but they are only the body of it:
the soul of the song was the dear old woman's sweet face,
and sweet voice, and the sweet old air to which she sang;
and that, alas! one cannot put on paper. And at last she
grew so stiff and lame, that the angels were forced to carry
her; and they helped her on with her wedding-dress, and
carried her up over Harthover Fells, and a long way
beyond that too; and there was a new schoolmistress in
Vendale, and we will hope that she was not certificated.

And all the while Tom was swimming about in the river,
with a pretty little lace-collar of gills about his neck as
lively as a grig, and as clean as a fresh-run salmon.

Now if you don't like my story, then go to the school-
room and learn your multiplication table, and see if you
like that better. Some people, no doubt, would do so.
So much the better for us, if not for them. It takes all
sorts, they say, to make a world.

CHAPTER THREE

He prayeth well who loveth well,
Both men and bird and beast;
He prayeth best who loveth best,
All things both great and small:
For the dear God who loveth us,
He made and loveth all.
                                    COLERIDGE.

TOM was now quite amphibious. You do not know what
that means? You had better, then, ask the nearest
Government pupil-teacher, who may possibly answer you
smartly enough, thus:

"Amphibious. Adjective, derived from two Greek
words, *amphi*, a fish, and *bios*, a beast. An animal supposed
by our ignorant ancestors to be compounded of a fish and
a beast; which therefore, like the hippopotamus, can't live
on the land, and dies in the water."

However that may be, Tom was amphibious; and what
is better still, he was clean. For the first time in his life
he felt how comfortable it was to have nothing on him but
himself. But he only enjoyed it; he did not know it, or
think about it; just as you enjoy life and health, and yet
never think about being alive and healthy: and may it be
long before you have to think about it!

He did not remember having ever been dirty. Indeed,
he did not remember any of his old troubles, being tired,
or hungry, or beaten, or sent up dark chimneys. Since that
sweet sleep, he had forgotten all about his master, and
Harthover Place, and the little white girl, and in a word,
all that had happened to him when he lived before; and
what was best of all, he had forgotten all the bad words
which he had learnt from Grimes, and the rude boys with
whom he used to play.

That is not strange: for you know, when you came into
this world, and became a land baby, you remembered

nothing. So why should he, when he became a water baby?

Then have you lived before?

My dear child, who can tell? One can only tell that, by remembering something which happened where we lived before; and as we remember nothing, we know nothing about it; and no book, and no man, can ever tell us certainly.

There was a wise man once, a very wise man, and a very good man, who wrote a poem about the feelings which some children have about having lived before; and this is what he said:

> Our birth is but a sleep and a forgetting;
> The soul that rises with us, our life's star,
>   Hath elsewhere had its setting,
>   And cometh from afar:
> Not in entire forgetfulness,
> And not in utter nakedness,
> But trailing clouds of glory, do we come
>   From God, who is our home.

There, you can know no more than that. But if I was you, I would believe that. For then the great fairy Science, who is likely to be queen of all the fairies for many a year to come, can only do you good, and never do you harm; and instead of fancying, with some people, that your body makes your soul, as if a steam-engine could make its own coke; or, with some other people, that your soul has nothing to do with your body, but is only stuck into it like a pin into a pin-cushion, to fall out with the first shake—you will believe the one true,

orthodox,	inductive,
rational,	deductive,
philosophical,	seductive,
logical,	productive,
irrefragable,	salutary,
nominalistic,	comfortable,
realistic,	
and on-all-accounts-to-be-received	

doctrine of this wonderful fairy tale; which is, that your soul makes your body, just as a snail makes his shell. For the rest, it is enough for us to be sure that whether or not we lived before, we shall live again; though not, I hope, as poor little heathen Tom did. For he went downward into the water: but we, I hope, shall go upward to a very different place.

But Tom was very happy in the water. He had been sadly overworked in the land-world; and so now, to make up for that, he had nothing but holidays in the water-world for a long, long time to come. He had nothing to do now but enjoy himself, and look at all the pretty things which are to be seen in the cool clear water-world, where the sun is never too hot, and the frost is never too cold.

And what did he live on? Water-cresses, perhaps; or perhaps water-gruel, and water-milk: too many land babies do so likewise. But we do not know what one-tenth of the water things eat; so we are not answerable for the water babies.

Sometimes he went along the smooth gravel waterways, looking at the crickets which ran in and out among the stones, as rabbits do on land; or he climbed over the ledges of rock, and saw the sand-pipes hanging in thousands, with every one of them a pretty little head and legs peeping out; or he went into a still corner, and watched the caddises eating dead sticks as greedily as you would eat plum-pudding, and building their houses with silk and glue. Very fanciful ladies they were; none of them would keep to the same materials for a day. One would begin with some pebbles; then she would stick on a piece of green weed; then she found a shell, and stuck it on too; and the poor shell was alive, and did not like at all being taken to build houses with: but the caddis did not let him have any voice in the matter, being rude and selfish, as vain people are apt to be; then she stuck on a piece of rotten wood, then a very smart pink stone, and so on, till she was patched all over like an Irishman's coat. Then she found a long straw, five times as long as herself, and said, "Hurrah! my sister has a tail, and I'll have one too"; and she stuck it on her back, and marched about with it quite proud, though it was very inconvenient indeed. And, at that, tails became all the fashion among the caddis-baits in that pool, as they were at the end of the Long Pond last May, and they all toddled about with long straws sticking out behind, getting between each other's legs, and tumbling over each other, and looking so ridiculous, that Tom laughed at them till he cried, as we did. But they were quite right, you know; for people must always follow the fashion, even if it be spoon-bonnets.

Then sometimes he came to a deep still reach; and there he saw the water-forests. They would have looked to you only little weeds; but Tom, you must remember, was so little that everything looked a hundred times as big to him as it does to you, just as things do to a minnow, who sees and catches the little water-creatures which you can only see in a microscope.

And in the water-forest he saw the water-monkeys and water-squirrels (they had all six legs, though; everything almost has six legs in the water, except efts and water babies); and nimbly enough they ran among the branches. There were water-flowers there, too, in thousands; and Tom tried to pick them: but as soon as he touched them, they drew themselves in and turned into knots of jelly; and then Tom saw that they were all alive—bells, and stars, and wheels, and flowers, of all beautiful shapes and colours; and all alive and busy, just as Tom was. So now he found that there was a great deal more in the world than he had fancied at first sight.

There was one wonderful little fellow, too, who peeped out of the top of a house built of round bricks. He had two big wheels, and one little one, all over teeth, spinning round and round like the wheels in a thrashing-machine; and Tom stood and stared at him, to see what he was going to make with his machinery. And what do you think he was doing? Brick-making. With his two big wheels he swept together all the mud which floated in the water: all that was nice in it he put into his stomach and ate; and all the mud he put into the little wheel on his breast, which really was a round hole set with teeth; and there he spun it into a neat hard round brick; and then he took it and stuck it on the top of his house-wall, and set to work to make another. Now was not he a clever little fellow?

Tom thought so: but when he wanted to talk to him, the brick-maker was much too busy and proud of his work to take notice of him.

Now you must know that all the things under the water talk: only not such a language as ours; but such as horses, and dogs, and cows, and birds talk to each other; and Tom soon learned to understand them and talk to them; so that he might have had very pleasant company if he had only been a good boy. But I am sorry to say, he was too like some other little boys, very fond of hunting and tormenting creatures for mere sport. Some people say that boys cannot help it; that it is nature, and only a proof that we are all originally descended from beasts of prey. But whether it is nature or not, little boys can help it, and must help it. For if they have naughty, low, mischievous tricks in their nature, as monkeys have, that is no reason why they should give way to those tricks like monkeys, who know no better. And therefore they must not torment dumb creatures; for if they do, a certain old lady who is coming will surely give them exactly what they deserve.

But Tom did not know that; and he pecked and howked the poor water things about sadly, till they were all afraid of him, and got out of his way, or crept into their shells; so he had no one to speak to or play with.

The water-fairies, of course, were very sorry to see him so unhappy, and longed to take him, and tell him how naughty he was, and teach him to be good, and to play and romp with him too: but they had been forbidden to do that. Tom had to learn his lesson for himself by sound and sharp experience, as many another foolish person has to do, though there may be many a kind heart yearning over them all the while, and longing to teach them what they can only teach themselves.

At last one day he found a caddis, and wanted it to peep out of its house: but its house-door was shut. He had never seen a caddis with a house-door before: so what must he do, the meddlesome little fellow, but pull it open, to see what the poor lady was doing inside. What a shame! How should you like to have any one breaking your bed-room door in, to see how you looked when you were in bed? So Tom broke to pieces the door, which was the prettiest little grating of silk stuck all over with shining bits of crystal; and when he looked in, the caddis poked out her head, and it had turned into just the shape of a bird's. But when Tom spoke to her she could not answer; for her mouth and face were tight tied up in a new night-cap of neat pink skin. However, if she didn't answer, all the other caddises did; for they held up their hands and shrieked like the cats in *Struwelpeter*: "Oh, you nasty, horrid boy; there you are at it again! And she had just laid herself up for a fortnight's sleep, and then she would have come out with such beautiful wings, and flown about, and laid such lots of eggs: and now you have broken her door, and she can't mend it because her mouth is tied up for a fort-night, and she will die. Who sent you here to worry us out of our lives?"

So Tom swam away. He was very much ashamed of himself, and felt all the naughtier; as little boys do when they have done wrong, and won't say so.

Then he came to a pool full of little trout, and began tormenting them, and trying to catch them: but they slipt through his fingers, and jumped clean out of the water in their fright. But as Tom chased them, he came close to a great dark hover under an alder root, and out floushed a huge old brown trout ten times as big as he was, and ran right against him, and knocked all the breath out of his body; and I don't know which was the more frightened of the two.

Then he went on sulky and lonely, as he deserved to be; and under a bank he saw a very ugly dirty creature sitting, about half as big as himself; which had six legs, and a big stomach, and a most ridiculous head with two great eyes and a face just like a donkey's.

"Oh," said Tom, "you are an ugly fellow to be sure!"

and he began making faces at him; and put his nose close to him, and halloed at him, like a very rude boy.

When, hey presto! all the thing's donkey-face came off in a moment, and out popped a long arm with a pair of pincers at the end of it, and caught Tom by the nose. It did not hurt him much; but it held him quite tight.

"Yah, ah! Oh, let me go!" cried Tom.

"Then let me go," said the creature. "I want to be quiet. I want to split."

Tom promised to let him alone, and he let go. "Why do you want to split?" said Tom.

"Because my brothers and sisters have all split, and turned into beautiful creatures with wings; and I want to split too. Don't speak to me. I am sure I shall split. I will split!"

Tom stood still, and watched him. And he swelled himself, and puffed, and stretched himself out stiff, and at last—crack, puff, bang—he opened all down his back, and then up to the top of his head.

And out of his inside came the most slender, elegant, soft creature, as soft and smooth as Tom: but very pale and weak, like a little child who has been ill a long time in a dark room. It moved its legs very feebly; and looked about it half ashamed, like a girl when she goes for the first time into a ball-room; and then it began walking slowly up a grass stem to the top of the water.

Tom was so astonished that he never said a word: but he stared with all his eyes. And he went up to the top of the water too, and peeped out to see what would happen.

And as the creature sat in the warm bright sun, a wonderful change came over it. It grew strong and firm; the most lovely colours began to show on its body, blue and yellow and black, spots and bars and rings; out of its back rose four great wings of bright brown gauze; and its eyes grew so large that they filled all its head, and shone like ten thousand diamonds.

"Oh, you beautiful creature!" said Tom; and he put out his hand to catch it.

But the thing whirled up into the air, and hung poised on its wings a moment, and then settled down again by Tom quite fearless.

" No! " it said, " you cannot catch me. I am a dragon-fly now, the king of all the flies; and I shall dance in the sunshine, and hawk over the river, and catch gnats, and have a beautiful wife like myself. I know what I shall do. Hurrah! " And he flew away into the air, and began catching gnats.

" Oh! come back, come back," cried Tom, " you beautiful creature. I have no one to play with, and I am so lonely here. If you will but come back I will never try to catch you."

" I don't care whether you do or not," said the dragon-fly; " for you can't. But when I have had my dinner, and looked a little about this pretty place, I will come back; and have a little chat about all I have seen in my travels. Why, what a huge tree this is! and what huge leaves on it! "

It was only a big dock: but you know the dragon-fly had never seen any but little water-trees: a starwort, and milfoil, and water-crowfoot, and such like; so it did look very big to him. Besides, he was very short-sighted, as all dragon-flies are; and never could see a yard before his nose; any more than a great many other folks, who are not half as handsome as he.

The dragon-fly did come back, and chatted away with Tom. He was a little conceited about his fine colours and his large wings; but you know, he had been a poor dirty ugly creature all his life before; so there were great excuses for him. He was very fond of talking about all the wonderful things he saw in the trees and the meadows; and Tom liked to listen to him, for he had forgotten all about them. So in a little while they became great friends.

And I am very glad to say that Tom learnt such a lesson that day, that he did not torment creatures for a long time after. And then the caddises grew quite tame, and used to tell him strange stories about the way they built their houses, and changed their skins, and turned at last into winged flies; till Tom began to long to change his skin, and have wings like them some day.

And the trout and he made it up (for trout very soon forget, if they have been frightened and hurt). So Tom used to play with them at hare and hounds, and great fun they had; and he used to try to leap out of the water, head over heels, as they did before a shower came on: but somehow he never could manage it. He liked most, though, to see them rising at the flies, as they sailed round and round under the shadow of the great oak, where the beetles fell flop into the water, and the green caterpillars let themselves down from the boughs by silk ropes for no reason at all; and then changed their foolish minds for no reason at all either; and hauled themselves up again into the tree, rolling up the rope in a ball between their paws; which is a very clever rope-dancer's trick, and neither Blondin nor Leotard could do it: but why they should take so much trouble about it no one can tell; for they cannot get their living, as Blondin and Leotard do, by trying to break their necks on a string.

And very often Tom caught them just as they touched the water; and caught the alder flies, and the caperers, and the cock-tailed duns and spinners, yellow, and brown, and claret, and grey, and gave them to his friends the trout. Perhaps he was not quite kind to the flies; but one must do a good turn to one's friends when one can.

And at last he gave up catching even the flies; for he made acquaintance with one by accident, and found him a very merry little fellow. And this was the way it happened; and it is all quite true.

He was basking at the top of the water one hot day in July, catching duns and feeding the trout, when he saw a new sort, a dark grey little fellow with a brown head. He was a very little fellow indeed: but he made the most of himself, as people ought to do. He cocked up his head and he cocked up his wings, and he cocked up his tail, and he cocked up the two whisks at his tail-end, and, in short, he looked the cockiest little man of all little men. And so he proved to be; for instead of getting away, he hopped upon Tom's finger, and sat there as bold as nine tailors; and he cried out in the tiniest, shrillest, squeakiest little voice you ever heard.

" Much obliged to you, indeed; but I don't want it yet."

" Want what? " said Tom, quite taken aback by his impudence.

" Your leg, which you are kind enough to hold out for me to sit on. I must just go and see after my wife for a few minutes. Dear me! what a troublesome business a family is! " (though the idle little rogue did nothing at all, but left his poor wife to lay all the eggs by herself). " When I come back, I shall be glad of it, if you'll be so good as to keep it sticking out just so "; and off he flew.

Tom thought him a very cool sort of personage; and still more so, when in five minutes he came back, and said, " Ah, you were tired waiting? Well, your other leg will do as well."

And he popped himself down on Tom's knee, and began chatting away in his squeaking voice.

" So you live under the water? It's a low place. I lived there for some time; and was very shabby and dirty. But I didn't choose that that should last. So I turned respectable, and came up to the top, and put on this grey suit. It's a very business-like suit, you think, don't you? "

" Very neat and quiet indeed," said Tom.

" Yes, one must be quiet, and neat, and respectable, and all that sort of thing for a little, when one becomes a family man. But I'm tired of it, that's the truth. I've done quite enough business, I consider, in the last week, to last me my life. So I shall put on a ball-dress, and go out and be a smart man, and see the gay world, and have a dance or two. Why shouldn't one be jolly if one can? "

" And what will become of your wife? "

" Oh! she is a very plain stupid creature, and that's the truth; and thinks about nothing but eggs. If she chooses to come, why, she may; and if not, why, I go without her—and here I go."

And, as he spoke, he turned quite pale, and then quite white.

"Why, you're ill!" said Tom. But he did not answer.

"You're dead," said Tom, looking at him as he stood on his knee as white as a ghost.

"No, I ain't!" answered a little squeaking voice over his head. "This is me up here, in my ball-dress: and that's my skin. Ha, ha! you could not do such a trick as that!"

And no more Tom could, nor Houdin, nor Robin, nor Frikell, nor all the conjurors in the world. For the little rogue had jumped clean out of his own skin, and left it standing on Tom's knee, eyes, wings, legs, tails, exactly as if it had been alive.

"Ha, ha!" he said, and he jerked and skipped up and down, never stopping an instant, just as if he had St. Vitus's dance. "Ain't I a pretty fellow now?"

And so he was; for his body was white, and his tail orange, and his eyes all the colours of a peacock's tail. And what was the oddest of all, the whisks at the end of his tail had grown five times as long as they were before.

"Ah!" said he, "now I will see the gay world. My living won't cost me much, for I have no mouth, you see, and no inside; so I can never be hungry, nor have the stomach-ache neither."

No more he had. He had grown as dry and hard and empty as a quill, as such silly shallow-hearted fellows deserve to grow.

But, instead of being ashamed of his emptiness, he was quite proud of it, as a good many fine gentlemen are, and began flirting and flipping up and down, and singing:

"My wife shall dance, and I shall sing,
    So merrily pass the day;
For I hold it one of the wisest things,
    To drive dull care away."

And he danced up and down for three days and three nights, till he grew so tired, that he tumbled into the water, and floated down. But what became of him Tom never knew, and he himself never minded; for Tom heard him singing to the last, as he floated down:

" To drive dull care away-ay-ay! "

And if he did not care, why nobody else cared either.

But one day Tom had a new adventure. He was sitting on a water-lily leaf, he and his friend the dragon-fly, watching the gnats dance. The dragon-fly had eaten as many as he wanted, and was sitting quite still and sleepy, for it was very hot and bright. The gnats (who did not care the least for their poor brothers' death), danced a foot over his head quite happily, and a large black fly settled within an inch of his nose, and began washing his own face and combing his hair with his paws: but the dragon-fly never stirred, and kept on chatting to Tom about the times when he lived under the water.

Suddenly, Tom heard the strangest noise up the stream; cooing, and grunting, and whining, and squeaking, as if you had put into a bag two stock-doves, nine mice, three guinea-pigs, and a blind puppy, and left them there to settle themselves and make music.

He looked up the water, and there he saw a sight as strange as the noise; a great ball rolling over and over down the stream, seeming one moment of soft brown fur, and the next of shining glass: and yet it was not a ball; for sometimes it broke up and streamed away in pieces, and then it joined again; and all the while the noise came out of it louder and louder.

Tom asked the dragon-fly what it could be: but, of course, with his short sight, he could not even see it, though it was not ten yards away. So he took the neatest little header into the water, and started off to see for himself; and, when he came near, the ball turned out to be four or five beautiful creatures, many times larger than Tom, who were swimming about, and rolling, and diving, and twisting, and wrestling, and cuddling, and kissing, and biting, and scratching, in the most charming fashion that ever was seen. And if you don't believe me, you may go to the Zoological Gardens (for I am afraid that you won't see it nearer, unless, perhaps, you get up at five in the morning, and go down to Cordery's Moor, and watch by the great withy pollard which hangs over the backwater, where the otters breed sometimes), and then say, if otters at play in the water are not the merriest, lithest, gracefullest creatures you ever saw.

But, when the biggest of them saw Tom, she darted out from the rest, and cried in the water-language sharply enough, " Quick, children, here is something to eat, indeed! " and came at poor Tom, showing such a wicked pair of eyes, and such a set of sharp teeth in a grinning mouth, that Tom, who had thought her very handsome, said to himself, Handsome is that handsome does, and slipt in between the water-lily roots as fast as he could, and then turned round and made faces at her.

" Come out," said the wicked old otter, " or it will be worse for you."

But Tom looked at her from between two thick roots, and shook them with all his might, making horrible faces all the while, just as he used to grin through the railings at the old women, when he lived before. It was not quite well-bred, no doubt; but you know, Tom had not finished his education yet.

" Come away, children," said the otter in disgust, " it is not worth eating, after all. It is only a nasty eft, which nothing eats, not even those vulgar pike in the pond."

" I am not an eft! " said Tom; " efts have tails."

" You are an eft," said the otter, very positively; " I see your two hands quite plain, and I know you have a tail."

" I tell you I have not," said Tom. " Look here! " and he turned his pretty little self quite round; and, sure enough, he had no more tail than you.

The otter might have got out of it by saying that Tom was a frog: but, like a great many other people, when she had once said a thing, she stood to it, right or wrong; so she answered:

" I say you are an eft, and therefore you are, and not fit food for gentlefolk like me and my children. You may stay there till the salmon eat you " (she knew the salmon would not, but she wanted to frighten poor Tom). " Ha! ha! they will eat you, and we will eat them "; and the otter laughed such a wicked cruel laugh—as you may hear them do sometimes; and the first time that you hear it you will probably think it is bogies.

" What are salmon? " asked Tom.

" Fish, you eft, great fish, nice fish to eat. They are the lords of the fish, and we are the lords of the salmon "; and she laughed again. " We hunt them up and down the pools, and drive them up into a corner, the silly things; they are so proud, and bully the little trout, and the minnows, till they see us coming, and then they are so meek all at once; and we catch them, but we disdain to eat them all; we just bite out their soft throats and suck their sweet juice—Oh, so good! "—(and she licked her wicked lips)—" and then throw them away, and go and catch another. They are coming soon, children, coming soon; I can smell the rain coming up off the sea, and then hurrah for a fresh, and salmon, and plenty of eating all day long."

And the otter grew so proud that she turned head over heels twice, and then stood upright half out of the water, grinning like a Cheshire cat.

" And where do they come from? " asked Tom, who kept himself very close, for he was considerably frightened.

" Out of the sea, eft, the great wide sea, where they might stay and be safe if they liked. But out of the sea the silly things come, into the great river down below, and we come up to watch for them; and when they go down again we go down and follow them. And there we fish for the bass and the pollock, and have jolly days along the shore, and toss the roll in the breakers, and sleep snug in the warm dry drags. Ah, that is a merry life too, children, if it were not for those horrid men."

" What are men? " asked Tom; but somehow he seemed to know before he asked.

" Two-legged things, eft: and, now I come to look at you, they are actually something like you, if you had not a tail " (she was determined that Tom should have a tail), " only a great deal bigger, worse luck for us; and they catch the fish with hooks and lines, which get into our feet sometimes, and set pots along the rocks to catch lobsters. They speared my poor dear husband as he went out to find something for me to eat. I was laid up among the crags then, and we were very low in the world, for the sea was so rough that no fish would come in shore. But they speared him, poor fellow, and I saw them carrying him away upon a pole. Ah, he lost his life for your sakes, my children, poor dear obedient creature that he was."

And the otter grew so sentimental (for otters can be very sentimental when they choose, like a good many people who are both cruel and greedy, and no good to anybody at all) that she sailed solemnly away down the burn, and Tom saw her no more for that time. And lucky it was for her that she did so; for no sooner was she gone, than down the bank came seven little rough terrier dogs, snuffing and yapping, and grubbing and splashing, in full cry after the otter. Tom hid among the water-lilies till they were gone; for he could not guess that they were the water fairies come to help him.

But *He* could not help thinking of what the otter had said about the great river and the broad sea. And, as he thought, he longed to go and see them. He could not tell why; but the more he thought, the more he grew discontented with the narrow little stream in which he lived, and all his companions there; and wanted to get out into the wide wide world, and enjoy all the wonderful sights of which he was sure it was full.

And once he set off to go down the stream. But the stream was very low; and when he came to the shallows he could not keep under water, for there was no water left to keep under. So the sun burnt his back and made him sick; and he went back again and lay quiet in the pool for a whole week more.

And then, on the evening of a very hot day, he saw a sight.

He had been very stupid all day, and so had the trout; for they would not move an inch to take a fly, though there were thousands on the water, but lay dozing at the bottom under the shade of the stones; and Tom lay dozing too, and was glad to cuddle their smooth cool sides, for the water was quite warm and unpleasant.

But toward evening it grew suddenly dark, and Tom looked up and saw a blanket of black clouds lying right across the valley above his head, resting on the crags right and left. He felt not quite frightened, but very still; for everything was still. There was not a whisper of wind, nor a chirp of a bird to be heard; and next a few great drops of rain fell plop into the water, and one hit Tom on the nose and made him pop his head down quickly enough.

And then the thunder roared, and the lightning flashed, and leapt across Vendale and back again, from cloud to cloud, and cliff to cliff, till the very rocks in the stream seemed to shake; and Tom looked up at it through the water, and thought it the finest thing he ever saw in his life.

But out of the water he dared not put his head; for the rain came down by bucketsful, and the hail hammered like shot on the stream, and churned it into foam; and soon the stream rose, and rushed down, higher and higher, and fouler and fouler, full of beetles, and sticks, and straws, and worms, and addle-eggs, and wood-lice, and leeches, and odds and ends, and omniumgatherums, and this, that, and the other, enough to fill nine museums.

Tom could hardly stand against the stream, and hid behind a rock. But the trout did not; for out they rushed from among the stones, and began gobbling the beetles and leeches in the most greedy and quarrelsome way, and swimming about with great worms hanging out of their mouths, tugging and kicking to get them away from each other.

And now, by the flashes of the lightning, Tom saw a new sight—all the bottom of the stream alive with great eels, turning and twisting along, all down stream and away. They had been hiding for weeks past in the cracks of the rocks, and in burrows in the mud; and Tom had hardly ever seen them, except now and then at night: but now they were all out, and went hurrying past him so fiercely and wildly that he was quite frightened. And as they hurried past he could hear them say to each other, " We must run, we must run. What a jolly thunder-storm! Down to the sea, down to the sea! "

And then the otter came by with all her brood, twining and sweeping along as fast as the eels themselves; and she spied Tom as she came by, and said:

" Now is your time, eft, if you want to see the world. Come along, children, never mind those nasty eels: we shall breakfast on salmon to-morrow. Down to the sea, down to the sea! "

Then came a flash brighter than all the rest, and by the light of it—in the thousandth part of a second they were gone again—but he had seen them, he was certain of it— three beautiful little white girls, with their arms twined round each other's necks, floating down the torrent, as they sang, " Down to the sea, down to the sea! "

" Oh stay! Wait for me! " cried Tom; but they were gone: yet he could hear their voices clear and sweet through the roar of thunder and water and wind, singing as they died away, " Down to the sea! "

" Down to the sea? " said Tom; " everything is going to the sea, and I will go too. Good-bye, trout." But the trout were so busy gobbling worms that they never turned to answer him; so that Tom was spared the pain of bidding them farewell.

And now, down the rushing stream, guided by the bright flashes of the storm; past tall birch-fringed rocks, which shone out one moment as clear as day, and the next were dark as night; past dark hovers under swirling banks, from which great trout rushed out on Tom, thinking him to be good to eat, and turned back sulkily, for the fairies sent them home again with a tremendous scolding, for daring to meddle with a water baby; on through narrow strids and roaring cataracts, where Tom was deafened and blinded for a moment by the rushing waters; along deep reaches, where the white water-lilies tossed and flapped beneath the wind and hail; past sleeping villages; under

Jean Cruikshanks.

dark bridge-arches, and away and away to the sea. And Tom could not stop, and did not care to stop; he would see the great world below, and the salmon, and the breakers, and the wide, wide sea.

And when the daylight came, Tom found himself out in the salmon river.

And what sort of a river was it? Was it like an Irish stream, winding through the brown bogs, where the wild ducks squatter up from among the white water-lilies, and the curlews flit to and fro, crying " Tullie-wheep, mind your sheep"; and Dennis tells you strange stories of the Peishta-more, the great bogy-snake which lies in the black peat pools, among the old pine steams, and puts his head out at night to snap at the cattle as they come down to drink?— But you must not believe all that Dennis tells you, mind; for if you ask him:

" Is there a salmon here, do you think, Dennis? "

" Is it salmon, thin, your honour manes? Salmon? Cart-loads it is of thim, thin, an' ridgmens, shouldthering ache other out of water, av' ye'd but the luck to see thim."

Then you fish the pool all over, and never get a rise.

" But there can't be a salmon here, Dennis! and, if you'll but think, if one had come up last tide, he'd be gone to the higher pools by now."

" Shure thin, and your honour's the thrue fisherman, and understands it all like a book. Why, ye spake as if ye'd known the wather a thousand years! As I said, how could there be a fish here at all, just now? "

" But you said just now they were shouldering each other out of water? "

And then Dennis will look up at you with his handsome, sly, soft, sleepy, good-natured, untrustable, Irish grey eye, and answer with the prettiest smile:

" Shure, and didn't I think your honour would like a pleasant answer? "

So you must not trust Dennis, because he is in the habit of giving pleasant answers: but, instead of being angry with him, you must remember that he is a poor Paddy, and knows no better; so you must just burst out laughing; and then he will burst out laughing too, and slave for you, and trot about after you, and show you good sport if he can—for he is an affectionate fellow, and as fond of sport as you are—and if he can't, tell you fibs instead, a hundred an hour; and wonder all the while why poor ould Ireland does not prosper like England and Scotland, and some other places, where folk have taken up a ridiculous fancy that honesty is the best policy.

Or was it like a Welsh salmon river, which is remarkable chiefly (at least, till this last year) for containing no salmon, as they have been all poached out by the enlightened peasantry, to prevent the Cythrawl Sassenach (which means you, my little dear, your kith and kin, and signifies much the same as the Chinese Fan Quei) from coming bothering into Wales, with good tackle, and ready money, and civilization, and common honesty, and other like things of which the Cymry stand in no need whatsoever?

Or was it such a salmon stream as I trust you will see among the Hampshire water-meadows before your hairs are grey, under the wise new fishing laws?—when Winchester apprentices shall covenant, as they did three hundred years ago, not to be made to eat salmon more than three days a week; and fresh-run fish shall be as plentiful under Salisbury spire as they are in Hollyhole at Christchurch; in the good time coming, when folks shall see that, of all Heaven's gifts of food, the one to be protected most carefully is that worthy gentleman salmon, who is generous enough to go down to the sea weighing five ounces, and to come back next year weighing five pounds, without having cost the soil or the State one farthing?

Or was it like a Scotch stream, such as Arthur Clough drew in his *Bothie*:

> Where over a ledge of granite
> Into a granite bason the amber torrent descended. . . .
> Beautiful there for the colour derived from green rocks under;
> Beautiful most of all, where beads of foam uprising

Mingle their clouds of white with the delicate hue of the
    stillness. . . .
Cliff over cliff for its sides, with rowan and pendant birch
    boughs. . . .

Ah, my little man, when you are a big man, and fish
such a stream as that, you will hardly care, I think, whether
she be roaring down in full spate, like coffee covered with
scald cream, while the fish are swirling at your fly as an
oar-blade swirls in a boat-race, or flashing up the cataract
like silver arrows, out of the fiercest of the foam; or whether
the fall be dwindled to a single thread, and the shingle
below be as white and dusty as a turnpike road, while the
salmon huddle together in one dark cloud in the clear
amber pool, sleeping away their time till the rain creeps
back again off the sea. You will not care much, if you
have eyes and brains; for you will lay down your rod
contentedly, and drink in at your eyes the beauty of that
glorious place; and listen to the water-ouzel piping on the
stones, and watch the yellow roes come down to drink, and
look up at you with their great soft trustful eyes, as much
as to say, " You could not have the heart to shoot at us? "
And then, if you have sense, you will turn and talk to the
great giant of a gilly who lies basking on the stone beside
you. He will tell you no fibs, my little man; for he is a
Scotchman, and fears God, and not the priest; and, as
you talk with him, you will be surprised more and more
at his knowledge, his sense, his humour, his courtesy; and
you will find out—unless you have found it out before—
that a man may learn from his Bible to be a more thorough
gentleman than if he had been brought up in all the
drawing-rooms in London.

No. It was none of these, the salmon stream at Harthover. It was such a stream as you see in dear old Bewick;
Bewick, who was born and bred upon them. A full
hundred yards broad it was, sliding on from broad pool to
broad shallow, and broad shallow to broad pool, over
great fields of shingle, under oak and ash coverts, past low
cliffs of sandstone, past green meadows, and fair parks,

and a great house of grey stone, and brown moors above, and here and there against the sky the smoking chimney of a colliery. You must look at Bewick to see just what it was like, for he has drawn it a hundred times with the care and the love of a true north countryman; and, even if you do not care about the salmon river, you ought, like all good boys, to know your Bewick.

At least, so old Sir John used to say, and very sensibly he put it too, as he was wont to do:

" If they want to describe a finished young gentleman in France, I hear, they say of him, ' Il sait son Rabelais.' But if I want to describe one in England, I say, ' He knows his Bewick." And I think that is the higher compliment."

But Tom thought nothing about what the river was like. All his fancy was, to get down to the wide wide sea.

And after a while he came to a place where the river spread out into broad still shallow reaches, so wide that little Tom, as he put his head out of the water, could hardly see across.

And there he stopped. He got a little frightened. " This must be the sea," he thought. " What a wide place it is. If I go on into it I shall surely lose my way, or some strange thing will bite me. I will stop here and look out for the otter, or the eels, or someone to tell me where I shall go."

So he went back a little way, and crept into a crack of the rock, just where the river opened out into the wide shallows, and watched for someone to tell him his way: but the otter and the eels were gone on miles and miles down the stream.

There he waited, and slept too, for he was quite tired with his night's journey: and, when he woke, the stream was clearing to a beautiful amber hue, though it was still very high. And after a while he saw a sight which made him jump up; for he knew in a moment it was one of the things which he had come to look for.

Such a fish! ten times as big as the biggest trout, and a hundred times as big as Tom, sculling up the stream past him, as easily as Tom had sculled down.

Such a fish! shining silver from head to tail, and here and there a crimson dot; with a grand hooked nose, and grand curling lip, and a grand bright eye, looking round him as proudly as a king, and surveying the water right and left as if it all belonged to him. Surely he must be the salmon, the king of all the fish.

Tom was so frightened that he longed to creep into a hole; but he need not have been; for salmon are all true gentlemen, and, like true gentlemen, they look noble and proud enough, and yet, like true gentlemen, they never harm or quarrel with any one, but go about their own business, and leave rude fellows to themselves.

The salmon looked him full in the face, and then went on without minding him, with a swish or two of his tail which made the stream boil again. And in a few minutes came another, and then four or five, and so on; and all passed Tom, rushing and plunging up the cataract with strong strokes of their silver tails, now and then leaping clean out of water and up over a rock, shining gloriously for a moment in the bright sun; while Tom was so delighted that he could have watched them all day long.

And at last one came up bigger than all the rest; but he came slowly, and stopped, and looked back, and seemed very anxious and busy. And Tom saw that he was helping another salmon, an especially handsome one, who had not a single spot upon it, but was clothed in pure silver from nose to tail.

" My dear," said the great fish to his companion, " you really look dreadfully tired, and you must not over-exert yourself at first. Do rest yourself behind this rock; " and he shoved her gently with his nose, to the rock where Tom sat.

You must know that this was the salmon's wife. For salmon, like other true gentlemen, always choose their lady, and love her, and are true to her, and take care of her, and work for her, and fight for her, as every true gentleman ought; and are not like vulgar chub and roach and pike, who have no high feelings, and take no care of their wives.

Then he saw Tom, and looked at him very fiercely one moment, as if he was going to bite him.

" What do you want here? " he said, very fiercely.

" Oh, don't hurt me! " cried Tom. " I only want to look at you; you are so handsome."

" Ah? " said the salmon, very stately but very civilly. " I really beg your pardon; I see what you are, my little dear. I have met one or two creatures like you before, and found them very agreeable and well-behaved. Indeed, one of them showed me a great kindness lately, which I hope to be able to repay. I hope we shall not be in your way here. As soon as this lady is rested, we shall proceed on our journey."

What a well-bred old salmon he was!

" So you have seen things like me before? " asked Tom.

" Several times, my dear. Indeed, it was only last night that one at the river's mouth came and warned me and my wife of some new stake-nets which had got into the stream, I cannot tell how, since last winter, and showed us the way round them, in the most charmingly obliging way."

" So there are babies in the sea? " cried Tom, and clapped his little hands. " Then I shall have someone to play with there? How delightful! "

" Were there no babies up this stream? " asked the lady salmon.

" No; and I grew so lonely. I thought I saw three last night: but they were gone in an instant, down to the sea. So I went too; for I had nothing to play with but caddises and dragon-flies and trout."

" Ugh! " cried the lady, " what low company! "

" My dear, if he has been in low company, he has certainly not learnt their low manners," said the salmon.

" No, indeed, poor little dear: but how sad for him to live among such people as caddises, who have actually six legs, the nasty things; and dragon-flies, too! why they are not even good to eat; for I tried them once, and they are all hard and empty; and, as for trout, every one knows what they are." Whereon she curled up her lip, and looked dreadfully scornful, while her husband curled up his too, till he looked as proud as Alcibiades.

" Why do you dislike the trout so? " asked Tom.

" My dear, we do not even mention them, if we can help it; for I am sorry to say they are relations of ours who do us no credit. A great many years ago they were just like us; but they were so lazy, and cowardly, and greedy, that instead of going down to the sea every year to see the world and grow strong and fat, they chose to stay and poke about in the little streams and eat worms and grubs: and they are very properly punished for it; for they have grown ugly and brown and spotted and small; and are actually so degraded in their tastes, that they will eat our children."

" And then they pretend to scrape acquaintance with us again," said the lady. " Why, I have actually known one of them propose to a lady salmon, the little impudent little creature."

" I should hope," said the gentleman, " that there are very few ladies of our race who would degrade themselves by listening to such a creature for an instant. If I saw such a thing happen, I should consider it my duty to put them both to death upon the spot." So the old salmon said, like an old blue-blooded hidalgo of Spain: and what is more, he would have done it too. For you must know, no enemies are so bitter against each other as those who are of the same race; and a salmon looks on a trout, as some great folks look on some little folks, as something just too much like himself to be tolerated.

CHAPTER FOUR

Sweet is the lore which Nature brings;
Our meddling intellect
Mis-shapes the beauteous forms of things
We murder to dissect.

Enough of science and of art:
Close up these barren leaves;
Come forth, and bring with you a heart
That watches and receives.

WORDSWORTH.

So the salmon went up, after Tom had warned them of the wicked old otter; and Tom went down, but slowly and cautiously, coasting along the shore. He was many days about it, for it was many miles down to the sea; and perhaps he would never have found his way, if the fairies had not guided him, without his seeing their fair faces, or feeling their gentle hands.

And, as he went, he had a very strange adventure. It was a clear still September night, and the moon shone so brightly down through the water, that he could not sleep, though he shut his eyes as tight as possible. So at last he came up to the top, and sat upon a little point of rock, and looked up at the broad yellow moon, and wondered what she was, and thought that she looked at him. And he watched the moonlight on the rippling river, and the black heads of the firs, and the silver-frosted lawns, and listened to the owl's hoot, and the snipe's bleat, and the fox's bark, and the otter's laugh; and smelt the soft perfume of the birches, and the wafts of heather honey off the grouse-moor far above; and felt very happy, though he could not well tell why. You, of course, would have been very cold sitting there on a September night, without the least bit of clothes on your wet back; but Tom was a water baby, and therefore felt cold no more than a fish.

Suddenly, he saw a beautiful sight. A bright red light moved along the river side, and threw down into the water a long tap-root of flame. Tom, curious little rogue that he was, must needs go and see what it was; so he swam to the shore, and met the light as it stopped over a shallow run at the edge of a low rock.

And there, underneath the light, lay five or six great salmon, looking up at the flame with their great goggle eyes, and wagging their tails, as if they were very much pleased at it.

Tom came to the top, to look at this wonderful light nearer, and made a splash.

And he heard a voice say:

"There was a fish rose."

He did not know what the words meant: but he seemed to know the sound of them, and to know the voice which spoke them; and he saw on the bank three great two-legged creatures, one of whom held the light, flaring and spluttering, and another a long pole. And he knew that they were men, and was frightened, and crept into a hole in the rock, from which he could see what went on.

The man with the torch bent down over the water, and looked earnestly in; and then he said:

"Take that muckle fellow, lad; he's ower fifteen punds; and haud your hand steady."

Tom felt that there was some danger coming, and longed to warn the foolish salmon, who kept staring up at the light as if he was bewitched. But, before he could make up his mind, down came the pole through the water; there was a fearful splash and struggle, and Tom saw that the poor salmon was speared right through, and was lifted out of the water.

And then, from behind, there sprung on these three men three other men; and there was shouts, and blows, and words which Tom recollected to have heard before; and he shuddered and turned sick at them now, for he felt somehow that they were strange, and ugly, and wrong, and horrible. And it all began to come back to him. They were men; and they were fighting; savage, desperate, up-and-down fighting, such as Tom had seen too many times before.

And he stopped his little ears, and longed to swim away; and was very glad that he was a water baby, and had nothing to do any more with horrid dirty men, with foul clothes on their backs, and foul words on their lips: but he dared not stir out of his hole; while the rock shook over his head with the trampling and struggling of the keepers and the poachers.

All of a sudden there was a tremendous splash, and a frightful flash, and a hissing, and all was still.

For into the water, close to Tom, fell one of the men; he who held the light in his hand. Into the swift river he sank, and rolled over and over in the current. Tom heard the men above run along, seemingly looking for him: but he drifted down into the deep hole below, and there lay quite still, and they could not find him.

Tom waited a long time, till all was quiet; and then he peeped out, and saw the man lying. At last he screwed up his courage, and swam down to him. "Perhaps," he thought, "the water has made him fall asleep, as it did me."

Then he went nearer. He grew more and more curious, he could not tell why. He must go and look at him. He would go very quietly, of course; so he swam round and round him, closer and closer; and, as he did not stir, at last he came quite close and looked him in the face.

The moon shone so bright that Tom could see every feature; and, as he saw, he recollected, bit by bit. It was his old master, Grimes.

Tom turned tail, and swam away as fast as he could.

"Oh dear me!" he thought, "now he will turn into a water baby. What a nasty troublesome one he will be! And perhaps he will find me out, and beat me again."

So he went up the river again a little way, and lay there the rest of the night under an alder root; but, when morning came, he longed to go down again to the big pool, and see whether Mr. Grimes had turned into a water baby yet.

Jean Cruickshanks.

So he went very carefully, peeping round all the rocks, and hiding under all the roots. Mr. Grimes lay there still; he had not turned into a water baby. In the afternoon Tom went back again. He could not rest till he had found out what had become of Mr. Grimes. But this time Mr Grimes was gone; and Tom made up his mind that he was turned into a water baby.

He might have made himself easy, poor little man; Mr. Grimes did not turn into a water baby, or anything like one at all. But he did not make himself easy; and a long time he was fearful lest he should meet Grimes suddenly in some deep pool. He could not know that the fairies had carried him away, and put him, where they put everything which falls into the water, exactly where it ought to be. But, do you know, what had happened to Mr. Grimes had such an effect on him, that he never poached salmon any more. And it is quite certain that, when a man becomes a confirmed poacher, the only way to cure him is to put him under water for twenty-four hours, like Grimes. So, when you grow to be a big man, do you behave as all honest fellows should; and never touch a fish or a head of game which belongs to another man without his express leave; and then people will call you a gentleman, and treat you like one; and perhaps give you good sport: instead of hitting you into the river, or calling you a poaching snob.

Then Tom went on down, for he was afraid of staying near Grimes; and as he went, all the vale looked sad. The red and yellow leaves showered down into the river; the flies and beetles were all dead and gone; the chill autumn fog lay low upon the hills, and sometimes spread itself so thickly on the river, that he could not see his way. But he felt his way instead, following the flow of the stream, day after day, past great bridges, past boats and barges, past the great town, with its wharfs, and mills, and tall smoking chimneys, and ships which rode at anchor in the stream; and now and then he ran against their hawsers, and wondered what they were, and peeped out, and saw the sailors lounging on board, smoking their pipes, and ducked under again, for he was terribly afraid of being caught by man and turned into a chimney-sweep once more. He did not know that the fairies were close to him always, shutting the sailors' eyes lest they should see him, and turning him aside from mill-races, and sewer-mouths, and all foul and dangerous things. Poor little fellow, it was a dreary journey for him; and more than once he longed to be back in Vendale, playing with the trout in the bright summer sun. But it could not be. What has been once can never come over again. And people can be little babies, even water babies, only once in their lives.

Besides, people who make up their minds to go and see the world, as Tom did, must needs find it a weary journey. Lucky for them if they do not lose heart and stop half way, instead of going on bravely to the end as Tom did. For then they will remain neither boys nor men, neither fish, flesh, nor good red herring; having learnt a great deal too much, and yet not enough; and sown their wild oats, without having the advantage of reaping them.

But Tom was always a brave, determined little English bulldog, who never knew when he was beaten; and on and on he held, till he saw a long way off the red buoy through the fog. And then he found, to his surprise, the stream turned round, and running up inland.

It was the tide, of course: but Tom knew nothing of the tide. He only knew that in a minute more the water, which had been fresh, turned salt all round him. And then there came a change over him. He felt as strong, and light, and fresh, as if his veins had run champagne; and gave, he did not know why, three skips out of the water, a yard high, and head over heels, just as the salmon do when they first touch the noble rich salt water, which, as some wise men tell us, is the mother of all living things.

He did not care now for the tide being against him. The red buoy was in sight, dancing in the open sea; and to the buoy he would go, and to it he went. He passed great shoals of bass and mullet, leaping and rushing in after the shrimps, but he never heeded them, or they him; and once he passed a great black shining seal, who was coming in after the mullet. The seal put his head and shoulders out of water, and stared at him, looking exactly like a fat old greasy negro with a grey pate. And Tom, instead of being frightened, said, " How d'ye do, sir; what a beautiful place the sea is! " And the old seal, instead of trying to bite him, looked at him with his soft sleepy winking eyes, and said, " Good tide to you, my little man; are you looking for your brothers and sisters? I passed them all at play outside."

" Oh, then," said Tom, " I shall have playfellows at last! " and he swam on to the buoy, and got upon it (for he was quite out of breath) and sat there, and looked round for water babies: but there were none to be seen.

The sea-breeze came in freshly with the tide, and blew the fog away; and the little waves danced for joy around the buoy, and the old buoy danced with them. The shadows of the clouds ran races over the bright blue bay, and yet never caught each other up; and the breakers plunged merrily upon the wide white sands, and jumped up over the rocks, to see what the green fields inside were like, and tumbled down and broke themselves all to pieces, and never minded it a bit, but mended themselves and jumped up again. And the terns hovered over Tom like huge white dragon-flies with black heads, and the gulls laughed like girls at play, and the sea-pies, with their red bills and legs, flew to and fro from shore to shore, and whistled sweet and wild. And Tom looked and looked, and listened; and he would have been very happy, if he could only have seen the water babies. Then, when the tide turned, he left the buoy, and swam round and round in search of them: but in vain. Sometimes he thought he heard them laughing: but it was only the laughter of the ripples. And sometimes he thought he saw them at the bottom: but it was only white and pink shells. And once he was sure he had found one, for he saw two bright eyes peeping out of the sand. So he dived down, and began scraping the sand away, and cried, " Don't hide; I do want someone to play with so much! " And out jumped a great turbot, with his ugly eyes and mouth all awry, and

flopped away along the bottom, knocking poor Tom over. And he sat down at the bottom of the sea, and cried salt tears from sheer disappointment.

To have come all this way, and faced so many dangers, and yet to find no water babies! How hard! Well, it did seem hard: but people, even little babies, cannot have all they want without waiting for it, and working for it too, my little man, as you will find out some day.

And Tom sat upon the buoy long days, long weeks, looking out to sea, and wondering when the water babies would come back; and yet they never came.

Then he began to ask all the strange things which came in out of the sea if they had seen any; and some said "Yes," and some said nothing at all.

He asked the bass and the pollock; but they were so greedy after the shrimps that they did not care to answer him a word.

Then there came in a whole fleet of purple sea-snails, floating along each on a sponge full of foam, and Tom said, "Where do you come from, you pretty creatures? and have you seen the water babies?"

And the sea-snails answered, "Whence we come we know not; and whither we are going, who can tell? We float out our little life in the mid ocean, with the warm sunshine above our heads, and the warm gulf stream below; and that is enough for us. Yes, perhaps we have seen the water babies. We have seen many strange things as we sailed along." And they floated away, the happy stupid things, and all went ashore upon the sands.

Then there came in a great lazy sunfish, as big as a fat pig cut in half; and he seemed to have been cut in half too, and squeezed in a clothes-press till he was flat; but to all his big body and big fins he had only a little rabbit's mouth, no bigger than Tom's; and, when Tom questioned him, he answered in a little squeaky, feeble voice:

"I'm sure I don't know, I've lost my way. I meant to go to the Chesapeake, and I'm afraid I've got wrong, somehow. Dear me! it was all by following that pleasant warm water. I'm sure I've lost my way."

And, when Tom asked him again, he could only answer,
" I've lost my way. Don't talk to me, I want to think."

But, like a good many other people, the more he tried
to think the less he could think; and Tom saw him blun-
dering about all day, till the coast-guardsmen saw his big
fin above the water, and rowed out, and struck a boat-hook
into him, and took him away. They took him up to the
town and showed him for a penny a head, and made a good
day's work of it. But of course Tom did not know that.

Then there came by a shoal of porpoises, rolling as they
went—papas, and mammas, and little children—and all
quite smooth and shiny, because the fairies french-polish
them every morning; and they sighed so softly as they
came by, that Tom took courage to speak to them: but all
they answered was, " Hush, hush, hush "; for that was all
they had learnt to say.

And then there came a shoal of basking sharks, some of
them as long as a boat, and Tom was frightened at them.
But they were very lazy, good-natured fellows, not greedy
tyrants, like white sharks and blue sharks and ground
sharks and hammer-heads, who eat men, or sawfish and
threshers and ice-sharks, who hunt the poor old whales.
They came and rubbed their great sides against the buoy,
and lay basking in the sun with their backfins out of water;
and winked at Tom: but he never could get them to speak.
They had eaten so many herrings that they were quite
stupid; and Tom was glad when a collier brig came by,
and frightened them all away; for they did smell most
horribly, certainly, and he had to hold his nose tight as
long as they were there.

And then there came by a beautiful creature, like
a ribbon of pure silver with a sharp head and very long
teeth: but seemed very sick and sad. Sometimes it rolled
helpless on its side; and then it dashed away glittering like
white fire; and then it lay sick again and motionless.

" Where do you come from? " asked Tom. " And why
are you so sick and sad? "

" I come from the warm Carolinas, and the sand-banks
fringed with pines; where the great owl-rays leap and flap,

like giant bats, upon the tide. But I wandered north and north, upon the treacherous warm gulf stream, till I met with the cold icebergs, afloat in the mid ocean. So I got tangled among the icebergs, and chilled with their frozen breath. But the water babies helped me from among them, and set me free again. And now I am mending every day; but I am very sick and sad; and perhaps I shall never get home again to play with the owl-rays any more."

"Oh!" cried Tom. "And you have seen water babies? Have you seen any near here?"

"Yes; they helped me again last night, or I should have been eaten by a great black porpoise."

How vexatious! The water babies close to him, and yet he could not find one.

And then he left the buoy, and used to go along the sands and round the rocks, and come out in the night—like the forsaken Merman in Mr. Arnold's beautiful, beautiful poem, which you must learn by heart some day—and sit upon a point of rock, among the shining seaweeds, in the low October tides, and cry and call for the water babies: but he never heard a voice call in return. And, at last, with his fretting and crying, he grew quite lean and thin.

But one day among the rocks he found a playfellow. It was not a water baby, alas! but it was a lobster; and a very distinguished lobster he was; for he had live barnacles on his claws, which is a great mark of distinction in lobster-dom, and no more to be bought for money than a good conscience or the Victoria Cross.

Tom had never seen a lobster before; and he was mightily taken with this one; for he thought him the most curious, odd, ridiculous creature he had ever seen; and there he was not far wrong; for all the ingenious men, and all the scientific men, and all the fanciful men, in the world, with all the old German bogy-painters into the bargain, could never invent, if all their wits were boiled into one, anything so curious, and so ridiculous, as a lobster.

He had one claw knobbed and the other jagged; and

Tom delighted in watching him hold on to the seaweed with his knobbed claw, while he cut up salads with his jagged one, and then put them in his mouth, after smelling at them, like a monkey. And always the little barnacles threw out their casting nets and swept the water, and came in for their share of whatever there was for dinner.

But Tom was most astonished to see how he fired himself off—snap! like the leap-frogs which you make out of a goose's breast-bone. Certainly he took the most wonderful shots, and backwards, too. For, if he wanted to go into a narrow crack ten yards off, what do you think he did? If he had gone in head foremost, of course he could not have turned round. So he used to turn his tail to it, and lay his long horns, which carry his sixth sense in their tips (and nobody knows what that sixth sense is), straight down his back to guide him, and twist his eyes back till they almost came out of their sockets, and then make ready, present, fire, sap!—and away he went, pop into the hole; and peeped out and twiddled his whiskers, as much as to say, " You couldn't do that."

Tom asked him about water babies. " Yes," he said. He had seen them often. But he did not think much of them. They were meddlesome little creatures, that went about helping fish and shells which got into scrapes. Well, for his part, he should be ashamed to be helped by little soft creatures that had not even a shell on their backs. He had lived quite long enough in the world to take care of himself.

He was a conceited fellow, the old lobster, and not very civil to Tom; and you will hear how he had to alter his mind before he was done, as conceited people generally have. But he was so funny, and Tom so lonely, that he could not quarrel with him; and they used to sit in holes in the rocks, and chat for hours.

And about this time there happened to Tom a very strange and important adventure—so important, indeed, that he was very near never finding the water babies at all; and I am sure you would have been sorry for that.

I hope that you have not forgotten the little white lady

all this while. At least, here she comes, looking like a clean white good little darling, as she always was, and always will be. For it befél in the pleasant short December days, when the wind always blows from the south-west, till Old Father Christmas comes and spreads the great white table-cloth, ready for little boys and girls to give the birds their Christmas dinner of crumbs—it befel (to go on) in the pleasant December days, that Sir John was so busy hunting that nobody at home could get a word out of him. Four days a week he hunted, and very good sport he had; and the other two he went to the bench and the board of guardians, and very good justice he did; and, when he got home in time, he dined at five; for he hated this absurd new fashion of dining at eight in the hunting season, which forces a man to make interest with the footman for cold beef and beer as soon as he comes in, and so spoil his appetite, and then sleep in an arm-chair in his bedroom, all stiff and tired, for two or three hours before he can get his dinner like a gentleman. And do you be like Sir John, my dear little man, when you are your own master; and, if you want either to read hard or ride hard, stick to the good old Cambridge hours of breakfast at eight and dinner at five, by which you may get two days' work out of one. But, of course, if you find a fox at three in the afternoon and run him till dark, and leave off twenty miles from home, why you must wait for your dinner till you can get it, as better men than you have done. Only see that, if you go hungry, your horse does not: but give him his warm gruel and beer, and take him gently home, remembering that good horses don't grow on the hedge like blackberries.

It befel (to go on a second time) that Sir John, hunting all day and dining at five, fell asleep every evening, and snored so terribly that all the windows in Harthover shook, and the soot fell down the chimneys. Whereon My Lady, being no more able to get conversation out of him than a song out of a dead nightingale, determined to go off and leave him, and the doctor, and Captain Swinger the agent, to snore in concert every evening to their hearts' content. So she started for the seaside with all the children, in order to put herself and them into condition by mild applications of iodine. She might as well have stayed at home and used Parry's liquid horse-blister, for there was plenty of it in the stables; and then she would have saved her money, and saved the chance, also of making all the children ill instead of well (as hundreds are made), by taking them to some nasty smelling undrained lodging, and then wondering how they caught scarlatina and diphtheria: but people won't be wise enough to understand that till they are all dead of bad smells, and then it will be too late: besides, you see, Sir John did certainly snore very loud.

But where she went to nobody must know, for fear young ladies should begin to fancy that there are water babies there; and so hunt and howk after them (besides raising the price of lodgings), and keep them in aquariums, as the ladies at Pompeii (as you may see by the paintings) used to keep Cupids in cages. But nobody ever heard that they starved the Cupids, or let them die of dirt and neglect, as English young ladies do by the poor sea-beasts. So nobody must know where My Lady went. Letting water babies die is as bad as taking singing-birds' eggs; for, though there are thousands, ay, millions, of both of them in the world, yet there is not one too many.

Now it befel that, on the very shore, and over the very rocks, where Tom was sitting with his friend the lobster, there walked one day the little white lady, Ellie herself, and with her a very wise man indeed—Professor Ptthml-lnsprts.

His mother was a Dutchwoman, and therefore he was born at Curacao (of course you have learnt your geography and therefore know why); and his father a Pole, and therefore he was brought up at Petropaulowski (of course you have learnt your modern politics, and therefore know why): but for all that he was as thorough an Englishman as ever coveted his neighbour's goods. And his name, as I said, was Professor Ptthmllnsprts, which is a very ancient and noble Polish name.

He was, as I said, a very great naturalist, and chief professor of Necrobioneopalaeonthydrochthonanthropopithekology in the new university which the king of the Cannibal Islands had founded; and, being a member of the Acclimatization Society, he had come here to collect all the nasty things which he could find on the coast of England, and turn them loose round the Cannibal Islands, because they had not nasty things enough there to eat what they left.

But he was a very worthy kind good-natured little old gentleman; and very fond of children (for he was not the least a cannibal himself); and very good to all the world as long as it was good to him. Only one fault he had, which cock robins have likewise, as you may see if you look out of the nursery window—that, when any one else found a curious worm, he would hop round them, and peck them, and set up his tail, and bristle up his feathers, just as a cock robin would; and declare that he found the worm first; and that it was his worm: and, if not, that then it was not a worm at all.

He had met Sir John at Scarborough, or Fleetwood, or somewhere or other (if you don't care where, nobody else does), and had made acquaintance with him, and become very fond of his children. Now, Sir John knew nothing about sea-cockyolybirds, and cared less, provided the fishmonger sent him good fish for dinner; and My Lady knew as little: but she thought it proper that the children should know something. For in the stupid old times, you must understand, children were taught to know one thing, and to know it well: but in these enlightened new times they are taught to know a little about everything, and to know it all ill; which is a great deal pleasanter and easier, and therefore quite right.

So Ellie and he were walking on the rocks, and he was showing her about one in ten thousand of all the beautiful and curious things which are to be seen there. But little Ellie was not satisfied with them at all. She liked much better to play with live children, or even with dolls, which she could pretend were alive; and at last she said honestly, "I don't care about all these things, because they can't play with me, or talk to me. If there were little children now in the water, as there used to be, and I could see them, I should like that."

" Children in the water, you strange little duck? " said the professor.

" Yes," said Ellie. " I know there used to be children in the water, and mermaids too, and mermen. I saw them all in a picture at home, of a beautiful lady sailing in a car drawn by dolphins, and babies flying round her, and one sitting in her lap; and the mermaids swimming and playing, and the mermen trumpeting on conch-shells; and it is called ' The Triumph of Galatea '; and there is a burning mountain in the picture behind. It hangs on the great staircase, and I have looked at it ever since I was a baby, and dreamt about it a hundred times; and it is so beautiful, that it must be true."

Ah, you dear little Ellie, fresh out of heaven! when will people understand that one of the deepest and wisest speeches which can come out of a human mouth is that— " It is so beautiful that it must be true."

Not till they give up believing that Mr. John Locke (good man and honest though he was) was the wisest man that ever lived on earth: and recollect that a wiser man than he lived long before him; and that his name was Plato the son of Ariston.

But the professor was not in the least of that opinion. He held very strange theories about a good many things. He had even got up once at the British Association, and declared that apes had hippopotamus majors in their brains just as men have. Which was a shocking thing to say; for, if it were so, what would become of the faith, hope, and charity of immortal millions? You may think that there are other more important differences between you and an ape, such as being able to speak, and make machines, and know right from wrong, and say your prayers, and other little matters of that kind: but that is a child's fancy, my dear. Nothing is to be depended on but the great hippopotamus test. If you have a hippopotamus major in your brain, you are no ape, though you had four hands, no feet, and were more apish than the apes of all aperies. But, if a hippopotamus major is discovered in one single ape's brain, nothing will save your great-great-great-great-great-great, great-great-great-great-great-greater-greatest-grand-mother from having been an ape too. No, my dear little man; always remember that the one true, certain, final and all-important difference between you and an ape is, that you have a hippopotamus major in your brain, and it has none; and that, therefore, to discover one in its brain will be a very wrong and dangerous thing, at which every one will be very much shocked, as we may suppose they were at the professor.—Though really, after all, it don't much matter: because—as Lord Dundreary and others would put it—nobody but men have hippopotamuses in their brains; so, if a hippopotamus was discovered in an ape's brain, why it would not be one, you know, but something else.

But the professor had gone, I am sorry to say, even further than that; for he had read at the British Association at Melbourne, Australia, in the year 1999, a paper, who assured every one who found himself the better or wiser for the news, that there were not, never had been, and could not be, any rational or half-rational beings except men, anywhere, anywhen, or anyhow; that nymphs, satyrs, fauns, inui, dwarfs, trolls, elves, gnomes, fairies, brownies, nixes, wilis, kobolds, leprechaunes, cluricaunes, banshees, will-o'-the-wisps, follets, lutins, magots, goblins, afrits, marids, jinns, ghouls, peris, deevs, angels, arch-angels, imps, bogies, or worse, were nothing at all, and pure bosh and wind. And he had to get up very early in the morning to prove that, and to eat his breakfast overnight: but he did it, at least to his own satisfaction. Whereon a certain great divine, and a very clever divine was he, called him a regular Sadducee; and probably he was quite right. Whereon the professor, in return, called him a regu-lar Pharisee; and probably he was quite right too. But they did not quarrel in the least; for, when men are men of the world, hard words run off them like water off a duck's back. So the professor and the divine met at dinner that evening, and sat together on the sofa afterwards for an hour, and talked over the state of female labour on the antarctic continent (for nobody talks shop after his claret), and each vowed that the other was the best company he ever met in his life. What an advantage it is to be men of the world!

From all which you may guess that the professor was not the least of little Ellie's opinion. So he gave her a succinct compendium of his famous paper at the British Association, in a form suited for the youthful mind. But, as we have gone over his arguments against water babies once already, which is once too often, we will not repeat them here.

Now little Ellie was, I suppose, a stupid little girl; for, instead of being convinced by Professor Ptthmllnsprts' arguments, she only asked the same question over again.

" But why are there not water babies? "

I trust and hope that it was because the professor trod at that moment on the edge of a very sharp mussel, and hurt one of his corns sadly, that he answered quite sharply, forgetting that he was a scientific man, and therefore ought to have known that he couldn't know; and that he was a logician, and therefore ought to have known that he could not prove an universal negative—I say, I trust and hope it was because the mussel hurt his corn, that the professor answered quite sharply:

" Because there ain't."

Which was not even good English, my dear little boy; for, as you must know from Aunt Agitate's Arguments, the professor ought to have said, if he was so angry as to say anything of the kind—Because there are not: or are none: or are none of them; or (if he had been reading Aunt Agitate too), because they do not exist.

And he groped with his net under the weeds so violently, that, as it befel, he caught poor little Tom.

He felt the net very heavy; and lifted it out quickly, with Tom all entangled in the meshes.

" Dear me! " he cried. " What a large pink Holo-thurian; with hands, too! It must be connected with Synapta."

And he took him out.

" It has actually eyes! " he cried. " Why, it must be a Cephalopod! This is most extraordinary! "

" No, I ain't! " cried Tom, as loud as he could; for he did not like to be called bad names.

" It is a water baby! " cried Ellie; and of course it was.

" Water fiddlesticks, my dear! " said the professor; and he turned away sharply.

There was no denying it. It was a water baby: and he had said a moment ago that there were none. What was he to do?

He would have liked, of course, to have taken Tom home in a bucket. He would not have put him in spirits. Of course not. He would have kept him alive, and petted him (for he was a very kind old gentleman), and written a book about him, and given him two long names, of which the first would have said a little about Tom, and the second all about himself; for of course he would have called him Hydrotecnon Ptthmllnsprtsianum, or some other long name like that; for they are forced to call everything by long names now, because they have used up all the short ones, ever since they took to making nine species out of one. But—what would all the learned men say to him after his speech at the British Association? And what would Ellie say, after what he had just told her?

There was a wise old heathen once, who said, " Maxima debetur pueris reverentia "—The greatest reverence is due to children; that is, that grown people should never say or do anything wrong before children, lest they should set them a bad example.—Cousin Cramchild says it means, " The greatest respectfulness is expected from little boys." But he was raised in a country where little boys are not expected to be respectful, because all of them are as good as the President:—Well, every one knows his own concerns best; so perhaps they are. But poor Cousin Cramchild, to do him justice, not being of that opinion, and having a moral mission, and being no scholar to speak of, and hard up for an authority—why, it was a very great temptation for him. But some people, and I am afraid the professor was one of them, interpret that in a more strange, curious, one-sided, left-handed, topsy-turvy, inside-out, behind-before fashion, than even Cousin Cramchild; for they make it mean, that you must show your respect for children, by never confessing yourself in the wrong to them, even if you know that you are so, lest they should lose confidence in their elders.

Now, if the professor had said to Ellie, " Yes, my darling, it is a water baby, and a very wonderful thing it is; and it shows how little I know of the wonders of nature, in spite of forty years' honest labour. I was just telling you that there could be no such creatures: and, behold! here is one come to confound my conceit, and show me that Nature can do, and has done, beyond all that man's poor fancy can imagine. So, let us thank the Maker, and Inspirer, and Lord of Nature for all His wonderful and glorious works, and try and find out something about this one ":—I think that, if the professor had said that, little Ellie would have believed him more firmly, and respected him more deeply, and loved him better, than ever she had done before. But he was of a different opinion. He hesitated a moment. He longed to keep Tom, and yet he half wished he never had caught him; and, at last, he quite longed to get rid of him. So he turned away, and poked Tom with his finger, for want of anything better to do; and said carelessly, " My dear little maid, you must have dreamt of water babies last night, your head is so full of them."

Now Tom had been in the most horrible and unspeakable fright all the while; and had kept as quiet as he could, though he was called a Holothurian and Cephalopod; for it was fixed in his little head that if a man with clothes on caught him, he might put clothes on him too, and make a dirty clack chimney-sweep of him again. But when the professor poked him, it was more than he could bear; and, between fright and rage, he turned to bay as valiantly as a mouse in a corner, and bit the professor's finger till it bled.

" Oh! ah! yah! " cried he; and glad of an excuse to be rid of Tom, dropped him on to the seaweed, and thence he dived into the water, and was gone in a moment.

" But it was a water baby, and I heard it speak! " cried

Ellie. "Ah, it is gone!" And she jumped down off the rock to try and catch Tom before he slipt into the sea.

Too late! and what was worse, as she sprang down, she slipped, and fell some six feet, with her head on a sharp rock and lay quite still.

The professor picked her up, and tried to waken her, and called to her, and cried over her, for he loved her very much: but she would not waken at all. So he took her up in his arms, and carried her to her governess, and they all went home; and little Ellie was put to bed, and lay there quite still; only now and then she woke up, and called out about the water baby: but no one knew what she meant, and the professor did not tell, for he was ashamed to tell.

And, after a week, one moonlight night, the fairies came flying in at the window, and brought her such a pretty pair of wings, that she could not help putting them on; and she flew with them out of the window, and over the land, and over the sea, and up through the clouds, and nobody heard or saw anything of her for a very long while.

And this is why they say that no one has ever yet seen a water baby. For my part, I believe that the naturalists get dozens of them when they are out dredging: but they say nothing about them, and throw them overboard again, for fear of spoiling their theories. But, you see the professor was found out, as every one is in due time. A very terrible old fairy found the professor out; she felt his bumps, and cast his nativity, and took the lunars of him carefully inside and out; and so she knew what he would do as well as if she had seen it in a print book, as they say in the dear old west country; and he did it; and so he was found out beforehand, as everybody always is; and the old fairy will find out the naturalists some day, and put them in *The Times*; and then on whose side will the laugh be?

So the old fairy took him in hand very severely there and then. But she says she is always most severe with the best people, because there is most chance of curing them, and therefore they are the patients who pay her best; for she has to work on the same salary as the Emperor of

China's physicians (it is a pity that all do not), no cure, no pay.

So she took the poor professor in hand: and because he was not content with things as they are, she filled his head with things as they are not, to try if he would like them better; and because he did not choose to believe in a water baby when he saw it, she made him believe in worse things than water babies—in unicorns, firedrakes, manticoras, basilisks, amphisboenas, griffins, phoenixes, rocs, orcs, dog-headed men, three-headed dogs, three-bodied geryons, and other pleasant creatures, which folks think never existed yet, and which folks hope never will exist, though they know nothing about the matter, and never will; and these creatures so upset, terrified, flustered, aggravated, confused, astounded, horrified, and totally flabbergasted the poor professor, that the doctors said that he was out of his wits for three months; and, perhaps, they were right, as they are now and then.

So all the doctors in the county were called in, to make a report on his case; and of course every one of them flatly contradicted the other: else what use is there in being men of science? But at last the majority agreed on a report, in the true medical language, one half bad Latin, the other half worse Greek, and the rest what might have been English if they had only learnt to write it. And this is the beginning thereof:

" The subanhypaposupernal anastomoses of peritomic diacellurite in the encephalo digital region of the distinguished individual of whose symptomatic phaenomena we had the melancholy honour (subsequently to a preliminary diagnostic inspection) of making an inspectorial diagnosis, presenting the interexclusively quadrilateral and antinomian diathesis known as Bumpsterhausen's blue follicles, we proceeded "—

But what they proceeded to do my lady never knew; for she was so frightened at the long words that she ran for her life, and locked herself into her bedroom, for fear of being squashed by the words and strangled by the sentence. A boa constrictor, she said, was bad company enough: but what was a boa constrictor made of paving-stones?

"It was quite shocking! What can they think is the matter with him?" said she to the old nurse.

"That his wit's just addled; may be wi' unbelief and heathenry," quoth she.

"Then why can't they say so?"

And the heaven, and the sea, and the rocks, and the vales re-echoed—"Why indeed?" But the doctors never heard them.

So she made Sir John write to *The Times* to command the Chancellor of the Exchequer for the time being to put a tax on long words:

A light tax on words over three syllables, which are necessary evils, like rats: but like them, must be kept down judiciously.

A heavy tax on words over four syllables, as heterodoxy, spontaneity, spiritualism, spuriosity, etc.

And on words over five syllables (of which I hope no one will wish to see any examples), a totally prohibitory tax.

And a similar prohibitory tax on words derived from three or more languages at once; words derived from two languages having become so common, that there was no more hope of rooting out them than of rooting out peth-winds.

The Chancellor of the Exchequer, being a scholar and a man of sense, jumped at the notion; for he saw in it the one and only plan for abolishing Schedule D: but when he brought in his Bill, most of the Irish members, and (I am sorry to say) some of the Scotch likewise, opposed it most strongly, on the ground that in a free country no man was bound either to understand himself or to let others understand him. So the bill fell through on the first reading; and the Chancellor, being a philosopher, comforted himself with the thought, that it was not the first time that a woman had hit off a grand idea, and the men turned up their stupid noses thereat.

Now the doctors had it all their own way; and to work

they went in earnest, and they gave the poor professor divers and sundry medicines, as prescribed by the ancient and moderns, from Hippocrates to Feuchtersleben, as below, viz.:

1. Hellebore, to wit—
   Hellebore of Aeta.
   Hellebore of Galatia.
   Hellebore of Sicily.
   And all other Hellebores, after the method of the Helleborizing Helleborists of the Helleboric era. But that would not do. Bumpsterhausen's blue follicles would not stir an inch out of his encephalo digital region.
2. Trying to find out what was the matter with him; after the method of—
   Hippocrates.
   Aretaeus.
   Celsus.
   Coelius Aurelianus.
   And Galen: but they found that a great deal too much trouble, as most people have since; and so had recourse to—
3. Borage.
   Cauteries.
   Boring a hole in his head to let out fumes, which (says Gordonius) " will, without doubt, do much good." But it didn't.
   Bezoar stone.
   Diamargaritum.
   A ram's brain boiled in spice.
   Oil of wormwood.
   Water of Nile.
   Capers.
   Good wine (but there was none to be got).
   The water of a smith's forge.
   Hops.
   Ambergris.
   Mandrake pillows.
   Dormouse' fat.

Hares' ears.

Starvation.

Camphor.

Salts and Senna.

Musk.

Opium.

Strait-waistcoats.

Bullyings.

Bumpings.

Blisterings.

Bleedings.

Bucketings with cold water.

Knockings down.

Kneeling on his chest till they broke it in, etc., etc., after the medieval or monkish method: but that would not do. Bumpsterhausen's blue follicles stuck there still.

Then—

4. Coaxing.

Kissing.

Champagne and turtle.

Red herrings and soda water.

Good advice.

Gardening.

Croquet.

Musical soirées.

Aunt Sally.

Mild tobacco.

The *Saturday Review.*

A carriage with outriders, etc., etc., after the modern method. But that would not do.

And if he had but been a convict lunatic, and had shot at the Queen, killed all his creditors to avoid paying them, or indulged in any other little amiable eccentricity of that kind, they would have given him in addition—

The healthiest situation in England, on Easthampstead Plain.

Free run of Windsor Forest.

The Times every morning.

A double-barrelled gun and pointers, and leave to shoot three Wellington College boys a week (not more) in case black game were scarce.

But as he was neither mad enough nor bad enough to be allowed such luxuries, they grew desperate, and fell into bad ways, viz. :

5. Suffumigations of sulphur.

Heerwiggius his " Incomparable drink for madmen ": only they could not find out what it was.

Suffumigation of the liver of the fish * * * only they had forgotten its name, so Dr. Gray could not well procure them a specimen.

Metallic tractors.

Holloway's Ointment.

Electro-biology.

Valentine Greatrakes his Stroking Cure.

Spirit-rapping.

Holloway's Pills.

Table-turning.

Morrison's Pills.

Homoeopathy.

Parr's Life Pills.

Mesmerism.

Pure Bosh.

Exorcisms, for which they read Malleus Maleficarum, Nideri Formicarium, Delrio, Wierus, etc., but could not get one that mentioned water babies.

Hydropathy.

Madame Rachel's Elixir of Youth.

The Ploughkeepsie Seer his Prophecies.

The distilled liquor of addle eggs.

Pyropathy, as successfully employed by the old inquisitors to cure the malady of thought, and now by the Persian Mollahs to cure that of rheumatism.

Geopathy, or burying him.

Atmopathy, or steaming him.

Sympathy, after the method of Basil Valentine his Triumph of Antimony, and Kenelm Digby his

Weapon-salve, which some call a hair of the dog that bit him.

Hermopathy, or pouring mercury down his throat, to move the animal spirits.

Meteoropathy, or going up to the moon to look for his lost wits, as Ruggiero did for Orlando Furioso's: only, having no hippogriff, they were forced to use a balloon; and, falling into the North Sea, were picked up by a Yarmouth herring-boat, and came home much the wiser, and all over scales.

Antipathy, or using him like " a man and a brother."

Apathy, or doing nothing at all.

With all other ipathies and opathies which Noodle has invented, and Foodle tried, since black-fellows chipped flints at Abbeyville—which is a considerable time ago, to judge by the Great Exhibition.

But nothing would do; for he screamed and cried all day for a water baby, to come and drive away the monsters; and of course they did not try to find one, because they did not believe in them, and were thinking of nothing but Bumpsterhausen's blue follicles; having, as usual, set the cart before the horse, and taken the effect for the cause.

So they were forced at last to let the poor professor ease his mind by writing a great book, exactly contrary to all his old opinions; in which he proved that the moon was made of green cheese, and that all the mites in it (which you may see sometimes quite plain through a telescope, if you will only keep the lens dirty enough, as Mr. Weekes kept his voltaic battery) are nothing in the world but little babies, who are hatching and swarming up there in millions, ready to come down into this world whenever children want a new little brother or sister.

Which must be a mistake, for this one reason: that, there being no atmosphere round the moon (though some-one or other says there is, at least on the other side, and that he has been round at the back of it to see, and found that the moon was just the shape of a Bath bun, and so wet that the man in the moon went about on Midsummer-day in Macintoshes and Cording's boots, spearing eels and sneezing); that therefore, I say, there being no atmosphere, there can be no evaporation; and, therefore, the dew-point can never fall below 71.5 below zero of Fahrenheit; and, therefore, it cannot be cold enough there about four o'clock in the morning to condense the babies' mesenteric apophthegms into their left ventricles; and, therefore, they can never catch the hooping-cough; and if they do not have hooping-cough, they cannot be babies at all; and, therefore, there are no babies in the moon.—Q. E. D.

Which may seem a roundabout reason; and so, perhaps, it is: but you will have heard worse ones in your time, and from better men than you are.

But one thing is certain; that, when the good old doctor got his book written, he felt considerably relieved from Bumpsterhausen's blue follicles, and a few things infinitely worse; to wit, from pride and vainglory, and from blindness and hardness of heart; which are the true causes of Bumpsterhausen's blue follicles, and of a good many other ugly things beside. Whereon the foul flood-water in his brains ran down, and cleared to a fine coffee colour, such as fish like to rise in, till very fine clean fresh-run fish did begin to rise in his brains; and he caught two or three of them (which is exceedingly fine sport, for brain rivers), and anatomized them carefully, and never mentioned what he found out from them, except to little children; and became ever after a sadder and a wiser man; which is a very good thing to become, my dear little boy, even though one has to pay a heavy price for the blessing.

CHAPTER FIVE

Stern Lawgiver! yet thou dost wear
The Godhead's most benignant grace;
Nor know we anything so fair
As is the smile upon they face:
Flowers laugh before thee on their beds;
And fragrance in thy footing treads;
Thou dost preserve the stars from wrong;
And the most ancient Heavens, through Thee are fresh
and strong.

WORDSWORTH, *Ode to Duty*.

BUT what became of little Tom?

He slipt away off the rocks into the water, as I said before. But he could not help thinking of little Ellie. He did not remember who she was; but he knew that she was a little girl, though she was a hundred times as big as he. This is not surprising: size has nothing to do with kindred. A tiny weed may be first cousin to a great tree; and a little dog like Vick knows that Lioness is a dog too, though she is twenty times larger than herself. So Tom knew that Ellie was a little girl, and thought about her all that day, and longed to have her to play with; but he had very soon to think of something else. And here is the account of what happened to him, as it was published next morning in the *Waterproof Gazette*, on the finest watered paper, for the use of the great fairy, Mrs. Bedonebyasyoudid, who reads the news very carefully every morning, and especially the police cases, as you will hear very soon.

He was going along the rocks in three-fathom water, watching the pollock catch prawns, and the wrasses nibble barnacles off the rocks, shells and all, when he saw a round cage of green withes; and inside it, looking very much ashamed of himself, sat his friend the lobster, twiddling his horns, instead of thumbs.

" What, have you been naughty, and have they put you in the lock-up? " asked Tom.

The lobster felt a little indignant at such a notion, but he was too much depressed in spirits to argue; so he only said, " I can't get out."

" Why did you get in? "

" After that nasty piece of dead fish." He had thought it looked and smelt very nice when he was outside, and so it did, for a lobster: but now he turned round and abused it because he was angry with himself.

" Where did you get in? "

" Through that round hole at the top."

" Then why don't you get out through it? "

" Because I can't "; and the lobster twiddled his horn more fiercely than ever, but he was forced to confess.

" I have jumped upwards, downwards, backwards, and sideways, at least four thousand times; and I can't get out: I always get up underneath there, and can't find the hole."

Tom looked at the trap, and having more wit than the lobster, he saw plainly enough what was the matter; as you may if you will look at a lobster-pot.

" Stop a bit," said Tom. " Turn your tail up to me, and I'll pull you through hindforemost, and then you won't stick in the spikes."

But the lobster was so stupid and clumsy that he couldn't hit the hole. Like a great many fox-hunters, he was very sharp as long as he was in his own country: but as soon as they get out of it they lose their heads; and so the lobster, so to speak, lost his tail.

Tom reached and clawed down the hole after him, till he caught hold of him; and then, as was to be expected the clumsy lobster pulled him in head foremost.

" Hullo! here is a pretty business," said Tom. " Now take your great.claws, and break the points off those spikes, and then we shall both get out easily."

" Dear me, I never thought of that," said the lobster; " and after all the experience of life that I have had! "

You see, experience is of very little good unless a man, or a lobster, has wit enough to make use of it. For a good many people, like old Polonius, have seen all the world, and yet remain little better than children after all.

But they had not got half the spikes away, when they saw a great dark cloud over them; and lo and behold, it was the otter.

How she did grin and grin when she saw Tom. " Yar! " said she, " you little meddlesome wretch, I have you now! I will serve you out for telling the salmon where I was! " And she crawled all over the pot to get in.

Tom was horribly frightened, and still more frightened when she found the hole in the top, and squeezed herself right down through it, all eyes and teeth. But no sooner was her head inside than valiant Mr. Lobster caught her by the nose, and held on.

And there they were all three in the pot, rolling over and over, and very tight packing it was. And the lobster tore at the otter, and the otter tore at the lobster, and both squeezed and thumped poor Tom till he had no breath left in his body; and I don't know what would have happened to him if he had not at last got on the otter's back, and safe out of the hole.

He was right glad when he got out: but he would not desert his friend who had saved him; and the first time he saw his tail uppermost he caught hold of it, and pulled with all his might.

But the lobster would not let go.

" Come along," said Tom; " don't you see she is dead? " And so she was, quite drowned and dead.

And that was the end of the wicked otter.

But the lobster would not let go.

" Come along, you stupid old stick-in-the-mud," cried Tom, " or the fisherman will catch you! " And that was true, for Tom felt someone above beginning to haul up the pot.

But the lobster would not let go.

Tom saw the fisherman haul him up to the boat-side, and thought it was all up with him. But when Mr. Lobster saw the fisherman, he gave such a furious and tremendous snap, that he snapped out of his hand, and out of the pot, and safe into the sea. But he left his knobbed claw behind him; for it never came into his stupid head to let go after all, so he just shook his claw off as the easier method. It was something of a bull, that; but you must know the lobster was an Irish lobster, and was hatched off Island Magee at the mouth of Belfast Lough.

Tom asked the lobster why he never thought of letting go. He said very determinedly that it was a point of honour among lobsters. And so it is, as the mayor of Plymouth found out once to his cost—eight or nine hundred years ago, of course; for if it had happened lately it would be personal to mention it.

For one day he was so tired with sitting on a hard chair, in a grand furred gown, with a gold chain round his neck, hearing one policeman after another come in and sing, " What shall we do with the drunken sailor, so early in the morning? " and answering them each exactly alike—" Put him in the round house till he gets sober, so early in the morning "—

That, when it was over, he jumped up, and played leap-frog with the town clerk till he burst his buttons, and then had his luncheon, and burst some more buttons, and then said, " It is a low spring tide; I shall go out this afternoon and cut my capers."

Now he did not mean to cut such capers as you eat with boiled mutton. It was the commandant of artillery at Valetta who used to amuse himself with cutting them, and who stuck upon one of the bastions a notice, " No one allowed to cut capers here but me," which greatly edified the midshipmen in port, and the Maltese on the Nix Mangiare stairs. But all that the mayor meant was that he would go and have an afternoon's fun, like any schoolboy, and catch lobsters with an iron hook.

So to the Mewstone he went, and for lobsters he looked. And, when he came to a certain crack in the rocks, he was so excited, that, instead of putting in his hook, he put in his hand; and Mr. Lobster was at home, and caught him by the finger, and held on.

" Yah! " said the mayor, and pulled as hard as he dared: but the more he pulled the more the lobster pinched, till he was forced to be quiet.

Then he tried to get his hook in with his other hand; but the hole was too narrow.

Then he pulled again, but he could not stand the pain.

Then he shouted and bawled for help: but there was no one nearer him than the men-of-war inside the breakwater.

Then he began to turn a little pale; for the tide flowed, and still the lobster held on.

Then he turned quite white; for the tide was up to his knees, and still the lobster held on.

Then he thought of cutting off his finger; but he wanted two things to do it with—courage and a knife; and he had got neither.

Then he turned quite yellow; for the tide was up to his waist, and still the lobster held on.

Then he thought over all the naughty things he ever had done: all the sand which he had put in the sugar, and the sloe leaves in the tea, and the water in the treacle, and the salt in the tobacco (because his brother was a brewer, and a man must help his own kin).

Then he turned quite blue; for the tide was up to his breast, and still the lobster held on.

Then, I have no doubt, he repented fully of all the said naughty things which he had done, and promised to mend his life, as too many do when they think they have no life left to mend. Whereby, as they fancy, they make a very cheap bargain. But the old fairy with the birch-rod soon undeceives them.

And then he grew all colours at once, and turned up his eyes like a duck in thunder; for the water was up to his chin, and still the lobster held on.

And then came a man-of-war's boat round the Mew-stone, and saw his head sticking up out of the water. One said it was a keg of brandy, and another that it was a coco-nut, and another that it was a buoy loose, and another that it was a black diver, and wanted to fire at it, which would not have been pleasant for the mayor: but just then such a yell came out of a great hole in the middle of it, that the midshipman in charge guessed what it was, and bade pull up to it as fast as they could. So somehow or other the Jack-tars got the lobster out, and set the mayor free, and put him ashore at the Barbican. He never went lobster-catching again; and we will hope he put no more salt in the tobacco, not even to sell his brother's beer.

And that is the story of the mayor of Plymouth, which has two advantages—first, that of being quite true; and second, that of having (as folks say all good stories ought to have) no moral whatsoever: no more, indeed, has any part of this book, because it is a fairy tale, you know.

And now happened to Tom a most wonderful thing; for he had not left the lobster five minutes before he came upon a water baby.

A real live water baby, sitting on the white sand, very busy about a little point of rock. And when it saw Tom it looked up for a moment, and then cried, " Why, you are not one of us. You are a new baby! Oh, how delightful! "

And it ran to Tom, and Tom ran to it, and they hugged and kissed each other for ever so long, they did not know why. But they did not want any introductions there under the water.

At last Tom said, " Oh, where have you been all this while? I have been looking for you so long, and I have been so lonely."

" We have been here for days and days. There are hundreds of us about the rocks. How was it you did not see us, or hear us when we sing and romp every evening before we go home? "

Tom looked at the baby again, and then he said:

" Well, this is wonderful! I have seen things just like you again and again, but I thought you were shells, or sea-creatures. I never took you for water babies like myself."

Now, was not that very odd? So odd, indeed, that you will, no doubt, want to know how it happened, and why Tom could never find a water baby till after he had got the lobster out of the pot. And, if you will read this story nine times over, and then think for yourself, you will find out why. It is not good for little boys to be told everything, and never to be forced to use their own wits. They would learn, then, no more than they do at Dr. Dulcimer's famous suburban establishment for the idler members of the youthful aristocracy, where the masters learn the lessons, and the boys hear them—which saves a great deal of trouble—for the time being.

"Now," said the baby, "come and help me, or I shall not have finished before my brothers and sisters come, and it is time to go home."

"What shall I help you at?"

"At this poor dear little rock; a great clumsy boulder came rolling by in the last storm, and knocked all its head off, and rubbed off all its flowers. And now I must plant it again with seaweeds, and coralline, and anemones, and I will make it the prettiest little rock-garden on all the shore.

So they worked away at the rock, and planted it, and smoothed the sand down round it, and capital fun they had till the tide began to turn. And then Tom heard all the other babies coming, laughing and singing and shouting and romping; and the noise they made was just like the noise of the ripple. So he knew that he had been hearing and seeing the water babies all along; only he did not know them, because his eyes and ears were not opened.

And in they came, dozens and dozens of them, some bigger than Tom and some smaller, all in the neatest little white bathing dresses; and when they found that he was a new baby they hugged him and kissed him, and then put him in the middle and danced round him on the sand, and there was no one ever so happy as poor little Tom.

"Now then," they cried all at once, "we must come away home, we must come away home, or the tide will leave us dry. We have mended all the broken seaweed, and put all the rock pools in order, and planted all the shells again in the sand, and nobody will see where the ugly storm swept in last week."

And this is the reason why the rock pools are always so neat and clean; because the water babies come in shore after every storm, to sweep them out, and comb them down, and put them all to rights again.

Only where men are wasteful and dirty, and let sewers

run into the sea, instead of putting the stuff upon the fields like thrifty reasonable souls; or throw herrings' heads, and dead dog-fish, or any other refuse, into the water; or in any way make a mess upon the clean shore, there the water babies will not come, sometimes not for hundreds of years (for they cannot abide anything smelly or foul): but leave the sea-anemones and the crabs to clear away everything, till the good tidy sea has covered up all the dirt in soft mud and clean sand, where the water babies can plant live cockles and whelks and razor shells and sea-cucumbers and golden-combs, and make a pretty live garden again, after man's dirt is cleared away. And that, I suppose, is the reason why there are no water babies at any watering place which I have ever seen.

And where is the home of the water babies? In St. Brandan's fairy isle.

Did you never hear of the blessed St. Brandan, how he preached to the wild Irish, on the wild wild Kerry coast; he and five other hermits, till they were weary, and longed to rest? For the wild Irish would not listen to them, or come to confession and to mass, but liked better to brew potheen, and dance the pater o'pee, and knock each other over the head with shillelaghs, and shoot each other from behind turf-dykes, and steal each other's cattle, and burn each other's homes; till St. Brandan and his friends were weary of them, for they would not learn to be peaceable Christians at all.

So St. Brandan went out to the point of old Dunmore, and looked over the tideway roaring round the Blasquets, at the end of all the world, and away into the ocean, and sighed, " Ah that I had wings as a dove! " And far away, before the setting sun, he saw a blue fairy sea, and golden fairy islands, and he said, " Those are the islands of the blest." Then he and his friends got into a hooker, and sailed away and away to the westward, and were never heard of more. But the people who would not hear him were changed into gorillas, and gorillas they are until this day.

And when St. Brandan and the hermits came to that

fairy isle, they found it overgrown with cedars, and full of
beautiful birds; and he sat down under the cedars, and
preached to all the birds in the air. And they liked his
sermons so well that they told the fishes in the sea; and
they came, and St. Brandan preached to them; and the
fishes told the water babies, who live in the caves under
the isle; and they came up by hundreds every Sunday,
and St. Brandan got quite a neat little Sunday school.
And there he taught the water-babies for a great many
hundred years, till his eyes grew too dim to see, and his
beard grew so long that he dared not walk for fear of
treading on it, and then he might have tumbled down.
And at last he and the five hermits fell fast asleep under the
cedar shades, and there they sleep unto this day. But the
fairies took to the water babies, and taught them their
lessons themselves.

And some say that St. Brandan will awake, and begin to
teach the babies once more: but some think that he will
sleep on, for better for worse, till the coming of the Cocqcigrues. But, on still clear summer evenings, when the sun
sinks down into the sea, among golden cloud-capes and
cloud-islands, and locks and friths of azure sky, the sailors
fancy that they see, away to westward, St. Brandan's fairy
isle.

But whether men can see it or not, St. Brandan's Isle
once actually stood there; a great land out in the ocean,
which has sunk and sunk beneath the waves. Old Plato
called it Atlantis, and told strange tales of the wise men
who lived therein, and of the wars they fought in the old
times. And from off that island came strange flowers,
which linger still about this land: the Cornish heath, and
Cornish moneywort, and the delicate Venus's hair, and
the London-pride which covers the Kerry mountains, and
the little pink butterwort of Devon, and the great blue
butterwort of Ireland, and the Connemara heath, and the
bristle-fern of the Turk waterfall, and many a strange plant
more; all fairy tokens left for wise men and good children
from off St. Brandan's Isle.

Now when Tom got there, he found that the isle stood

all on pillars, and that its roots were full of caves. There were pillars of black basalt, like Staffa; and pillars of green and crimson serpentine, like Kynance; and pillars ribboned with red and white and yellow sandstone, like Livermead; and there were blue grottoes, like Capri; and white grottoes, like Adelsberg; all curtained and draped with seaweeds, purple and crimson, green and brown; and strewn with soft white sand, on which the water babies sleep every night. But, to keep the place clean and sweet, the crabs picked up all the scraps off the floor, and ate them like so many monkeys; while the rocks were covered with ten thousand sea-anemones, and corals and madrepores, who scavenged the water all day long, and kept it nice and pure. But, to make up to them for having to do such nasty work, they were not left black and dirty, as poor chimney-sweeps and dustmen are. No; the fairies are more considerate and just than that; and have dressed them all in the most beautiful colours and patterns, till they look like vast flower-beds of gay blossoms. If you think I am talking nonsense, I can only say that it is true; and that an old gentleman named Fourier used to say that we ought to do the same by chimney-sweeps and dustmen, and honour them instead of despising them; and he was a very clever old gentleman: but unfortunately for him and the world, as mad as a March hare.

And, instead of watchmen and policemen to keep out nasty things at night, there were thousands and thousands of water-snakes, and most wonderful creatures they were. They were all named after the Nereids, the sea fairies who took care of them, Eunice and Polynoe, Phyllodoce and Psamathe, and all the rest of the pretty darlings who swim round their Queen Amphitrite, and her car of cameo shell. They were dressed in green velvet, and black velvet, and purple velvet; and were all jointed in rings; and some of them had three hundred brains apiece, so that they must have been uncommonly shrewd detectives; and some had eyes in their tails; and some had eyes in every joint, so that they kept a very sharp look-out; and when they wanted a baby-snake, they just grew one at the end of their own tails, and when it was able to take care of itself it dropped off; so that they brought up their families very cheaply. But if any nasty thing came by, out they rushed upon it; and then out of each of their hundreds of feet there sprang a whole cutler's shop of

Scythes,	Javelins,
Billhooks,	Lances,
Pickaxes,	Halberts,
Forks,	Gisarines,
Penknives,	Poleaxes,
Rapiers,	Fishhooks,
Sabres,	Bradawls,
Yataghans,	Gimblets,
Creeses,	Corkscrews,
Ghoorka swords,	Pins,
Tucks,	Needles,

And so forth,

which stabbed, shot, poked, pricked, scratched, ripped, pinked, and crimped those naughty beasts so terribly, that they had to run for their lives, or else be chopped into small pieces and be eaten afterwards. And, if that is not all, every word, true, then there is no faith in microscopes, and all is over with the Linnaean Society.

And there were the water babies in thousands, more than Tom, or you either, could count. All the little children whom the good fairies take to, because their cruel mothers and fathers will not; all who are untaught and brought up heathens, and all who come to grief by ill-usage or ignorance or neglect; all the little children who are overlaid, or given gin when they are young, or are let to drink out of hot kettles, or to fall into the fire; all the little children in alleys and courts, and tumbledown cottages, who die by fever, and cholera, and measles, and scarlatina, and nasty complaints which no one has any business to have, and which no one will have some day, when folks have common sense; and all the little children who have been killed by cruel masters, and wicked soldiers; they were all there, except, of course, the babes of Bethlehem who were killed by wicked King Herod; for they were taken straight to heaven long ago, as everybody knows, and we call them the Holy Innocents.

But I wish Tom had given up all his naughty tricks, and left off tormenting dumb animals, now that he had plenty of playfellows to amuse him. Instead of that, I am sorry to say, he would meddle with the creatures, all but the water-snakes, for they would stand no nonsense. So he tickled the madrepores, to make them shut up; and frightened the crabs, to make them hide in the sand and peep out at him with the tips of their eyes; and put stones into the anemones' mouths to make them fancy that their dinner was coming.

The other children warned him, and said, " Take care what you are at. Mrs. Bedonebyasyoudid is coming." But Tom never heeded them, being quite riotous with high spirits and good luck, till, one Friday morning early, Mrs. Bedonebyasyoudid came indeed.

A very tremendous lady she was; and when the children saw her, they all stood in a row, very upright indeed, and smoothed down their bathing dresses, and put their hands behind them, just as if they were going to be examined by the inspector.

And she had on a black bonnet, and a black shawl, and no crinoline at all; and a pair of large green spectacles, and a great hooked nose, hooked so much that the bridge of it stood quite up above her eyebrows; and under her arm she carried a great birch-rod. Indeed, she was so ugly, that Tom was tempted to make faces at her: but did not; for he did not admire the look of the birch-rod under her arm.

And she looked at the children one by one, and seemed very much pleased with them, though she never asked them one question about how they were behaving; and then began giving them all sorts of nice sea-things—sea-cakes, sea-apples, sea-oranges, sea-bullseyes, sea-toffee; and to the very best of all she gave sea-ices, made out of sea-cows' cream, which never melt under water.

And, if you don't quite believe me, then just think—

What is more cheap and plentiful than sea-rock? Then why should there not be sea-toffee as well? And every one can find sea-lemons (ready quartered too) if they will look for them at low tide; and sea-grapes too sometimes, hanging in bunches; and, if you will go to Nice, you will find the fish-market full of sea-fruit, which they call "frutta di mare": though I suppose they call them "fruits de mer" now, out of compliment to that most successful, and therefore most immaculate, potentate who is seemingly desirous of inheriting the blessing pronounced on those who remove their neighbours' landmark. And, perhaps, that is the very reason why the place is called Nice, because there are so many nice things in the sea there: at least, if it is not, it ought to be.

Now little Tom watched all these sweet things given away, till his mouth watered, and his eyes grew as round as an owl's. For he hoped that his turn would come at last; and so it did. For the lady called him up, and held out her fingers with something in them, and popped it into his mouth; and, lo and behold, it was a nasty cold hard pebble.

"You are a very cruel woman," said he, and began to whimper.

"And you are a very cruel boy; who puts pebbles into the sea-anemones' mouths, to take them in, and make them fancy that they had caught a good dinner? As you did to them, so I must do to you."

"Who told you that?" said Tom.

"You did yourself, this very minute."

Tom had never opened his lips; so he was very much taken aback indeed.

"Yes; every one tells me exactly what they have done wrong; and that without knowing it themselves. So there is no use trying to hide anything from me. Now go, and be a good boy, and I will put no more pebbles in your mouth, if you put none in other creatures'."

"I did not know there was any harm in it," said Tom.

"Then you know now. People continually say that to me: but I tell them, if you don't know that fire burns, that

is no reason that it should not burn you; and if you don't
know that dirt breeds fever, and that is no reason why the
fevers should not kill you. The lobster did not know that
there was any harm in getting into the lobster pot; but it
caught him all the same."

"Dear me," thought Tom, "she knows everything!"
And so she did, indeed.

"And so, if you do not know that things are wrong, that
is no reason why you should not be punished for them;
though not as much, not as much, my little man" (and,
the lady looked very kindly, after all), "as if you did
know."

"Well, you are a little hard on a poor lad," said Tom.

"Not at all; I am the best friend you ever had in all
your life. But I will tell you; I cannot help punishing
people when they do wrong. I like it no more than they
do; I am often very, very sorry for them, poor things: but
I cannot help it. If I tried not to do it, I should do it all
the same. For I work by machinery, just like an engine;
and am full of wheels and springs inside; and am wound
up very carefully, so that I cannot help going."

"Was it long ago since they wound you up?" asked
Tom. For he thought, the cunning little fellow, "She will
run down some day: or they may forget to wind her up,
as old Grimes used to forget to wind up his watch when he
came in from the public-house: and then I shall be
safe."

"I was wound up once and for all, so long ago that I
forget all about it."

"Dear me," said Tom, "you must have been made a
long time!"

"I never was made, my child; and I shall go for ever
and ever; for I am as old as Eternity, and yet as young
as Time."

And there came over the lady's face a very curious
expression—very solemn, and very sad; and yet very,
very sweet. And she looked up and away, as if she were
gazing through the sea, and through the sky, at something
far, far off; and as she did so, there came such a quiet,

tender, patient, hopeful smile over her face, that Tom thought for the moment that she did not look ugly at all. And no more she did; for she was like a great many people who have not a pretty feature in their faces, and yet are lovely to behold, and draw little children's hearts to them at once; because, though the house is plain enough, yet from the windows a beautiful and good spirit is looking forth.

And Tom smiled in her face, she looked so pleasant for the moment. And the strange fairy smiled too, and said:

"Yes. You thought me very ugly just now, did you not?"

Tom hung down his head, and got very red about the ears.

"And I am very ugly. I am the ugliest fairy in the world; and I shall be, till people behave themselves as they ought to do. And then I shall grow as handsome as my sister, who is the loveliest fairy in the world; and her name is Mrs. Doasyouwouldbedoneby. So she begins where I end, and I begin where she ends; and those who will not listen to her must listen to me, as you will see. Now, all of you run away, except Tom; and he may stay and see what I am going to do. It will be a very good warning for him to begin with, before he goes to school.

"Now, Tom, every Friday I come down here and call up all who have ill-used little children, and serve them as they served the children."

And at that Tom was frightened, and crept under a stone; which made the two crabs who lived there very angry, and frightened their friend the butter-fish into flapping hysterics: but he would not move for them.

And first she called up all the doctors who give little children so much physic (they were most of them old ones; for the young ones have learnt better, all but a few army surgeons, who still fancy that a baby's inside is much like a Scotch grenadier's), and she set them all in a row; and very rueful they looked; for they knew what was coming.

And first she pulled all their teeth out; and then she bled them all round; and then she dosed them with calomel, and jalap, and salts and senna, and brimstone and treacle; and horrible faces they made; and then she gave them a great emetic of mustard and water, and no basons; and began all over again; and that was the way she spent the morning.

And then she called up a whole troop of foolish ladies, who pinch up their children's waists and toes; and she laced them all up in tight stays, so that they were choked and sick, and their noses grew red, and their hands and feet swelled; and then she crammed their poor feet into the most dreadfully tight boots, and made them all dance, which they did most clumsily indeed; and then she asked them how they liked it; and when they said not at all, she let them go: because they had only done it out of foolish fashion, fancying it was for their children's good, as if wasps' waists and pigs' toes could be pretty, or wholesome, or of any use to anybody.

Then she called up all the careless nurserymaids, and stuck pins into them all over, and wheeled them about in perambulators with tight straps across their stomachs and their heads and arms hanging over the side, till they were quite sick and stupid, and would have had sun-strokes: but, being under the water, they could only have water-strokes; which, I assure you, are nearly as bad, as you will find if you try to sit under a mill wheel. And mind—when you hear a rumbling at the bottom of the sea, sailors will tell you that it is a ground-swell: but now you know better. It is the old lady wheeling the maids about in perambulators.

And by that time she was so tired, she had to go to luncheon.

And after luncheon she set to work again, and called up all the cruel schoolmasters—whole regiments and brigades of them; and, when she saw them, she frowned most terribly, and set to work in earnest, as if the best part of the day's work was to come. More than half of them were nasty, dirty, frowzy, grubby, smelly old monks, who, because they dare not hit a man of their own size, amused themselves with beating little children instead; as you may see in the picture of old Pope Gregory (good man and true though he was, when he meddled with things which he did understand), teaching children to sing their fa-fa-mi-fa with a cat-o'-nine-tails under his chair; but, because they never had any children of their own, they took into their heads (as some folks do still) that they were the only people in the world who knew how to manage children; and they first brought into England, in the old Anglo-Saxon times, the fashion of treating free boys, and girls too, worse than you would treat a dog or a horse: but Mrs. Bedonebyasyoudid has caught them all long ago; and given them many a taste of their own rods; and much good may it do them.

And she boxed their ears, and thumped them over the head with rulers, and pandied their hands with canes, and told them that they told stories, and were this and that bad sort of people; and the more they were very indignant, and stood upon their honour, and declared they told the truth, the more she declared they were not, and that they were only telling lies; and at last she birched them all round soundly with her great birch-rod, and set them each an imposition of three hundred thousand lines of Hebrew to learn by heart before she came back next Friday. And at that they all cried and howled so, that their breaths came all up through the sea like bubbles out of soda-water; and that is one reason of the bubbles in the sea. There are others: but that is the one which principally concerns little boys. And by that time she was so tired that she was glad to stop; and, indeed, she had done a very good day's work.

Tom did not quite dislike the old lady: but he could not help thinking her a little spiteful—and no wonder if she was, poor old soul; for, if she has to wait to grow handsome till people do as they would be done by, she will have to wait a very long time.

Poor old Mrs. Bedonebyasyoudid! she has a great deal of hard work before her, and had better have been born a washerwoman, and stood over a tub all day: but, you see, people cannot always choose their own profession.

But Tom longed to ask her one question; and after all,

whenever she looked at him, she did not look cross at all; and now and then there was a funny smile in her face, and she chuckled to herself in a way which gave Tom courage, and at last he said:

"Pray, ma'am, may I ask you a question?"

"Certainly, my little dear."

"Why don't you bring all the bad masters here, and serve them out too? The butties that knock about the poor collier-boys; and the nailers that file off their lads' noses and hammer their fingers; and all the master sweeps, like my master Grimes? I saw him fall into the water long ago; so I surely expected he would have been here. I'm sure he was bad enough to me."

Then the old lady looked so very stern that Tom was quite frightened, and sorry that he had been so bold. But she was not angry with him. She only answered, "I look after them all the week round; and they are in a very different place from this, because they knew that they were doing wrong."

She spoke very quietly; but there was something in her voice which made Tom tingle from head to foot, as if he had got into a shoal of sea-nettles.

"But these people," she went on, "did not know that they were doing wrong: they were only stupid and impatient; and therefore I only punish them till they become patient, and learn to use their common sense like reasonable beings. But as for chimney-sweeps, and collier-boys, and nailer lads, my sister has set good people to stop all that sort of thing; and very much obliged to her I am; for if she could only stop the cruel masters from ill-using poor children, I should grow handsome at least a thousand years sooner. And now do you be a good boy, and do as you would be done by, which they did not; and then, when my sister, Madame Doasyouwouldbedoneby, comes on Sunday, perhaps she will take notice of you, and teach you how to behave. She understands that better than I do." And so she went.

Tom was very glad to hear that there was no chance of meeting Grimes again, though he was a little sorry for him, considering that he used sometimes to give him the leavings of the beer: but he determined to be a very good boy all Saturday; and he was; for he never frightened one crab, nor tickled any live corals, nor put stones into the sea-anemones' mouths, to make them fancy they had got a dinner; and, when Sunday morning came, sure enough Mrs. Doasyouwouldbedoneby came too. Whereat all the little children began dancing and clapping their hands, and Tom danced too with all his might.

And as for the pretty lady, I cannot tell you what the colour of her hair was, or of her eyes: no more could Tom; for, when any one looks at her, all they can think of is, that she has the sweetest, kindest, tenderest, funniest, merriest face they ever saw, or want to see. But Tom saw that she was a very tall woman, as tall as her sister: but instead of being gnarly, and horny, and scaly, and prickly, like her, she was the most nice, soft, fat, smooth, pussy, cuddly, delicious creature who ever nursed a baby; and she understood babies thoroughly, for she had plenty of her own, whole rows and regiments of them, and has to this day. And all her delight was, whenever she had a spare moment, to play with babies, in which she showed herself a woman of sense; for babies are the best company, and the pleasantest playfellows, in the world; at least, so all the wise people in the world think. And therefore when the children saw her, they naturally all caught hold of her, and pulled her till she sat down on a stone, and climbed into her lap, and clung round her neck, and caught hold of her hands; and then they all put their thumbs into their mouths, and began cuddling and purring like so many kittens, as they ought to have done. While those who could get nowhere else sat down on the sand, and cuddled her feet—for no one, you know, wears shoes in the water, except horrid old bathing-women, who are afraid of the water babies pinching their horny toes. And Tom stood staring at them; for he could not understand what it was all about.

" And who are you, you little darling? " she said.

" Oh, that is the new baby! " they all cried, pulling their

thumbs out of their mouths; "and he never had any mother," and they all put their thumbs back again, for they did not wish to lose any time.

"Then I will be his mother, and he shall have the very best place; so get out all of you, this moment."

And she took up two great armfuls of babies—nine hundred under one arm, and thirteen hundred under the other—and threw them away, right and left, into the water. But they minded it no more than the naughty boys in *Struwelpeter* minded when St. Nicholas dipped them in his ink-stand; and did not even take their thumbs out of their mouths, but came paddling and wriggling back to her like so many tadpoles, till you could see nothing of her from head to foot for the swarm of little babies.

But she took Tom in her arms, and laid him in the softest place of all, and kissed him, and patted him, and talked to him, tenderly and low, such things as he had never heard before in his life; and Tom looked up into her eyes, and loved her, and loved, till he fell fast asleep from pure love.

And when he awoke, she was telling the children a story. And what story did she tell them? One story she told them which begins every Christmas Eve, and yet never ends at all for ever and ever; and, as she went on, the children took their thumbs out of their mouths, and listened quite seriously; but not sadly at all; for she never told them anything sad; and Tom listened too, and never grew tired of listening. And he listened so long that he fell fast asleep again, and, when he woke, the lady was nursing him still.

"Don't go away," said little Tom. "This is so nice. I never had any one to cuddle me before."

"Don't go away," said all the children; "you have not sung us one song."

"Well, I have time for only one. So what shall it be?"

"The doll you lost! The doll you lost!" cried all the babies at once.

So the strange fairy sang:

"I once had a sweet little doll, dears,
    The prettiest doll in the world;
Her cheeks were so red and so white, dears,
    And her hair was so charmingly curled.
But I lost my poor little doll, dears,
    As I played in the heath one day;
And I cried for her more than a week, dears;
    But I never could find where she lay.

I found my poor little doll, dears,
    As I played in the heath one day:
Folks say she is terribly changed, dears,
    For her paint is all washed away,
And her arm trodden off by the cows, dears,
    And her hair not the least bit curled:
Yet for old sakes' sake she is still, dears,
    The prettiest doll in the world."

What a silly song for a fairy to sing!

And what silly water babies to be quite delighted at it!

Well, but you see they have not the advantage of Aunt Agitate's Arguments in the sea-land down below.

"Now," said the fairy to Tom, "will you be a good boy for my sake, and torment no more sea-beasts, till I come back?"

"And you will cuddle me again?" said poor little Tom.

"Of course I will, you little duck. I should like to take you with me, and cuddle you all the way, only I must not"; and away she went.

So Tom really tried to be a good boy, and tormented no sea-beasts after that, as long as he lived; and he is quite alive, I assure you, still.

Oh, how good little boys ought to be, who have kind pussy mammas to cuddle them and tell them stories; and how afraid they ought to be of growing naughty, and bringing tears into their mammas' pretty eyes!

CHAPTER SIX

Thou little child, yet glorious in the might
Of heaven-born freedom on thy Being's height,
Why with such earnest pains dost thou provoke
The Years to bring the inevitable yoke—
Thus blindly with thy blessedness at strife?
Full soon thy soul shall have her earthly freight,
And custom lie upon thee with a weight
Heavy as frost, and deep almost as life.
WORDSWORTH.

HERE I come to the very saddest part of all my story. I know some people who will only laugh at it, and call it much ado about nothing. But I know one man who would not; and he was an officer with a pair of grey moustaches as long as your arm, who said once in company, that two of the most heart-rending sights in the world, which moved him most to tears, which he would do anything to prevent or remedy, were a child over a broken toy, and a child stealing sweets.

The company did not laugh at him; his moustaches were too long and too grey for that: but, after he was gone, they called him sentimental, and so forth, all but one dear little old Quaker lady with a soul as white as her cap, who was not, of course, generally partial to soldiers; and she said very quietly, like a Quaker:

"Friends, it is borne upon my mind that that is a truly brave man."

Now you may fancy that Tom was quite good, when he had everything that he could want or wish: but you would be very much mistaken. Being quite comfortable is a very good thing; but it does not make people good. Indeed, it sometimes makes them naughty, as it has made the people in America; and as it made the people in the Bible, who waxed fat and kicked, like horses overfed and underworked. And I am very sorry to say that this happened to little Tom.

For he grew so fond of the sea-bull's-eyes and sea-lollipops, that his foolish little head could think of nothing else: and he was always longing for more, and wondering when the strange lady would come again and give him some, and what she would give him, and how much, and whether she would give him more than the others. And he thought of nothing but lollipops by day, and dreamt of nothing else by night—and what happened then?

That he began to watch the lady to see where she kept the sweet things; and began hiding, and sneaking, and following her about, and pretending to be looking the other way, or going after something else, till he found out that she kept them in a beautiful mother-of-pearl cabinet, away in a deep crack of the rocks.

And he longed to go to the cabinet, and yet he was afraid; and then he longed again, and was less afraid; and at last, by continual thinking about it, he longed so violently, that he was not afraid at all. And one night, when all the other children were asleep, and he could not sleep for thinking of lollipops, he crept away among the rocks, and got to the cabinet, and behold! it was open.

But, when he saw all the nice things inside, instead of being delighted, he was quite frightened, and wished he had never come there. And then he would only touch them, and he did; and then he would only taste one, and he did; and then he would only eat one, and he did; and then he would only eat two, and then three, and so on; and then he was terrified lest she should come and catch him, and began gobbling them down so fast that he did not taste them, or have any pleasure in them; and then he felt sick, and would have only one more; and then only one more again; and so on till he had eaten them all up.

And all the while, close behind him, stood Mrs. Bedone-byasyoudid.

Some people may say, But why did she not keep her cupboard locked? Well, I know. It may seem a very strange thing, but she never does keep her cupboard locked; every one may go and taste for themselves, and fare accordingly. It is very odd, but so it is; and I am quite sure that she knows best. Perhaps she wishes people to keep their fingers out of the fire, by having them burnt.

She took off her spectacles, because she did not like to see too much; and in her pity she arched up her eyebrows into her very hair, and her eyes grew so wide that they would have taken in all the sorrows of the world, and filled with great big tears, as they too often do.

But all she said was:

"Ah, you poor little dear! you are just like all the rest."

But she said it to herself, and Tom neither heard nor saw her. Now, you must not fancy that she was sentimental at all. If you do, and think that she is going to let off you, or me, or any human being when we do wrong, because she is too tender-hearted to punish us, then you will find yourself very much mistaken, as many a man does every year and every day.

But what did the strange fairy do when she saw all her lollipops eaten?

Did she fly at Tom, catch him by the scruff of the neck, hold him, howk him, hump him, hurry him, hit him, poke him, pull him, pinch him, pound him, put him in the corner, shake him, slap him, set him on a cold stone to reconsider himself, and so forth?

Not a bit. You may watch her at work, if you know where to find her. But you will never see her do that. For, if she had, she knew quite well, Tom would have fought, and kicked, and bit, and said bad words, and turned again that moment into a naughty little heathen chimney-sweep, with his hand, like Ishmael's of old, against every man, and every man's hand against him.

Did she question him, hurry him, frighten him, threaten him, to make him confess? Not a bit. You may see her, as I said, at her work often enough, if you know where to look for her: but you will never see her do that. For if she had, she would have tempted him to tell lies in his fright; and that would have been worse for him, if possible, than even becoming a heathen chimney-sweep again.

No. She leaves that for anxious parents and teachers

(lazy ones, some call them), who, instead of giving children a fair trial, such as they would expect and demand for themselves, force them by fright to confess their own faults —which is so cruel and unfair, that no judge on the bench dare do it to the wickedest thief or murderer, for the good British law forbids it—ay, and even punish them to make them confess, which is so detestable a crime, that it is never committed now, save by Inquisitors, and Kings of Naples, and a few other wretched people of whom the world is weary. And then they say, " We have trained up the child in the way he should go, and when he grew up he has departed from it. Why then did Solomon say that he would not depart from it? " But perhaps the way of beating, and hurrying, and frightening, and questioning, was not the way that the child should go; for it is not even the way in which a colt should go, if you want to break it in, and make it a quiet serviceable horse.

Some folks may say, " Ah! but the fairy does not need to do that, if she knows everything already." True. But if she did not know, she would not surely behave worse than a British judge and jury; and no more should parents and teachers either.

So she just said nothing at all about the matter, not even when Tom came next day with the rest for sweet things. He was horribly afraid of coming: but he was still more afraid of staying away, lest any one should suspect him. He was dreadfully afraid, too, lest there should be no sweets—as was to be expected, he having eaten them all— and lest then the fairy should inquire who had taken them. But, behold! she pulled out just as many as ever, which astonished Tom, and frightened him still more.

And, when the fairy looked him full in the face, he shook from head to foot: however, she gave him his share like the rest, and he thought within himself that she could not have found him out.

But, when he put the sweets into his mouth, he hated the taste of them; and they made him so sick, that he had to get away as fast as he could; and terribly sick he was, and very cross and unhappy, all the week after.

Then, when next week came, he had his share again; and again the fairy looked him full in the face; but more sadly than she had ever looked. And he could not bear the sweets: but took them again in spite of himself.

And, when Mrs. Doasyouwouldbedoneby came, he wanted to be cuddled like the rest; but she said very seriously:

"I should like to cuddle you; but I cannot, you are so horny and prickly."

And Tom looked at himself: and he was all over prickles, just like a sea-egg.

Which was quite natural; for you must know and believe that people's souls make their bodies, just as a snail makes its shell (I am not joking, my little man; I am in serious, solemn earnest). And, therefore, when Tom's soul grew all prickly with naughty tempers, his body could not help growing prickly too, so that nobody would cuddle him, or play with him, or even like to look at him.

What could Tom do now, but go away and hide in a corner, and cry? For nobody would play with him, and he knew full well why.

And he was so miserable all that week that, when the ugly fairy came, and looked at him once more full in the face, more seriously and sadly than ever, he could stand it no longer, and thrust the sweetmeats away, saying, "No, I don't want any; I can't bear them now," and then burst out crying, poor little man, and told Mrs. Bedonebyas-youdid every word as it happened.

He was horribly frightened when he had done so; for he expected her to punish him very severely. But, instead, she only took him up and kissed him, which was not quite pleasant, for her chin was very bristly indeed; but he was so lonely hearted, he thought that rough kissing was better than none.

"I will forgive you, little man," she said. "I always forgive every one the moment they tell me the truth of their own accord."

"Then you will take away all these nasty prickles?"

" That is a very different matter. You put them there yourself, and only you can take them away."

" But how can I do that? " asked Tom, crying afresh.

" Well, I think it is time for you to go to school; so I shall fetch you a schoolmistress, who will teach you how to get rid of your prickles." And so she went away.

Tom was frightened at the notion of a schoolmistress; for he thought she would certainly come with a birch-rod or a cane; but he comforted himself, at last, that she might be something like the old woman in Vendale—which she was not in the least; for, when the fairy brought her, she was the most beautiful little girl that ever was seen, with long curls floating behind her like a golden cloud, and long robes floating all round her like a silver one.

" There he is," said the fairy; " and you must teach him to be good, whether you like or not."

" I know," said the little girl; but she did not seem quite to like, for she put her finger in her mouth, and looked at Tom under her brows; and Tom put his finger to his mouth, and looked at her under his brows, for he was horribly ashamed of himself.

The little girl seemed hardly to know how to begin; and perhaps she would never have begun at all, if poor Tom had not burst out crying, and begged her to teach him to be good, and help him to cure his prickles; and at that she grew so tender-hearted, that she began teaching him as prettily as ever child was taught in the world.

And what did the little girl teach Tom? She taught him, first, what you have been taught ever since you said your first prayers at your mother's knees; but she taught him much more simply. For the lessons in that world, my child, have no such hard words in them as the lessons in this, and therefore the water babies like them better than you like your lessons, and long to learn them more and more; and grown men cannot puzzle nor quarrel over their meaning, as they do here on land; for those lessons all rise clear and pure, like the Test out of Overton Pool, out of the everlasting ground of all life and truth.

So she taught Tom every day in the week; only on

Sundays she always went away home, and the kind fairy took her place. And, before she had taught Tom many Sundays, his prickles had vanished quite away, and his skin was smooth and clean again.

"Dear me!" said the little girl; "why, I know you now. You are the very same little chimney-sweep who came into my bedroom."

"Dear me!" cried Tom. "And I know you, too, now. You are the very little white lady whom I saw in bed." And he jumped at her, and longed to hug and kiss her; but did not, remembering that she was a lady born; so he only jumped round and round her, till he was quite tired.

And then they began telling each other all their story— how he had got into the water, and she had fallen over the rock; and how he had swam down to the sea, and how she had flown out of the window; and how this, that, and the other, till it was all talked out: and then they both began over again, and I can't say which of the two talked fastest.

And then they set to work at their lessons again, and both liked them so well, that they went on well till seven full years were past and gone.

You may fancy that Tom was quite content and happy all those seven years; but the truth is, he was not. He had always one thing on his mind, and that was—where little Ellie went, when she went home on Sundays.

To a very beautiful place, she said.

But what was the beautiful place like, and where was it?

Ah! that is just what she could not say. And it is strange, but true, that no one can say; and that those who have been oftenest in it, or even nearest to it, can say least about it, and make people understand least what it is like. There are a good many folks about the Other-end-of-Nowhere (where Tom went afterwards), who pretend to know it from north to south as well as if they had been penny postmen there; but, as they are safe at the Other-end-of-Nowhere, nine hundred and ninety-nine million miles away, what they say cannot concern us.

But the dear, sweet, loving, wise, good, self-sacrificing people, who really go there, can never tell you anything about it, save that it is the most beautiful place in all the world; and, if you ask them more, they grow modest, and hold their peace, for fear of being laughed at; and quite right they are.

So all that good little Ellie could say was, that it was worth all the rest of the world put together. And of course that only made Tom the more anxious to go likewise.

" Miss Ellie," he said, at last, " I will know why I cannot go with you when you go home, on Sundays, or I shall have no peace, and give you none either."

" You must ask the fairies that."

So when the fairy, Mrs. Bedonebyasyoudid, came next, Tom asked her.

" Little boys who are only fit to play with sea-beasts cannot go there," she said. " Those who go there must go first where they do not like, and do what they do not like, and help somebody they do not like."

" Why, did Ellie do that? "

" Ask her."

And Ellie blushed, and said, " Yes, Tom; I did not like coming here at first; I was so much happier at home, where it is always Sunday. And I was afraid of you, Tom, at first, because—because——"

" Because I was all over prickles? But I am not prickly now, am I, Miss Ellie? "

" No," said Ellie. " I like you very much now; and I like coming here, too."

" And perhaps," said the fairy, " you will learn to like going where you don't like, and helping someone that you don't like, as Ellie has."

But Tom put his finger in his mouth, and hung his head down; for he did not see that at all.

So when Mrs. Doasyouwouldbedoneby came, Tom asked her; for he thought in his little head, She is not so strict as her sister, and perhaps she may let me off more easily.

Ah, Tom, Tom, silly fellow! and yet I don't know why I should blame you, while so many grown people have got the very same notion in their heads.

But, when they try it, they get just the same answer as

Tom did. For, when he asked the second fairy, she told him just what the first did, and in the very same words.

Tom was very unhappy at that. And, when Ellie went home on Sunday, he fretted and cried all day, and did not care to listen to the fairy's stories about good children, though they were prettier than ever. Indeed, the more he overheard of them, the less he liked to listen, because they were all about children who did what they did not like, and took trouble for other people, and worked to feed their little brothers and sisters, instead of caring only for their play. And, when she began to tell a story about a holy child in old times, who was martyred by the heathen because it would not worship idols, Tom could bear no more, and ran away and hid among the rocks.

And, when Ellie came back, he was shy with her, because he fancied she looked down on him, and thought him a coward. And then he grew quite cross with her, because she was superior to him, and did what he could not do. And poor Ellie was quite surprised and sad; and at last Tom burst out crying; but he would not tell her what was really in his mind.

And all the while he was eaten up with curiosity to know where Ellie went to; so that he began not to care for his playmates, or for the sea-palace, or anything else. But perhaps that made matters all the easier for him; for he grew so discontented with everything round him, that he did not care to stay, and did not care where he went.

"Well," he said, at last, "I am so miserable here, I'll go; if only you will go with me."

"Ah!" said Ellie, "I wish I might; but the worst of it is, that the fairy says, that you must go alone, if you go at all. Now don't poke that poor crab about, Tom" (for he was feeling very naughty and mischievous), "or the fairy will have to punish you."

Tom was very nearly saying, "I don't care if she does"; but he stopped himself in time.

"I know what she wants me to do," he said, whining most dolefully. "She wants me to go after that horrid old Grimes. I don't like him, that's certain. And if I find him, he will turn me into a chimney-sweep again, I know. That's what I have been afraid of all along."

"No, he won't—I know as much as that. Nobody can turn water-babies into sweeps, or hurt them at all, as long as they are good."

"Ah," said naughty Tom, "I see what you want; you are persuading me all along to go, because you are tired of me, and want to get rid of me."

Little Ellie opened her eyes very wide at that, and they were all brimming over with tears.

"Oh, Tom, Tom!" she said, very mournfully—and then she cried, "Oh, Tom! where are you?"

And Tom cried, "Oh, Ellie, where are you?"

For neither of them could see each other—not the least. Little Ellie vanished quite away, and Tom heard her voice calling him, and growing smaller and smaller, and fainter and fainter, till all was silent.

Who was frightened then but Tom? He swam up and down among the rocks, into all the halls and chambers, faster than ever he swam before, but could not find her. He shouted after her, but she did not answer; he asked all the other children, but they had not seen her; and at last he went up to the top of the water and began crying and screaming for Mrs. Doasyouwouldbedoneby, but she did not come. Then he began crying and screaming for Mrs. Bedonebyasyoudid—which perhaps was the best thing to do—for she came in a moment.

"Oh!" said Tom. "Oh dear, oh dear! I have been naughty to Ellie, and I have killed her—I know I have killed her."

"Not quite that," said the fairy; "but I have sent her away home, and she will not come back again for I do not know how long."

And at that Tom cried so bitterly, that the salt sea was swelled with his tears, and the tide was .3954620819 of an inch higher than it had been the day before: but perhaps that was owing to the waxing of the moon. It may have been so; but it is considered right in the new philosophy, you know, to give spiritual causes for physical phenomena

Jean Cruickshanks.

—especially in parlour-tables; and of course, physical causes for spiritual ones, like thinking, and praying, and knowing right from wrong. And so they odds it till it comes even as folks say down in Berkshire.

"How cruel of you to send Ellie away!" sobbed Tom. "However, I will find her again, if I go to the world's end to look for her."

The fairy did not slap Tom, and tell him to hold his tongue: but she took him on her lap very kindly, just as her sister would have done; and put him in mind how it was not her fault, because she was wound up inside, like watches, and could not help doing things whether she liked or not. And then she told him how he had been in the nursery long enough, and must go out now and see the world, if he intended ever to be a man; and how he must go all alone by himself, as every one else that ever was born has to go, and see with his own eyes, and smell with his own nose, and make his own bed and lie on it, and burn his own fingers if he put them into the fire. And then she told him how many fine things there were to be seen in the world, and what an odd, curious, pleasant, orderly respectable, well-managed, and, on the whole, successful (as, indeed, might have been expected) sort of a place it was, if people would only be tolerably brave and honest and good in it; and then she told him not to be afraid of anything he met, for nothing would harm him if he remembered all his lessons, and did what he knew was right. And at last she comforted poor little Tom so much, that he was quite eager to go, and wanted to set out that minute. "Only," he said, "if I might see Ellie once before I went!"

"Why do you want that?"

"Because—because I should be so much happier if I thought she had forgiven me."

And in the twinkling of an eye there stood Ellie, smiling and looking so happy that Tom longed to kiss her; but was still afraid it would not be respectful, because she was a lady born.

"I am going, Ellie!" said Tom. "I am going, if it is to

the world's end. But I don't like going at all, and that's the truth."

"Pooh! pooh! pooh!" said the fairy. "You will like it very well indeed, you little rogue, and you know that at the bottom of your heart. But if you don't, I will make you like it. Come here, and see what happens to people who do only what is pleasant."

And she took out of one of her cupboards (she had all sorts of mysterious cupboards in the cracks of the rocks) the most wonderful waterproof book, full of such photographs as never were seen. For she had found out photography (and this is a fact) more than 13,598,000 years before anybody was born; and, what is more, her photographs did did not merely represent light and shade, as ours do, but colour also, and all colours, as you may see if you look at a black cock's tail, or a butterfly's wing, or, indeed, most things that are or can be, so to speak. And, therefore, her photographs were very curious and famous, and the children looked with great delight for the opening of the book.

And on the title-page was written, "The History of the great and famous nation of the Doasyoulikes, who came away from the country of Hardwork, because they wanted to play on the Jews'-harp all day long."

In the first picture they saw these Doasyoulikes living in the land of Readymade, at the foot of the Happygolucky Mountains, where flapdoodle grows wild; and if you want to know what that is, you must read *Peter Simple*.

They lived very much such a life as those jolly old Greeks in Sicily, whom you may see painted on the ancient vases, and really there seemed to be great excuses for them, for they had no need to work.

Instead of houses, they lived in the beautiful caves of tufa, and bathed in the warm springs three times a day; and, as for clothes, it was so warm there that the gentlemen walked about in little beside a cocked hat and a pair of straps, or some light summer tackle of that kind; and the ladies all gathered gossamer in autumn (when they were not too lazy) to make their winter dresses.

They were very fond of music, but it was too much trouble to learn the piano or the violin; and, as for dancing, that would have been too great an exertion. So they sat on ant-hills all day long, and played on the Jews'-harp; and, if the ants bit them, why they just got up and went to the next ant-hill, till they were bitten there likewise.

And they sat under the flapdoodle-trees, and let the flapdoodle drop into their mouths; and under the vines, and squeezed the grape-juice down their throats; and, if any little pigs ran about ready roasted, crying, " Come and eat me," as was their fashion in that country, they waited till the pigs ran against their mouths, and then took a bite, and were content, just as so many oysters would have been.

They needed no weapons, for no enemies ever came near their land; and no tools, for everything was ready-made to their hand; and the stern old fairy Necessity never came near them to hunt them up, and make them use their wits, or die.

And so on, and so on, and so on, till there were never such comfortable, easy-going, happy-go-lucky people in the world.

" Well, that is a jolly life," said Tom.

" You think so? " said the fairy. " Do you see that great peaked mountain there behind," said the fairy, " with smoke coming out of its top? "

" Yes."

"And do you see all those ashes, and slag, and cinders, lying about? "

" Yes."

" Then turn over the next five hundred years, and you will see what happens next."

And behold the mountain had blown up like a barrel of gunpowder, and then boiled over like a kettle; whereby one-third of the Doasyoulikes were blown into the air, and another third were smothered in ashes; so that there was only one-third left.

" You see," said the fairy, " what comes of living on a burning mountain."

" Oh, why did you not warn them? " said little Ellie.

" I did warn them all that I could. I let the smoke come out of the mountain; and wherever there is smoke there is fire. And I laid the ashes and cinders all about; and wherever there are cinders, cinders may be again. But they did not like to face facts, my dears, as very few people do; and so they invented a cock-and-bull story, which, I am sure, I never told them, that the smoke was the breath of a giant, whom some gods or other had buried under the mountain; and that the cinders were what the dwarfs roasted the little pigs whole with; and other nonsense of that kind. And, when folks are in that humour, I cannot teach them, save by the good old birch-rod."

And then she turned over the next five hundred years: and there were the remnant of the Doasyoulikes, doing as they liked, as before. They were too lazy to move away from the mountains; so they said, If it has blown up once, that is all the more reason that it should not blow up again. And they were few in number: but they only said, The more the merrier, but the fewer the better fare. However, that was not quite true; for all the flapdoodle-trees were killed by the volcano, and they had eaten all the roast pigs, who, of course, could not be expected to have little ones. So they had to live very hard, on nuts and roots which they scratched out of the ground with sticks. Some of them talked of sowing corn, as their ancestors used to do, before they came into the land of Readymade; but they had forgotten how to make ploughs (they had forgotten even how to make Jews'-harps by this time), and had eaten all the seed-corn which they brought out of the land of Hardwork years since; and of course it was too much trouble to go away and find more. So they lived miserably on roots and nuts, and all the weakly little children had great stomachs, and then died.

" Why," said Tom, " they are growing no better than savages."

" And look how ugly they are all getting," said Ellie.

" Yes; when people live on poor vegetables instead of roast beef and plum-pudding, their jaws grow large, and

6

their lips grow coarse, like the poor Paddies who eat potatoes."

And she turned over the next five hundred years. And there they were all living up in trees, and making nests to keep off the rain. And underneath the trees lions were prowling about.

"Why," said Ellie, "the lions seem to have eaten a good many of them, for there are very few left now."

"Yes," said the fairy; "you see it was only the strongest and most active ones who could climb the trees, and so escape."

"But what great, hulking, broad-shouldered chaps they are," said Tom; "they are a rough lot as ever I saw."

"Yes, they are getting very strong now; for the ladies will not marry any but the very strongest and fiercest gentlemen, who can help them up the trees out of the lions' way."

And she turned over the next five hundred years. And in that they were fewer still, and stronger, and fiercer; but their feet had changed shape very oddly, for they laid hold of the branches with their great toes, as if they had been thumbs, just as a Hindoo tailor uses his toes to thread his needle.

The children were very much surprised, and asked the fairy whether that was her doing.

"Yes, and no," she said, smiling. "It was only those who could use their feet as well as their hands who could get a good living: or, indeed, get married; so that they got the best of everything, and starved out all the rest; and those who are left keep up a regular breed of toe-thumb-men, as a breed of shorthorns, or skye-terriers, or fancy pigeons is kept up."

"But there is a hairy one among them," said Ellie.

"Ah!" said the fairy, "that will be a great man in his time, and chief of all the tribe."

And, when she turned over the next five hundred years, it was true.

For this hairy chief had had hairy children, and they hairier children still; and every one wished to marry hairy husbands, and have hairy children too; for the climate was growing so damp that none but the hairy ones could live: all the rest coughed and sneezed, and had sore throats, and went into consumptions, before they could grow up to be men and women.

Then the fairy turned over the next five hundred years. And they were fewer still.

"Why, there is one on the ground picking up roots," said Ellie, "and he cannot walk upright."

No more he could; for in the same way that the shape of their feet had altered, the shape of their backs had altered also.

"Why," cried Tom, "I declare they are all apes."

"Something fearfully like it, poor foolish creatures," said the fairy. "They are grown so stupid now, that they can hardly think: for none of them have used their wits for many hundred years. They have almost forgotten, too, how to talk. For each stupid child forgot some of the words it heard from its stupid parents, and had not wits enough to make fresh words for itself. Beside, they are grown so fierce and suspicious and brutal that they keep out of each other's way, and mope and sulk in the dark forests, never hearing each other's voice, till they have forgotten almost what speech is like. I am afraid they will all be apes very soon, and all by doing only what they liked."

And in the next five hundred years they were all dead and gone, by bad food and wild beasts and hunters; all except one tremendous old fellow with jaws like a jack, who stood full seven feet high; and M. du Chaillu came up to him, and shot him, as he stood roaring and thumping his breast. And he remembered that his ancestors had once been men, and tried to say, "Am I not a man and a brother?" but had forgotten how to use his tongue; and then he had tried to call for a doctor, but he had forgotten the word for one. So all he said was, "Ubboboo!" and died.

And that was the end of the great and jolly nation of the Doasyoulikes. And, when Tom and Ellie came to the end of the book, they looked very sad and solemn; and they had good reason so to do, for they really fancied that the men were apes, and never thought, in their simplicity, of asking whether the creatures had hippopotamus majors in their brains or not; in which case, as you have been told already, they could not possibly have been apes, though they were more apish than the apes of all aperies.

"But could you not have saved them from becoming apes?" said little Ellie, at last.

"At first, my dear; if only they would have behaved like men, and set to work to do what they did not like. But the longer they waited, and behaved like the dumb beasts, who only do what they like, the stupider and clumsier they grew; till at last they were past all cure, for they had thrown their own wits away. It is such things as this that help to make me so ugly, that I know not when I shall grow fair."

"And where are they all now?" asked Ellie.

"Exactly where they ought to be, my dear.

"Yes!" said the fairy, solemnly, half to herself, as she closed the wonderful book. "Folks say now that I can make beasts into men, by circumstance, and selection, and competition, and so forth. Well, perhaps they are right; and perhaps, again, they are wrong. That is one of the seven things which I am forbidden to tell, till the coming of the Cocqcigrues; and, at all events, it is no concern of theirs. Whatever their ancestors were, men they are; and I advise them to behave as such, and act accordingly. But let them recollect this, that there are two sides to every question, and a downhill as well as an uphill road; and, if I can turn beasts into men, I can, by the same laws of circumstance, and slection, and competition, turn men into beasts. You were very near being turned into a beast once or twice, little Tom. Indeed, if you had not made up your mind to go on this journey, and see the world, like an Englishman, I am not sure but that you would have ended as an eft in a pond."

"Oh, dear me!" said Tom; "sooner than that, and be all over slime, I'll go this minute, if it is to the world's end."

CHAPTER SEVEN

And Nature, the old Nurse, took
    The child upon her knee,
Saying " Here is a story book
    Thy father hath written for thee.

" Come wander with me," she said,
    " Into regions yet untrod,
And read what is still unread
    In the Manuscripts of God."

And he wandered away and away
    With Nature, the dear old Nurse,
Who sang to him night and day
    The rhymes of the universe.
                        LONGFELLOW.

" Now," said Tom, " I am ready to be off, if it's to the world's end."

" Ah! " said the fairy, " that is a brave, good boy. But you must go further than the word's end, if you want to find Mr. Grimes; for he is at the Other-end-of-Nowhere. You must go to Shiny Wall, and through the white gate that never was opened; and then you will come to Peace-pool, and Mother Carey's Haven, where the good whales go when they die. And there Mother Carey will tell you the way to the Other-end-of-Nowhere, and there you will find Mr. Grimes."

" Oh, dear! " said Tom. " But I do not know my way to Shiny Wall, or where it is at all."

" Little boys must take the trouble to find out things for themselves, or they will never grow to be men; so that you must ask all the beasts in the sea and the birds in the air, and if you have been good to them, some of them will tell you the way to Shiny Wall."

" Well," said Tom, " it will be a long journey, so I had better start at once. Good-bye, Miss Ellie; you know I am getting a big boy, and I must go out and see the world."

"I know you must," said Ellie; "but you will not forget me, Tom. I shall wait here till you come."

And she shook hands with him, and bade him good-bye. Tom longed very much again to kiss her; but he thought it would not be respectful, considering she was a lady born; so he promised not to forget her: but his little whirl-about of a head was so full of the notion of going out to see the world, that it forgot her in five minutes: however, though his head forgot her, I am glad to say his heart did not.

So he asked all the beasts in the sea, and all the birds in the air, but none of them knew the way to Shiny Wall. For why? He was still too far down south.

Then he met a ship, far larger than he had ever seen—a gallant ocean-steamer, with a long cloud of smoke trailing behind; and he wondered how she went on without sails, and swam up to her to see. A school of dolphins were running races round and round her, going three feet for her one, and Tom asked them the way to Shiny Wall; but they did not know. Then he tried to find out how she moved, and at last he saw her screw, and was so delighted with it that he played under her quarter all day, till he nearly had his nose knocked off by the fans, and thought it time to move. Then he watched the sailors upon deck, and the ladies, with their bonnets and parasols: but none of them could see him, because their eyes were not opened —as, indeed, most people's eyes are not.

At last there came out into the quarter-gallery a very pretty lady, in deep black window's weeds, and in her arms a baby. She leaned over the quarter-gallery, and looked back and back toward England far away; and as she looked she sang:

I

" Soft soft wind, from out the sweet south sliding,
Waft thy silver cloud-webs athwart the summer sea;
Thin thin threads of mist on dewy fingers twining
Weave a veil of dappled gauze to shade my babe and me.

II

" Deep deep Love, within thine own abyss abiding,
Pour Thyself abroad, O Lord, on earth and air and sea;
   Worn weary hearts within Thy holy temple hiding,
Shield from sorrow, sin, and shame my helpless babe and
   me."

Her voice was so soft and low, and the music of the air
so sweet, that Tom could have listened to it all day. But
as she held the baby over the gallery-rail, to show it the
dolphins leaping and the water gurgling in the ship's wake,
lo! and behold, the baby saw Tom.

He was quite sure of that; for when their eyes met, the
baby smiled and held out its hands; and Tom smiled and
held out his hands too; and the baby kicked and leaped, as
if it wanted to jump overboard to him.

" What do you see, my darling? " said the lady; and
her eyes followed the baby's till she too caught sight of
Tom, swimming among the foam-beads below.

She gave a little shriek and start; and then she said,
quite quietly, " Babies in the sea? Well, perhaps it is the
happiest place for them," and waved her hand to Tom, and
cried, " Wait a little, darling, only a little: and perhaps
we shall go with you and be at rest."

And at that an old nurse, all in black, came out and
talked to her, and drew her in. And Tom turned away
northward, sad and wondering; and watched the great
steamer slide away into the dusk, and the lights on board
peep out one by one, and die out again, and the long bar
of smoke fade away into the evening mist, till all was out
of sight.

And he swam northward again, day after day, till at
last he met the King of the Herrings, with a currycomb
growing out of his nose, and a sprat in his mouth for a
cigar, and asked him the way to Shiny Wall; so he bolted
his sprat head foremost, and said:

" If I were you, young gentleman, I should go to the
Allalonestone, and ask the last of the Gairfowl. She is of
a very ancient clan, very nearly as ancient as my own; and

knows a good deal which these modern upstarts don't, as ladies of old houses are likely to do."

Tom asked his way to her, and the King of the Herrings told him very kindly; for he was a courteous old gentleman of the old school, though he was horribly ugly, and strangely bedizened too, like the old dandies who lounge in the clubhouse windows.

But just as Tom had thanked him and set off, he called after him: "Hi! I say, can you fly?"

"I never tried," says Tom. "Why?"

"Because, if you can, I should advise you to say nothing to the old lady about it. There; take a hint. Good-bye."

And away Tom went for seven days and seven nights due north-west, till he came to a great cod-bank, the like of which he never saw before. The great cod lay below in tens of thousands, and gobbled shell-fish all day long; and the blue sharks roved above in hundreds, and gobbled them when they came up. So they ate, and ate, and ate each other, as they had done since the making of the world; for no man had come here yet to catch them, and find out how rich old Mother Carey is.

And there he saw the last of the Gairfowl, standing up on the Allalonestone, all alone. And a very grand old lady she was, full three feet high, and bolt upright, like some old Highland chieftainess. She had on a black velvet gown, and a white pinner and apron, and a very high bridge to her nose (which is a sure mark of high breeding), and a large pair of white spectacles on it, which made her look rather odd: but it was the ancient fashion of her house.

And instead of wings, she had two little feathery arms, with which she fanned herself, and complained of the dreadful heat; and she kept on crooning an old song to herself, which she learnt when she was a little baby-bird, long ago:

"Two little birds, they sat on a stone,
One swam away, and then there was one;
With a fal-lal-la-lady.

The other swam after, and then there was none,
And so the poor stone was left all alone;
    With a fal-lal-la-lady."

It was " flew " away, properly, and not " swam " away:
but, as she could not fly, she had a right to alter it. However, it was a very fit song for her to sing, because she was
a lady herself.

Tom came up to her very humbly, and made his bow;
and the first thing she said was:

" Have you wings? Can you fly? "

" Oh dear, no, ma'am; I should not think of such a
thing," said cunning little Tom.

" Then I shall have great pleasure in talking to you
my dear. It is quite refreshing nowadays to see anything
without wings. They must all have wings, forsooth, now,
every new upstart sort of bird, and fly. What can they
want with flying, and raising themselves above their proper
station in life? In the days of my ancestors no birds ever
thought of having wings, and did very well without; and
now they all laugh at me because I keep to the good old
fashion. Why, the very marrocks and dovekies have got
wings, the vulgar creatures, and poor little ones enough
they are; and my own cousins too, the razor-bills, who are
gentlefolk born, and ought to know better than to ape
their inferiors."

And so she was running on, while Tom tried to get in a
word edgeways; and at last he did, when the old lady got
out of breath, and began fanning herself again; and then he
asked if she knew the way to Shiny Wall.

" Shiny Wall? Who should know better than I? We
all came from Shiny Wall, thousands of years ago, when it
was decently cold, and the climate was fit for gentlefolk;
but now, what with the heat, and what with these vulgar
winged things who fly up and down and eat everything,
so that gentlepeople's hunting is all spoilt, and one really
cannot get one's living, or hardly venture off the rock for
fear of being flown against by some creature that would
not have dared to come within a mile of one a thousand

years ago—what was I saying? Why, we have quite gone down in the world, my dear, and have nothing left but our honour. And I am the last of my family. A friend of mine and I came and settled on this rock when we were young, to be out of the way of low people. Once we were a great nation, and spread over all the Northern Isles. But men shot us so, and knocked us on the head, and took our eggs —why, if you will believe it, they say that on the coast of Labrador the sailors used to lay a plank from the rock on board the thing they called their ship, and drive us along the plank by hundreds, till we tumbled down into the ship's waist in heaps; and then, I suppose, they ate us, the nasty fellows! Well—but—what was I saying? At last there were none of us left, except on the old Gairfowlskerry, just off the Iceland coast, up which no man could climb. Even there we had no peace; for one day, when I was quite a young girl, the land rocked, and the sea boiled, and the sky grew dark, and all the air was filled with smoke and dust, and down tumbled the old Gairfowlskerry into the sea. The dovekies and marrocks, of course, all flew away; but we were too proud to do that. Some of us were dashed to pieces, and some drowned; and those who were left got away to Eldey, and the dovekies tell me they are all dead now, and that another Gairfowlskerry has risen out of the sea close to the old one, but that it is such a poor flat place that it is not safe to live on: and so here I am left alone."

This was the Gairfowl's story, and, strange as it may seem, it is every word of it true.

"If you only had had wings!" said Tom; "then you might all have flown away too."

"Yes, young gentleman: and if people are not gentlemen and ladies, and forget that *noblesse oblige*, they will find it as easy to get on in the world as other people who don't care what they do. Why, if I had not recollected that *noblesse oblige*, I should not have been all alone now." And the poor old lady sighed.

"How was that, ma'am?"

"Why, my dear, a gentleman came hither with me, and

after we had been here some time, he wanted to marry—in fact, he actually proposed to me. Well, I can't blame him; I was young, and very handsome then, I don't deny: but you see, I could not hear of such a thing, because he was my deceased sister's husband, you see?"

"Of course not, ma'am," said Tom; though, of course, he knew nothing about it. "She was very much diseased, I suppose?"

"You do not understand me, my dear. I mean, that being a lady, and with right and honourable feelings, as our house always has had, I felt it my duty to snub him, and howk him, and peck him continually, to keep him at his proper distance; and, to tell the truth, I once pecked him a little too hard, poor fellow, and he tumbled backwards off the rock, and—really, it was very unfortunate, but it was not my fault—a shark coming by saw him flapping, and snapped him up. And since then I have lived all alone—

With a fal-lal-la-lady.

And soon I shall be gone, my little dear, and nobody will miss me; and then the poor stone will be left all alone."

"But, please, which is the way to Shiny Wall?" said Tom.

"Oh, you must go, my little dear—you must go. Let me see—I am sure—that is—really, my poor old brains are getting quite puzzled. Do you know, my little dear, I am afraid, if you want to know, you must ask some of these vulgar birds about, for I have quite forgotten."

And the poor old Gairfowl began to cry tears of pure oil; and Tom was quite sorry for her; and for himself too, for he was at his wit's end whom to ask.

But by there came a flock of petrels, who are Mother Carey's own chickens; and Tom thought them much prettier than Lady Gairfowl, and so perhaps they were; for Mother Carey had had a great deal of fresh experience between the time that she invented the Gairfowl and the time that she invented them. They flitted along like a flock of black swallows, and hopped and skipped from wave to wave, lifting up their little feet behind them so daintily, and whistling to each other so tenderly, that Tom fell in love with them at once, and called them to know the way to Shiny Wall.

"Shiny Wall? Do you want Shiny Wall? Then come with us, and we will show you. We are Mother Carey's own chickens, and she sends us out over all the seas, to show the good birds the way home."

Tom was delighted, and swam off to them, after he had made his bow to the Gairfowl. But she would not return his bow: but held herself bolt upright, and wept tears of oil as she sang:

> "And so the poor stone was left all alone;
> With a fal-lal-la-lady."

But she was wrong there; for the stone was not left all alone: and the next time that Tom goes by it, he will see a sight worth seeing.

The old Gairfowl is gone already: but there are better things come in her place; and when Tom comes he will see the fishing-smacks anchored there in hundreds, from Scotland, and from Ireland, and from the Orkneys, and the Shetlands, and from all the Northern ports, full of the children of the old Norse Vikings, the masters of the sea. And the men will be hauling in the great cod by thousands, till their hands are sore from the lines; and they will be making cod-liver oil and guano, and salting down the fish; and there will be a man-of-war steamer there to protect them, and a lighthouse to show them the way; and you and I, perhaps, shall go some day to the Allalonestone to the great summer sea-fair, and dredge strange creatures such as man never saw before; and we shall hear the sailors boast that it is not the worst jewel in Queen Victoria's crown, for there are eighty miles of cod-bank, and food for all the poor folk in the land. That is what Tom will see, and perhaps you and I shall see it too. And then we shall not be sorry because we cannot get a Gairfowl to stuff, much less find gairfowl enough to drive them into stone pens and slaughter them, as the old Norsemen did, or drive them on board along a plank till the ship was victualled with them, as the old English and French rovers used to do, of whom dear old Hakluyt tells: but we shall remember what Mr. Tennyson says, how

> The old order changeth, giving place to the new,
> And God fulfils Himself in many ways.

And now Tom was all agog to start for Shiny Wall; but the petrels said no. They must go first to Allfowlsness, and wait there for the great gathering of all the sea-birds, before they start for their summer breeding-places far away in the Northern isles; and there they would be sure to find some birds which were going to Shiny Wall: but where Allfowlsness was, he must promise never to tell, lest men should go there and shoot the birds, and stuff them, and put them into stupid museums, instead of leaving them to play and breed and work in Mother Carey's water-garden, where they ought to be.

So where Allfowlsness is nobody must know; and all that is to be said about it is, that Tom waited there many days; and as he waited, he saw a very curious sight. On the rabbit burrows on the shore there gathered hundreds and hundreds of hoodie-crows, such as you see in Cambridgeshire. And they made such a noise, that Tom came on shore and went up to see what was the matter.

And there he found them holding their great caucus, which they hold every year in the North; and all their stump-orators were speechifying; and for a tribune, the speaker stood on an old sheep's skull.

And they cawed and cawed, and boasted of all the clever things they had done; how many lambs' eyes they had picked out, and how many dead bullocks they had eaten, and now many young grouse they had swallowed whole, and how many grouse-eggs they had flown away with, stuck on the the point of their bills, which is the hoodie-crow's particularly clever feat, of which he is as proud as a gipsy is of doing the hokany-baro; and what that is, I won't tell you.

And at last they brought out the prettiest, neatest young lady-crow that ever was seen, and set her in the middle, and all began abusing and vilifying, and rating, and bully-ragging at her, because she had stolen no grouse-eggs, and had actually dared to say that she would not steal any. So she was to be tried publicly by their laws (for the hoodies always try some offenders in their great yearly parliament) And there she stood in the middle, in her black gown and grey hood, looking as meek and as neat as a Quakeress, and they all bawled at her at once—

And it was in vain that she pleaded

That she did not like grouse-eggs;

That she could get her living very well without them;

That she was afraid to eat them, for fear of the game-keepers;

That she had not the heart to eat them, because the grouse were such pretty, kind, jolly birds;

And a dozen reasons more.

For all the other scaul-crows set upon her, and pecked her to death there and then, before Tom could come to help her; and then flew away, very proud of what they had done.

Now, was not this a scandalous transaction?

But they are true republicans, these hoodies, who do every one just what he likes, and make other people do so too, so that, for any freedom of speech, thought, or action, which is allowed among them, they might as well be American citizens of the new school.

But the fairies took the good crow, and gave her nine new sets of feathers running, and turned her at last into the most beautiful bird of paradise with a green velvet suit and a long tail, and sent her to eat fruit in the Spice Islands, where cloves and nutmegs grow.

And Mrs. Bedonebyasyoudid settled her account with the wicked hoodies. For, as they flew away, what should they find but a nasty dead dog?—on which they all set to work, pecking and gobbling and cawing and quarrelling, to their hearts' content. But the moment afterwards, they all threw up their bills into the air, and gave one screech; and then turned head over heels backward, and fell down dead, one hundred and twenty-three of them at once. For why? The fairy had told the gamekeeper in a dream, to fill the dead dog full of strychnine; and so he did.

And after a while the birds began to gather at Allfowlsness in thousands and tens of thousands, blackening all the air; swans and brant geese, harlequins and eiders, harelds and garganeys, smews and goosanders, divers and loons, grebes and dovekies, auks and razor-bills, gannets and petrels, skuas and terns, with gulls beyond all naming or numbering; and they paddled and washed and splashed and combed and brushed themselves on the sand, till the shore was white with feathers; and they quacked and clucked and gabbled and chattered and screamed and whooped as they talked over matters with their friends, and settled where they were to go and breed that summer, till you might have heard them ten miles off; and lucky it was for them that there was no one to hear them but the old keeper, who lived all alone upon the Ness, in a turf hut thatched with heather and fringed round with great stones slung across the roof by bent-ropes, lest the winter gales should blow the hut right away. But he never minded the birds nor hurt them, because they were not in season: indeed, he minded but two things in the whole world, and those were, his Bible and his grouse; for he was as good an old Scotchman as ever knit stockings on a winter's night: only, when all the birds were going, he toddled out, and took off his cap to them, and wished them a merry journey and a safe return; and then gathered up all the feathers which they had left, and cleaned them to sell down south, and make feather-beds for stuffy people to lie on.

Then the petrels asked this bird and that whether they would take Tom to Shiny Wall: but one set was going to Sutherland, and one to the Shetlands, and one to Norway, and one to Spitzbergen, and one to Iceland, and one to Greenland; but none would go to Shiny Wall. So the good-natured petrels said that they would show him part of the way themselves, but they were only going as far as Jan Mayen's land; and after that he must shift for himself.

And then all the birds rose up, and streamed away in long black lines, north, and north-east, and north-west, across the bright blue summer sky; and their cry was like ten thousand packs of hounds, and ten thousand peals of bells. Only the puffins stayed behind, and killed the young rabbits, and laid their eggs in the rabbit-burrows; which was rough practice, certainly: but a man must see to his own family.

And, as Tom and the petrels went north-eastward, it began to blow right hard; for the old gentleman in the grey greatcoat, who looks after the big copper boiler in the gulf of Mexico, had got behindhand with his work; so Mother Carey had sent an electric message to him for more steam; and now the steam was coming, as much in an hour as ought to have come in a week, puffing and roaring and swishing and swirling, till you could not see where the sky ended and the sea began. But Tom and the petrels never cared, for the gale was right abaft and away they went over the crests of the billows, as merry as so many flying-fish.

And at last they saw an ugly sight—the black side of a great ship, waterlogged in the trough of the sea. Her funnel and her masts were overboard, and swayed and surged under her lee; her decks were swept as clean as a barn floor, and there was no living soul on board.

The petrels flew up to her, and wailed round her; for they were very sorry indeed, and also they expected to find some salt pork; and Tom scrambled on board of her and looked round, frightened and sad.

And there, in a little cot, lashed tight under the bulwark, lay a baby fast asleep: the very same baby, Tom saw at once, which he had seen in the singing lady's arms.

He went up to it, and wanted to wake it: but behold, from under the cot out jumped a little black and tan terrier dog, and began barking and snapping at Tom, and would not let him touch the cot.

Tom knew the dog's teeth could not hurt him: but at

least it could shove him away, and did; and he and the dog fought and struggled, for he wanted to help the baby, and did not want to throw the poor dog overboard; but, as they were struggling, there came a tall green sea, and walked in over the weather side of the ship, and swept them all into the waves.

"Oh, the baby, the baby!" screamed Tom: but the next moment he did not scream at all; for he saw the cot settling down through the green water, with the baby smiling in it, fast asleep; and he saw the fairies come up from below, and carry baby and cradle gently down in their soft arms; and then he knew it was all right, and that there would be a new water baby in St. Brandan's Isle.

And the poor little dog?

Why, after he had kicked and coughed a little, he sneezed so hard, that he sneezed himself clean out of his skin, and turned into a water-dog, and jumped and danced round Tom, and ran over the crests of the waves, and snapped at the jelly-fish and the mackerel, and followed Tom the whole way to the Other-end-of-Nowhere.

Then they went on again, till they began to see the peak of Jan Mayen's Land, standing up like a white sugar-loaf, two miles above the clouds.

And there they fell in with a whole flock of molly-mocks, who were feeding on a dead whale.

"These are the fellows to show you the way," said Mother Carey's chickens; "we cannot help you further north. We don't like to get among the ice pack, for fear it should nip our toes; but the mollys dare fly anywhere."

So the petrels called to the mollys: but they were so busy and greedy, gobbling and pecking and spluttering and fighting over the blubber, that they did not take the least notice.

"Come, come," said the petrels, "you lazy greedy lubbers, this young gentleman is going to Mother Carey, and if you don't attend on him, you won't earn your discharge from her, you know."

"Greedy we are," says a great fat old molly, "but lazy

we ain't; and, as for lubbers, we're no more lubbers than you. Let's have a look at the lad."

And he flapped right into Tom's face, and stared at him in the most impudent way (for the mollys are audacious fellows, as all whalers know), and then asked him where he hailed from, and what land he sighted last.

And, when Tom told him, he seemed pleased, and said he was a good plucked one to have got so far.

" Come along, lads," he said to the rest, " and give this little chap a cast over the pack, for Mother Carey's sake. We've eaten blubber enough for to-day, and we'll e'en work out a bit of our time by helping the lad."

So the mollys took Tom up on their backs, and flew off with him, laughing and joking—and oh, how they did smell of train oil!

" Who are you, you jolly birds? " asked Tom.

" We are the spirits of the old Greenland skippers (as every sailor knows), who hunted here, right whales and horse-whales, full hundreds of years agone. But, because we were saucy and greedy, we were all turned into mollys, to eat whale's blubber all our days. But lubbers we are none, and could sail a ship against any man in the North Seas, though we don't hold with this new-fangled steam. And it's a shame of those black imps of petrels to call us so; but because they're her grace's pets, they think they may say anything they like."

" And who are you? " asked Tom of him, for he saw that he was the king of all the birds.

" My name is Hendrick Hudson, and a right good skipper was I; and my name will last to the world's end, in spite of all the wrong I did. For I discovered Hudson River, and I named Hudson's Bay; and many have come in my wake that dared not have shown me the way. But I was a hard man in my time, that's truth, and stole the poor Indians off the coast of Maine, and sold them for slaves down in Virginia; and at last I was so cruel to my sailors, here in these very seas, that they set me adrift in an open boat, and I never was heard of more. So now I'm the king of all the mollys, till I've worked out my time."

Jean Cruickshanks

And now they came to the edge of the pack, and beyond it they could see Shiny Wall looming, through mist, and snow, and storm. But the pack rolled horribly upon the swell, and the ice giants fought and roared, and leapt upon each other's backs, and ground each other to powder, so that Tom was afraid to venture among them, lest he should be ground to powder too. And he was the more afraid, when he saw lying among the ice pack the wrecks of many a gallant ship; some with masts and yards all standing some with the seamen frozen fast on board. Alas, alas, for them! They were all true English hearts; and they came to their end like good knights-errant, in searching for the white gate that never was opened yet.

But the good mollys took Tom and his dog up, and flew with them safe over the pack and the roaring ice giants, and set them down at the foot of Shiny Wall.

" And where is the gate? " asked Tom.

" There is no gate," said the mollys.

" No gate? " cried Tom aghast.

" None; never a crack of one, and that's the whole of the secret, as better fellows, lad, than you have found to their cost; and if there had been, they'd have killed by now every right whale that swims the sea."

" What am I to do, then? "

" Dive under the floe, to be sure, if you have pluck."

" I've not come so far to turn now," said Tom; " so here goes for a header."

" A lucky voyage to you, lad," said the mollys; " we knew you were one of the right sort. So good-bye."

" Why don't you come too? " asked Tom.

But the mollys only wailed sadly, " We can't go yet, we can't go yet," and flew over the pack.

So Tom dived under the great white gate which never was opened yet, and went on in black darkness, at the bottom of the sea, for seven days and seven nights. And yet he was not a bit frightened. Why should he be? He was a brave English lad, whose business is to go out and see all the world.

And at last he saw the lights, and clear clear water overhead; and up he came a thousand fathoms, among clouds of sea-moths, which fluttered round his head. There were moths with pink heads and wings and opal bodies, that flapped about slowly; moths with brown wings that flapped about quickly; yellow shrimps that hopped and skipped most quickly of all; and jellies of all the colours in the world, that neither hopped nor skipped, but only dawdled and yawned, and would not get out of his way. The dog snapped at them till his jaws were tired: but Tom hardly minded them at all, he was so eager to get to the top of the water, and see the pool where the good whales go.

And a very large pool it was, miles and miles across, though the air was so clear that the ice cliffs on the opposite side looked as if they were close at hand. All round it the ice cliffs rose, in walls and spires and battlements, and caves and bridges, and stories and galleries, in which the ice-fairies live, and drive away the storms and clouds, that Mother Carey's pool may lie calm from year's end to year's end. And the sun acted policeman, and walked round outside every day, peeping just over the top of the ice wall, to see that all went right; and now and then he played conjuring tricks, or had an exhibition of fireworks, to amuse the ice-fairies. For he would make himself into four or five suns at once, or paint the sky with rings and crosses and crescents of white fire, and stick himself in the middle of them, and wink at the fairies; and I dare say they were very much amused; for anything's fun in the country.

And there the good whales lay, the happy sleepy beasts, upon the still oily sea. They were all right whales, you must know, and finners, and razor-backs, and bottle-noses, and spotted sea-unicorns with long ivory horns. But the sperm whales are such raging, ramping, roaring rum-bustious fellows, that, if Mother Carey let them in, their would be no more peace in Peacepool. So she packs them away in a great pond by themselves at the South Pole, two hundred and sixty-three miles south-south-east of Mount Erebus, the great volcano in the ice; and there they butt each other with their ugly noses, day and night

from year's end to year's end. And if they think that
sport—why, so do their American cousins.

But here there were only good quiet beasts, lying about
like the black hulls of sloops, and blowing every now and
then jets of white steam, or sculling round with their huge
moths open, for the sea-moths to swim down their throats.
There were no threshers there to thresh their poor old
backs, or sword-fish to stab their stomachs, or saw-fish to
rip them up, or ice-sharks to bite lumps out of their sides,
or whalers to harpoon and lance them. They were quite
safe and happy there; and all they had to do was to wait
quietly in Peacepool, till Mother Carey sent for them to
make them out of old beasts into new.

Tom swam up to the nearest whale, and asked the way
to Mother Carey.

"There she sits in the middle," said the whale.

Tom looked; but he could see nothing in the middle of
the pool, but one peaked iceberg: and he said so.

"That's Mother Carey," said the whale, "as you will
find when you get to her. There she sits making old beasts
into new all the year round."

"How does she do that?"

"That's her concern, not mine," said the old whale;
and yawned so wide (for he was very large) that there
swam into his mouth 943 sea-moths, 13,846 jelly-fish no
bigger than pins' heads, a string of salpae nine yards long,
and forty-three little ice-crabs, who gave each other a
parting pinch all round, tucked their legs under their
stomachs, and determined to die decently, like Julius
Caesar.

"I suppose," said Tom, "she cuts up a great whale like
you into a whole shoal of porpoises?"

At which the old whale laughed so violently that he
coughed up all the creatures; who swam away again very
thankful at having escaped out of that terrible whalebone
net of his, from which bourne no traveller returns; and
Tom went on to the iceberg, wondering.

And, when he came near it, it took the form of the
grandest old lady he had ever seen—a white marble lady.

sitting on a white marble throne. And from the foot of the throne there swum away, out and out into the sea, millions of new-born creatures, of more shapes and colours than man ever dreamed. And they were Mother Carey's children, whom she makes out of the sea-water all day long.

He expected, of course—like some grown people who ought to know better—to find her snipping, piecing, fitting, stitching, cobbling, basting, filing, planing, hammering, turning, polishing, moulding, measuring, chiselling, slipping, and so forth, as men do when they go to work to make anything.

But, instead of that, she sat quite still with her chin upon her hand, looking down into the sea with two great grand blue eyes, as blue as the sea itself. Her hair was as white as the snow—for she was very very old—in fact, as old as anything which you are likely to come across, except the difference between right and wrong.

And, when she saw Tom, she looked at him very kindly.

"What do you want, my little man? It is long since I have seen a water baby here."

Tom told her his errand, and asked the way to the Other-end-of-Nowhere.

"You ought to know yourself, for you have been there already."

"Have I, ma'am? I'm sure I forget all about it."

"Then look at me."

And, as Tom looked into her great blue eyes, he recollected the way perfectly.

Now, was not that strange?

"Thank you, ma'am," said Tom. "Then I won't trouble your ladyship any more; I hear you are very busy."

"I am never more busy than I am now," she said, without stirring a finger.

"I heard, ma'am, that you were always making new beasts out of old."

"So people fancy. But I am not going to trouble myself to make things, my little dear. I sit here and make them make themselves."

"You are a clever fairy, indeed," thought Tom. And he was quite right.

That is a grand trick of good old Mother Carey's, and a grand answer, which she has had occasion to make several times to impertinent people.

There was once, for instance, a fairy who was so clever that she found out how to make butterflies. I don't mean sham ones; no: but real live ones, which would fly, and eat, and lay eggs, and do everything that they ought; and she was so proud of her skill that she went flying straight off to the North Pole, to boast to Mother Carey how she could make butterflies.

But Mother Carey laughed.

"Know, silly child," she said, "that any one can make things, if they will take time and trouble enough: but it is not every one who, like me, can make things make themselves."

But people do not yet believe that Mother Carey is as clever as all that comes to; and they will not till they, too, go the journey to the Other-end-of-Nowhere.

"And now, my pretty little man," said Mother Carey, "you are sure you know the way to the Other-end-of-Nowhere?"

Tom thought; and behold, he had forgotten it utterly.

"That is because you took your eyes off me."

Tom looked at her again, and recollected; and then looked away, and forgot in an instant.

"But what am I to do, ma'am? For I can't keep looking at you when I am somewhere else."

"You must do without me, as most people have to do, for nine hundred and ninety-nine thousandths of their lives; and look at the dog instead; for he knows the way well enough, and will not forget it. Besides, you may meet some very queer-tempered people there, who will not let you pass without this passport of mine, which you must hang round your neck and take care of; and, of course, as the dog will always go behind you, you must go the whole way backward."

" Backward! " cried Tom. " Then I shall not be able to see my way."

" On the contrary, if you look forward, you will not see a step before you, and be certain to go wrong; but, if you look behind you, and watch carefully whatever you have passed, and especially keep your eye on the dog, who goes by instinct, and therefore can't go wrong, then you will know what is coming next as plainly as if you saw it in a looking-glass."

Tom was very much astonished: but he obeyed her, for he had learnt always to believe what the fairies told him.

" So it is, my dear child," said Mother Carey; " and I will tell you a story, which will show you that I am perfectly right, as it is my custom to be."

" Once on a time, there were two brothers. One was called Prometheus, because he always looked before him, and boasted that he was wise beforehand. The other was called Epimetheus, because he always looked behind him, and did not boast at all; but said humbly, like the Irishman, that he had sooner prophesy after the event.

" Well, Prometheus was a very clever fellow, of course, and invented all sorts of wonderful things. But unfortunately, when they were set to work, to work was just what they would not do: wherefore very little has come of them, and very little is left of them; and now nobody knows what they were, save a few archaelogical old gentlemen who scratch in queer corners, and find little there save Ptinum Furem, Blaptem Mortisagam, Acarum Horridum, and Tineam Laciniarum.

" But Epimetheus was a very slow fellow, certainly, and went among men for a clod, and a muff, and a milksop, and a slowcoach, and a bloke, and a boodle, and so forth. And very little he did, for many years: but what he did, he never had to do over again.

" And what happened at last? There came to the two brothers the most beautiful creature that ever was seen, Pandora by name; which means, All the gifts of the Gods. But because she had a strange box in her hand, this fanciful forecasting, suspicious, prudential, theoretical, deductive, prophesying Prometheus, who was always settling what was going to happen, would have nothing to do with pretty Pandora and her box.

"But Epimetheus took her and it, as he took everything that came; and married her for better for worse, as every man ought, whenever he has even the chance of a good wife. And they opened the box between them, of course, to see what was inside: for, else, of what possible use could it have been to them?

"And out flew all the ills which flesh is heir to; all the children of the four great bogies, Self-will, Ignorance, Fear, and Dirt—for instance:

Measles,	Famines,
Monks,	Quacks,
Scarlatina,	Unpaid bills,
Idols,	Tight stays,
Hooping-coughs,	Potatoes,
Popes,	Bad Wine,
Wars,	Despots,
Peacemongers,	Demagogues,

And, worst of all, Naughty Boys and Girls: But one thing remained at the bottom of the box, and that was, Hope.

"So Epimetheus got a great deal of trouble, as most men do in this world: but he got the three best things in the world into the bargain—a good wife, and experience, and hope: while Prometheus had just as much trouble, and a great deal more (as you will hear), of his own making; with nothing beside, save fancies spun out of his own brain, as a spider spins her web out of her stomach.

"And Prometheus kept on looking before him so far ahead, that as he was running about with a box of lucifers (which were the only useful things he ever invented, and do as much harm as good), he trod on his own nose, a tumbled down (as most deductive philosophers do), whereby he set the Thames on fire; and they have hardly put it out again yet. So he had to be chained to the top of a mountain, with a vulture by him to give him a peck whenever he stirred, lest he should turn the whole world upside down with his prophecies and his theories.

" But stupid old Epimetheus went working and grubbing on, with the help of his wife Pandora, always looking behind him to see what had happened, till he really learnt to know now and then what would happen next; and understood so well which side his bread was buttered, and which way the cat jumped, that he began to make things which would work, and go on working, too; to till and drain the ground, and to make looms, and ships, and railroads, and steam ploughs, and electric telegraphs, and all the things which you see in the Great Exhibition; and to foretell famine and bad weather, and the price of stocks, and the end of President Lincoln's policy; till at last he grew as rich as a Jew, and as fat as a farmer; and people thought twice before they meddled with him, and only once before they asked him to help them; for, because he earned his money well, he could afford to spend it well likewise.

" And his children are the men of science, who get good lasting work done in the world: but the children of Prometheus are the fanatics, and the theorists, and the bigots, and the bores, and the noisy windy people, who go telling silly folk what will happen, instead of looking to see what has happened already."

Now, was not Mother Carey's a wonderful story? And, I am happy to say, Tom believed it every word.

For so it happened to Tom likewise. He was very sorely tried; for though, by keeping the dog to heels (or rather to toes, for he had to walk backward), he could see pretty well which way the dog was hunting, yet it was much slower work to go backwards than to go forwards. But, what was more trying still, no sooner had he got out of Peacepool, than there came running to him all the conjurors, fortune-tellers, astrologers, prophesiers, projectors, prestigiators, as many as were in those parts (and there are too many of them everywhere), Old Mother Shipton on her broomstick, with Merlin, Thomas the Rhymer, Gerbertus, Rabanus Maurus, Nostradamus, Zadkiel, Raphael Moore, Old Nixon, and a good many in black coats and white ties who might have known better, considering in what century they were born, all bawling and screaming at him, " Look ahead, only look ahead; and we will show you what man never saw before, and right away to the end of the world! "

But I am proud to say that, though Tom had not been at Cambridge—for, if he had, he would have certainly been senior wrangler—he was such a little dogged, hard, gnarly, foursquare brick of an English boy, that he never turned his head round once all the way from Peacepool to the Other-end-of-Nowhere: but kept his eye on the dog, and let him pick out the scent, hot or cold, straight or crooked, set or dry, up hill or down dale; by which means he never made a single mistake, and saw all the wonderful and hitherto by-no-mortal-man-imagined things, which it is my duty to relate to you in the next chapter.

CHAPTER EIGHT AND LAST

Come to me, O ye children!
　For I hear you at your play;
And the questions that perplexed me
　Have vanished quite away.

Ye open the Eastern windows,
　That look towards the sun,
Where thoughts are singing swallows,
　And the brooks of morning run.

　　　★　　★　　★　　★

For what are all our contrivings
　And the wisdom of our books,
When compared with your caresses,
　And the gladness of your looks?

Ye are better than all the ballads
　That ever were sung or said;
For ye are living poems,
　And all the rest are dead.
						LONGFELLOW.

HERE begins the never-to-be-too-much-studied account of the nine-hundred-and-ninety-ninth part of the wonderful things which Tom saw, on his journey to the Other-end-of-Nowhere; which all good little children are requested to read; that, if ever they get to the Other-end-of-Nowhere, as they may very probably do, they may not burst out laughing, or try to run away, or do any other silly vulgar thing which may offend Mrs. Bedonebyasyoudid.

Now, as soon as Tom had left Peacepool, he came to the white lap of the great sea-mother, ten thousand fathoms deep; where she makes world-pap all day long, for the steam-giants to knead, and the fire-giants to bake, till it has risen and hardened into mountain-loaves and island-cakes.

And there Tom was very near being kneaded up in the

world-pap, and turned into a fossil water baby; which would have astonished the Geological Society of New Zealand some hundreds of thousands of years hence.

For, as he walked along in the silence of the sea-twilight, on the soft white ocean floor, he was aware of a hissing, and a roaring, and a thumping, and a pumping, as of all the steam-engines in the world at once. And, when he came near, the water grew boiling hot; not that that hurt him in the least: but it also grew as foul as gruel; and every moment he stumbled over dead shells, and fish, and sharks, and seals, and whales, which had been killed by the hot water.

And at last he came to the great sea-serpent himself lying dead at the bottom; and, as he was too thick to scramble over, Tom had to walk round him three-quarters of a mile and more, which put him out of his path sadly; and, when he had got round, he came to the place called Stop. And there he stopped, and just in time.

For he was on the edge of a vast hole in the bottom of the sea, up which was rushing and roaring clear steam enough to work all the engines in the world at once; so clear, indeed, that it was quite light at moments; and Tom could see almost up to the top of the water above, and down below into the pit for nobody knows how far.

But, as soon as he bent his head over the edge, he got such a rap on the nose from pebbles, that he jumped back again; for the steam, as it rushed up, rasped away the sides of the hole, and hurled it up into the sea in a shower of mud and gravel and ashes; and then it spread all around, and sank again, and covered in the dead fish so fast, that before Tom had stood there five minutes he was buried in silt up to his ankles, and began to be afraid that he should have been buried alive.

And perhaps he would have been, but that while he was thinking, the whole piece of ground on which he stood was torn off and blown upwards, and away flew Tom a mile up through the sea, wondering what was coming next.

At last he stopped—thump! and found himself tight in

the legs of the most wonderful bogy which he had ever seen.

It had I don't know how many wings, as big as the sails of a windmill, and spread out in a ring like them; and with them it hovered over the steam which rushed up, as a ball hovers over the top of a fountain. And for every wing above it had a leg below, with a claw like a comb at the tip, and a nostril at the root; and in the middle it had no stomach and one eye; and as for its mouth, that was all on one side, as the madreporiform tubercle in a star-fish is. Well, it was a very strange beast; but no stranger than some dozens which you may see.

"What do you want here," it cried quite peevishly, "getting in my way?" and it tried to drop Tom: but he held on tight to its claws, thinking himself safer where he was.

So Tom told him who he was, and what his errand was. And the thing winked its one eye, and sneered:

"I am too old to be taken in in that way. You are come after gold—I know you are."

"Gold! What is gold?" And really Tom did not know; but the suspicious old bogy would not believe him.

But after a while Tom began to understand a little. For, as the vapours came up out of the hole, the bogy smelt them with his nostrils, and combed them and sorted them with his combs; and then, when they steamed up through them against his wings, they were changed into showers and streams of metal. From one wing fell gold-dust, and from another silver, and from another copper, and from another tin, and from another lead, and so on, and sank into the soft mud, into veins and cracks, and hardened there. Whereby it comes to pass that the rocks are full of metal.

But, all of a sudden, somebody shut off the steam below, and the hole was left empty in an instant: and then down rushed the water into the hole, in such a whirlpool that the bogy spun round and round as fast as a teetotum. But that was all in his day's work, like a fair fall with the hounds; so all he did was to say to Tom:

" Now is your time, youngster, to get down, if you are in earnest, which I don't believe."

" You'll soon see," said Tom; and away he went, as bold as Baron Munchausen, and shot down the rushing cataract like a salmon at Ballisodare.

And, when he got to the bottom, he swam till he was washed on shore safe upon the Other-end-of-Nowhere; and he found it, to his surprise, as most other people do, much more like This-End-of-Somewhere than he had been in the habit of expecting.

And first he went through Waste-paper-land, where all the stupid books lie in heaps, up hill and down dale, like leaves in a winter wood; and there he saw people digging and grubbing among them, to make worse books out of bad ones, and thrashing chaff to save the dust of it; and a very good trade they drove thereby, especially among children.

Then he went by the sea of slops, to the mountain of messes, and the territory of tuck, where the ground was very sticky, for it was all made of bad toffee (not Everton toffee, of course), and full of deep cracks and holes choked with wind-fallen fruit, and green gooseberries, and sloes, and crabs, and whinberries, and hips and haws, and all the nasty things which little children will eat if they can get them. But the fairies hide them out of the way in that country as fast as they can, and very hard work they have, and of very little use it is. For as fast as they hide away the old trash, foolish and wicked people make fresh trash full of lime and poisonous paints, and actually go and steal receipts out of old Madame Science's big book to invent poisons for little children, and sell them at wakes and fairs and tuck-shops. Very well. Let them go on. Dr. Letheby and Dr. Hassall cannot catch them, though they are setting traps for them all day long. But the Fairy with the birch-rod will catch them all in time, and make them begin at one corner of their shops, and eat their way out at the other: by which time they will have got such stomach-aches as will cure them of poisoning little children.

Next day he saw all the little people in the world, writing

all the little books in the world, about all the other little people in the world; probably because they had no great people to write about: and if the names of the books were not *Squeeky*, nor the *Pumplighter*, nor the *Narrow Narrow World*, nor the *Hills of the Chattermuch*, nor the *Children's Twaddeday*, why then they were something else. And all the rest of the little people in the world read the books, and thought themselves each as good as the President; and perhaps they were right, for every one knows his own business best. But Tom thought he would sooner have a jolly good fairy tale, about Jack the Giant-killer or Beauty and the Beast, which taught him something that he didn't know already.

And next he came to the centre of Creation (the hub, they call it there), which lies in latitude 42.21 south, and longitude 108.56 east.

And there he found all the wise people instructing mankind in the science of spirit-rapping, while their house was burning over their heads: and when Tom told them of the fire, they held an indignation meeting forthwith, and unanimously determined to hang Tom's dog for coming into their country with gunpowder in his mouth. Tom couldn't help saying that though they did fancy they had carried all the wit away with them out of Lincolnshire two hundred years ago, yet if they had had one such Lincolnshire nobleman among them as good old Lord Yarborough, he would have called for the fire-engines before he hanged other people's dogs. But it was of no use, and the dog was hanged: and Tom couldn't even have his carcase; for they had abolished the have-his-carcase act in that country, for fear lest when rogues fell out, honest men should come by their own. And so they would have succeeded perfectly, as they always do, only that (as they also always do) they failed in one little particular, viz. that the dog would not die, being a water-dog, but bit their fingers so abominably that they were forced to let him go, and Tom likewise, as British subjects. Whereon they recommended rapping for the spirits of their fathers; and very much astonished the poor old spirits were when they came, and saw how, according to the laws of Mrs. Bedonebyasyoudid, their descendants had weakened their constitution by hard living.

Then came Tom to the Island of Polupragmosyne, which some call Rogues' Harbour (but they are wrong; for that is in the middle of Bramshill Bushes, and the county police have cleared it out long ago). There every one knows his neighbour's business better than his own; and a very noisy place it is, as might be expected, considering that all the inhabitants are ex-officio on the wrong side of the house in the "Parliament of Man, and the Federation of the World"; and are always making wry mouths, and crying that the fairies' grapes were sour.

There Tom saw ploughs drawing horses, nails driving hammers, birds' nest taking boys, books making authors, bulls keeping china-shops, monkeys shaving cats, dead dogs drilling live lions, blind brigadiers shelfed as principals of colleges, play-actors not in the least shelfed as popular preachers; and, in short, every one set to do something which he had not learnt, because in what he had learnt, or pretended to learn, he had failed.

There stands the Pantheon of the great Unsuccessful, from the builders of the Tower of Babel to those of the Trafalgar Fountains; in which politicians lecture on the constitutions which ought to have marched, conspirators on the revolutions which ought to have succeeded, economists on the schemes which ought to have made every one's fortune, projectors on the discoveries which ought to have set the Thames on fire; and (in due time) presidents on the union which ought to have reunited, and secretaries of state on the greenbacks which ought to have done just as well as hard money. There cobblers lecture on orthopedy (whatsoever that may be) because they cannot sell their shoes; and poets on Aesthetics (whatsoever that may be) because they cannot sell their poetry. There philosophers demonstrate that England would be the freest and richest country in the world, if she would only turn Papist again; penny-a-liners abuse *The Times*, because they have not wit enough to get on its staff; and young ladies walk about with lockets of Charles the First's hair (or of somebody else's, when the Jews' genuine stock is used up), inscribed with the neat and appropriate legend—which indeed is popular through all that land, and which, I hope, you will learn to translate in due time and perpend likewise:

Victrix causa diis placuit, sed victa puellis,

When he got into the middle of the town, they all set on him at once, to show him his way; or rather, to show him that he did not know his way; for as for asking him what way he wanted to go, no one ever thought of that.

But one pulled him hither, and another poked him thither, and a third cried:

"You mustn't go west, I tell you; it is destruction to go west."

"But I am not going west, as you may see," said Tom.

And another, "The east lies here, my dear; I assure you this is the east."

"But I don't want to go east," said Tom.

"Well then at all events, whichever way you are going, you are going wrong," cried they all with one voice—which was the only thing which they ever agreed about; and all pointed at once to all the thirty-and-two points of the compass, till Tom thought all the signposts in England had got together, and fallen fighting.

And whether he would have ever escaped out of the town, it is hard to say, if the dog had not taken it into his head that they were going to pull his master in pieces, and tackled them so sharply about the gastro-cnemius muscle, that he gave them some business of their own to think of at last; and while they were rubbing their bitten calves, Tom and the dog got safe away.

On the borders of that island he found Gotham, where the wise men live; the same who dragged the pond because the moon had fallen into it, and planted a hedge round the cuckoo, to keep spring all the year. And he found them bricking up the town gate, because it was so wide that little folks could not get through. And, when he asked why, they told him they were expanding their liturgy. So he went on; for it was no business of his: only he could not help saying that in his country, if the kitten could not get in at the same hole as the cat, she might stay outside and mew.

But he saw the end of such fellows, when he came to the island of the Golden Asses, where nothing but thistles grow. For there they were all turned into mokes with ears a yard long, for meddling with matters which they do not understand, as Lucius did in the story. And like him, mokes they must remain, till, by the laws of development, the thistles develop into roses. Till then, they must comfort themselves with the thought, that the longer theirs ear are, the thicker their hides; and so a good beating don't hurt them.

Then came Tom to the great land of Hearsay, in which are no less than thirty and odd kings, beside half a dozen Republics, and perhaps more by next mail.

And there he fell in with a deep, dark, deadly, and destructive war, waged by the princes and potentates of those parts, both spiritual and temporal, against what do you think? One thing I am sure of. That unless I told you, you would never know; nor how they waged that war either; for all their strategy and art military consisted in the safe and easy process of stopping their ears and screaming, " Oh, don't tell us! " and then running away.

So when Tom came into that land, he found them all, high and low, man, woman, and child, running for their lives day and night continually, and entreating not to be told they didn't know what: only the land being an island, and they having a dislike to the water (being a musty lot for the most part), they ran round and round the shore for ever, which (as the island was exactly of the same circumference as the planet on which we have the honour of living) was hard work, especially to those who had business to look after. But before them, as bandmaster and fugleman, ran a gentleman shearing a pig; the melodious strains of which animal led them for ever, if not to conquest, still to fight; and kept up their spirits mightily with the thought that they would at least have the pig's wool for their pains.

And running after them, day and night, came such a poor, lean, seedy, hard-worked old giant, as ought to have been cockered up, and had a good dinner given him, and a good wife found him, and been set to play with little children; and then he would have been a very presentable old fellow after all; for he had a heart, though it was considerably overgrown with brains.

He was made up principally of fish bones and parchment, put together with wire and Canada balsam; and smelt strongly of spirits, though he never drank anything but water: but spirits he used somehow, there was no denying. He had a great pair of spectacles on his nose, and a butterfly-net in one hand, and a geological hammer in the other; and was hung all over with pockets, full of collecting boxes, bottles, miscroscopes, telescopes, barometers, ordnance maps, scalpels, forceps, photographic apparatus, and all other tackle for finding out everything about everything, and a little more too. And, most strange of all, he was running not forwards but backwards, as fast as he could.

Away all the good folks ran from him, except Tom, who stood his ground and dodged between his legs; and the giant, when he had passed him, looked down, and cried, as if he was quite pleased and comforted:

" What? who are you? And you actually don't run away, like all the rest? " But he had to take his spectacles off, Tom remarked, in order to see him plainly.

Tom told him who he was; and the giant pulled out a bottle and a cork instantly, to collect him with.

But Tom was too sharp for that, and dodged between his legs and in front of him; and then the giant could not see him at all.

" No, no, no! " said Tom, " I've not been round the world, and through the world, and up to Mother Carey's haven, beside being caught in a net and called a Holothurian and a Cephalopod, to be bottled up by any old giant like you."

And when the giant understood what a great traveller Tom had been, he made a truce with him at once, and would have kept him there to this day to pick his brains,

THE WATER BABIES

so delighted was he at finding any one to tell him what he did not know before.

"Ah, you lucky little dog!" said he at last, quite simply—for he was the simplest, pleasantest, honestest, kindliest old Dominie Sampson of a giant that ever turned the world upside down without intending it—"Ah, you lucky little dog! If I had only been where you have been, to see what you have seen!"

"Well," said Tom, "if you want to do that, you had best put your head under water for a few hours, as I did, and turn into a water baby, or some other baby, and then you might have a chance."

"Turn into a baby, eh? If I could do that, and know what was happening to me for but one hour, I should know everything then, and be at rest. But I can't; I can't be a little child again; and I suppose if I could, it would be no use, because then I should know nothing about what was happening to me. Ah, you lucky little dog!" said the poor old giant.

"But why do you run after all these poor people?" said Tom, who liked the giant very much.

"My dear, it's they that have been running after me, father and son, for hundreds and hundreds of years, throwing stones at me till they have knocked off my spectacles fifty times, and calling me a malignant and a turbaned Turk, who beat a Venetian and traduced the state—goodness only knows what they mean, for I never read poetry—and hunting me round and round—though catch me they can't, for every time I go over the same ground, I go the faster, and grow the bigger. While all I want is to be friends with them, and to tell them something to their advantage, like Mr. Joseph Ady: only somehow they are so strangely afraid of hearing it. But, I suppose I am not a man of the world, and have no tact."

"But why don't you turn round and tell them so?"

"Because I can't. You see, I am one of the sons of Epimetheus, and must go backwards, if I am to go at all."

"But why don't you stop, and let them come up to you?"

198

" Why, my dear, only think. If I did, all the butterflies and cockyolybirds would fly past me, and then I should catch no more new species, and should grow rusty and mouldy, and die. And I don't intend to do that, my dear; for I have a destiny before me, they say: though what it is I don't know, and don't care."

" Don't care? " said Tom.

" No. Do the duty which lies nearest you, and catch the first beetle you come across, is my motto; and I have thriven by it for some hundred years. Now I must go on. Dear me, while I have been talking to you, at least nine new species have escaped me."

And on went the giant, behind before, like a bull in a china shop, till he ran into the steeple of the great idol temple (for they are all idolaters in those parts, of course, else they would never be afraid of giants), and knocked the upper half clean off, hurting himself horribly about the small of the back.

But little he cared; for as soon as the ruins of the steeple were well between his legs, he poked and peered among the falling stones, and shifted his spectacles, and pulled out his pocket-magnifier, and cried:

" An entirely new Oniscus, and three obscure Podurellae! Beside a moth which M. le Roi des Papillons (though he, like all Frenchmen, is given to hasty inductions) says is confined to the limits of the Glacial Drift. This is most important! "

And down he sat on the nave of the temple (not being a man of the world) to examine his Podurellae. Whereon (as was to be expected) the roof caved in bodily, smashing the idols, and sending the priests flying out of doors and windows, like rabbits out of a burrow when a ferret goes in.

But he never heeded; for out of the dust flew a bat, and the giant had him in a moment.

" Dear me! This is even more important! Here is a cognate species to that which Macgilliwaukie Brown insists is confined to the Buddhist Temples of Little Thibet; and now when I look at it, it may be only a variety produced by difference of climate! "

And having bagged his bat, up he got, and on he went; while all the people ran, being in none the better humour for having their temple smashed for the sake of three obscure species of Podurella, and a Buddhist bat.

"Well," thought Tom; "this is a very pretty quarrel, with a good deal to be said on both sides. But it is no business of mine."

And no more it was; because he was a water-baby, and had the original sow by the right ear; which you will never have, unless you be a baby, whether of the water, the land, or the air, matters not, provided you can only keep on continually being a baby.

So the giant ran round after the people, and the people ran round after the giant, and they are running unto this day for aught I know, or do not know; and will run till either he, or they, or both, turn into little children. And then, as Shakespeare says (and therefore it must be true):

> Jack shall have Gill
> Nought shall go ill
> The man shall have his mare again, and all go well.

Then Tom came to a very famous island, which was called, in the days of the great traveller Captain Gulliver, the Isle of Laputa. But Mrs. Bedonebyasyoudid has named it over again, the Isle of Tomtoddies, all heads and no bodies.

And when Tom came near it, he heard such a grumbling and grunting and growling and wailing and weeping and whining that he thought people must be ringing little pigs, or cropping puppies' ears, or drowning kittens: but when he came nearer still, he began to hear words among the noise; which was the Tomtoddies' song which they sing morning and evening, and all night too, to their great idol Examination:

"I can't learn my lesson: the examiner's coming!"

And that was the only song which they knew.

And when Tom got on shore the first thing he saw was a great pillar, on one side of which was inscribed, " Playthings not allowed here "; at which he was so shocked that he would not stay to see what was written on the other side. Then he looked round for the people of the island: but instead of men, women, and children, he found nothing but turnips and radishes, beet and mangold wurzel, without a single green leaf among them, and half of them burst and decayed, with toadstools growing out of them. Those which were left began crying to Tom, in half a dozen different languages at once, and all of them badly spoken, " I can't learn my lesson; do come and help me! " And one cried, " Can you show me how to extract this square root? "

And another, " Can you tell me the distance between α Lyrae and β Camelopardalis? "

And another, " What is the latitude and longitude of Snooksville, in Noman's County, Oregon, U.S.? "

And another, " What was the name of Mutius Scaevola's thirteenth cousin's grandmother's maid's cat? "

And another, " How long would it take a school inspector of average activity to tumble head over heels from London to York? "

And another, " Can you tell me the name of a place that nobody ever heard of, where nothing ever happened, in a country which has not been discovered yet? "

And another, " Can you show me how to correct this hopelessly corrupt passage of Graidiocolosyrtus Tabenniticus, on the cause why crocodiles have no tongues? "

And so on, and so on, and so on, till one would have thought they were all trying for tide-waiters' places, or cornetcies in the heavy dragoons.

" And what good on earth will it do you if I did tell you? " quoth Tom.

Well, they didn't know that: all they knew was the examiner was coming.

Then Tom stumbled on the hugest and softest nimble-comequick turnip you ever saw filling a hole in a crop of

swedes, and it cried to him, " Can you tell me anything
at all about anything you like ? "

" About what ? " says Tom.

" About anything you like; for as fast as I learn things
I forget them again. So my mamma says that my intellect
is not adapted for methodic science, and says that I must
go in for general information."

Tom told him that he did not know general information,
nor any officers in the army; only he had a friend once
that went for a drummer: but he could tell him a great
many strange things which he had seen in his travels.

So he told him prettily enough, while the poor turnip
listened very carefully; and the more he listened, the more
he forgot, and the more water ran out of him.

Tom thought he was crying: but it was only his poor
brains running away, from being worked so hard; and as
Tom talked, the unhappy turnip streamed down all over
with juice, and split and shrank till nothing was left of
him but rind and water; whereat Tom ran away in a
fright, for he thought he might be taken up for killing the
turnip.

But, on the contrary, the turnip's parents were highly
delighted, and considered him a saint and a martyr, and
put up a long inscription over his tomb about his wonderful
talents, early development, and unparalleled precocity.
Were they not a foolish couple ? But there was a still more
foolish couple next to them, who were beating a wretched
little radish, no bigger than my thumb, for sullenness and
obstinacy and wilful stupidity, and never knew that the
reason why it couldn't learn or hardly even speak was, that
there was a great worm inside it eating out all its brains.
But even they are no foolisher than some hundred score of
papas and mammas, who fetch the rod when they ought to
fetch a new toy, and send to the dark cupboard instead of
to the doctor.

Tom was so puzzled and frightened with all he saw, that
he was longing to ask the meaning of it; and at last he
stumbled over a respectable old stick lying half covered
with earth. But a very stout and worthy stick it was, for it

belonged to good Roger Ascham in old time, and had carved on its head King Edward the Sixth, with the Bible in his hand.

"You see," said the stick, "there were as pretty little children once as you could wish to see, and might have been so still if they had been only left to grow up like human beings, and then handed over to me; but their foolish fathers and mothers, instead of letting them pick flowers, and make dirt-pies, and get birds' nests, and dance round the gooseberry bush, as little children should, kept them always at lessons, working, working, working, learning weekday lessons all weekdays, and Sunday lessons all Sunday, and weekly examinations every Saturday, and monthly examinations every month, and yearly examinations every year, everything seven times over, as if once was not enough, and enough as good as a feast—till their brains grew big, and their bodies grew small, and they were all changed into turnips, with little but water inside; and still their foolish parents actually pick the leaves off them as fast as they grow, lest they should have anything green about them."

"Ah!" said Tom, "if dear Mrs. Doasyouwouldbedone-by knew of it she would send them a lot of tops, and balls, and marbles, and ninepins, and make them all as jolly as sandboys."

"It would be no use," said the stick. "They can't play now, if they tried. Don't you see how their legs have turned to roots and grown into the ground, by never taking any exercise, but sapping and moping always in the same place? But here comes the Examiner-of-all-Examiners. So you had better get away, I warn you, or he will examine you and your dog into the bargain, and set him to examine all the other dogs, and you to examine all the other water-babies. There is no escaping out of his hands, for his nose is nine thousand miles long, and can go down chimneys and through keyholes, upstairs, downstairs, in my lady's chamber, examining all little boys, and the little boys' tutors likewise. But when he is thrashed—so Mrs. Bedonebyasyoudid has promised me—I shall have the thrashing of him: and if I don't lay it on with a will it's a pity."

Tom went off: but rather slowly and surlily; for he was somewhat minded to face this same Examiner-of-all-Examiners, who came striding among the poor turnips, binding heavy burdens and grievous to be borne, and laying them on little children's shoulders, like the Scribes and Pharisees of old, and not touching the same with one of his fingers; for he had plenty of money, and a fine house to live in, and so forth; which was more than the poor little turnips had.

But when he got near, he looked so big and burly and dictatorial, and shouted so loud to Tom to come and be examined, that Tom ran for his life, and the dog too. And really it was time; for the poor turnips, in their hurry and fright, crammed themselves so fast to be ready for the Examiner, that they burst and popped by dozens all round him, till the place sounded like Aldershot on a field-day, and Tom thought he should be blown into the air, dog and all.

As he went down to the shore he passed the poor turnip's new tomb. But Mrs. Bedonebyasyoudid had taken away the epitaph about talents and precocity and development, and put up one of her own instead which Tom thought much more sensible:

> Instruction sore long time I bore,
>   And cramming was in vain;
> Till Heaven did please my woes to ease,
>   By water on the brain.' '

So Tom jumped into the sea, and swam on his way singing:

> " Farewell, Tomtoddies all; I thank my stars
>   That nought I know save those three royal r's:
> Reading and riting sure, with rithmetick,
>   Will help a lad of sense through thin and thick."

Whereby you may see that Tom was no poet: but no more was John Bunyan, though he was as wise a man as you will meet in a month of Sundays.

And next he came to Oldwivesfabledom, where the folks were all heathens, and worshipped a howling ape.

And there he found a little boy sitting in the middle of the road, and crying bitterly.

"What are you crying for?" said Tom.

"Because I am not as frightened as I could wish to be."

"Not frightened? You are a queer little chap: but, if you want to be frightened, here goes—Boo!"

"Ah," said the little boy, "that is very kind of you; but I don't feel that it has made any impression."

Tom offered to upset him, punch him, stamp on him, fettle him over the head with a brick, or anything else whatsoever which would give him the slightest comfort.

But he only thanked Tom very civilly, in fine long words which he had heard other folk use, and which, therefore, he thought were fit and proper to use himself; and cried on till his papa and mamma came, and sent off for the Powwow man immediately. And a very good-natured gentleman and lady they were, though they were heathens; and talked quite pleasantly to Tom about his travels, till the Powwow man arrived, with his thunder-box under his arm.

And a well-fed, ill-favoured gentleman he was, as ever served Her Majesty at Portland. Tom was a little frightened at first; for he thought it was Grimes. But he soon saw his mistake: for Grimes always looked a man in the face; and this fellow never did. And when he spoke, it was fire and smoke; and when he sneezed, it was squibs and crackers; and when he cried (which he did whenever it paid him), it was boiling pitch; and some of it was sure to stick.

"Here we are again!" cried he, like the clown in a pantomime. "So you can't feel frightened, my little dear —eh? I'll do that for you. I'll make an impression on you! Yah! Boo! Whirroo! Hullabaloo!"

And he rattled, thumped, brandished his thunder-box,

yelled, shouted, raved, roared, stamped, and danced corroboy like any black fellow; and then he touched a spring in the thunder-box, and out popped turnip-ghosts and magic-lanthorns and pasteboard bogies and spring-heeled Jacks and sallabalas, with such horrid din, clatter, clank, roll, rattle, and roar, that the little boy turned up the whites of his eyes, and fainted right away.

And at that his poor heathen papa and mamma were as much delighted as if they had found a gold mine; and fell down upon their knees before the Powwow man, and gave him a palanquin with a pole of solid silver and curtains of cloth of gold; and carried him about in it on their own backs: but as soon as they had taken him up, the pole stuck to their shoulders, and they could not set him down any more, but carried him on willy-nilly, as Sinbad carried the old man of the sea: which was a pitiable sight to see; for the father was a very brave officer, and wore two swords and a blue button; and the mother was as pretty a lady as ever had pinched feet like a Chinese. But you see, they had chosen to do a foolish thing just once too often; so by the laws of Mrs. Bedonebyasyoudid, they had to go on doing it whether they chose or not, till the coming of the Cocqcigrues.

Ah! don't you wish that someone would go and convert those poor heathens, and teach them not to frighten their little children into fits?

" Now, then," said the Powwow man to Tom, " wouldn't you like to be frightened, my little dear? For I can see plainly that you are a very wicked, naughty, graceless, reprobate boy."

" You're another," quoth Tom, very sturdily. And when the man ran at him, and cried " Boo! " Tom ran at him in return, and cried " Boo! " likewise, right in his face, and set the little dog upon him; and at his legs the dog went.

At which, if you will believe it, the fellow turned tail, thunder-box and all, with a " Woof! " like an old sow on the common; and ran for his life, screaming, " Help! thieves! murder! fire! He is going to kill me! I am a ruined man! He will murder me; and break, burn, and destroy my precious and invaluable thunder-box; and then you will have no more thunder showers in the land. Help! help! help!"

At which the papa and mamma and all the people of Oldwivesfabledom, flew at Tom, shouting, "Oh, the wicked, impudent, hard-hearted, graceless boy! Beat him, kick him, shoot him, drown him, hang him, burn him!" and so forth: but luckily they had nothing to shoot, hang, or burn him with, for the fairies had hid all the killing-tackle out of the way a little while before; so they could only pelt him with stones; and some of the stones went clean through him, and came out the other side. But he did not mind that a bit; for the holes closed up again as fast as they were made, because he was a water baby. However, he was very glad when he was safe out of the country, for the noise there made him all but deaf.

Then he came to a very quiet place, called Leaveheaven-alone. And there the sun was drawing water out of the sea to make steam-threads, and the wind was twisting them up to make cloud-patterns, till they had worked between them the loveliest wedding veil of Chantilly lace, and hung it up in their own Crystal Palace for any one to buy who could afford it, while the good old sea never grudged, for she knew they would pay her back honestly. So the sun span, and the wind wove, and all went well with the great steam-loom; as is likely, considering—and considering—and considering——

And at last, after innumerable adventures, each more wonderful than the last, he saw before him a huge building, much bigger, and—what is most surprising—a little uglier than a certain new lunatic asylum, but not built quite of the same materials. None of it, at least—or, indeed, for aught that I ever saw, any part of any other building whatsoever —is cased with nine-inch brick inside and out, and filled up with rubble between the walls, in order that any gentle-man who has been confined during Her Majesty's pleasure may be unconfined during his own pleasure, and take a walk in the neighbouring park to improve his spirits, after an hour's light and wholesome labour with his dinner-fork or one of the legs of his iron bedstead. No. The walls of this building were built on an entirely different principle, which need not be described, as it has not yet been discovered.

Tom walked towards this great building, wondering what it was, and having a strange fancy that he might find Mr. Grimes inside it, till he saw running toward him, and shouting "Stop!" three or four people, who, when they came nearer, were nothing else than policemen's truncheons, running along without legs or arms.

Tom was not astonished. He was long past that. Besides, he had seen the naviculae in the water move nobody knows how, a hundred times, without arms, or legs, or anything to stand in their stead. Neither was he frightened; for he had been doing no harm.

So he stopped; and, when the foremost truncheon came up and asked his business, he showed Mother Carey's pass; and the truncheon looked at it in the oddest fashion; for he had one eye in the middle of his upper end, so that when he looked at anything, being quite stiff, he had to slope himself, and poke himself, till it was a wonder why he did not tumble over; but, being quite full of the spirit of justice (as all policemen, and their truncheons, ought to be), he was always in a position of stable equilibrium, whichever way he put himself.

"All right—pass on," said he at last. And then he added, "I had better go with you, young man." And Tom had no objection, for such company was both respectable and safe; so the truncheon coiled its thong neatly round its handle, to prevent tripping itself up—for the thong had got loose in running—and marched on by Tom's side.

"Why have you no policeman to carry you?" asked Tom, after a while.

"Because we are not like those clumsy-made truncheons in the land world, which cannot go without having a whole man to carry them about. We do our own work for ourselves; and do it very well, though I say it who should not."

" Then why have you a thong to your handle? " asked Tom.

" To hang ourselves up by, of course, when we are off duty."

Tom had got his answer, and had no more to say, till they came up to the great iron door of the prison. And there the truncheon knocked twice, with its own head.

A wicket in the door opened, and out looked a tremendous old brass blunderbuss charged up to the muzzle with slugs, who was the porter; and Tom started back a little at the sight of him.

" What case is this? " he asked in a deep voice, out of his broad bell-mouth.

" If you please, sir, it is no case; only a young gentleman from her ladyship, who wants to see Grimes the master-sweep."

" Grimes? " said the blunderbuss. And he pulled in his muzzle, perhaps to look over his prison-lists.

" Grimes is up chimney No. 345," he said from inside. " So the young gentleman had better go on to the roof."

Tom looked up at the enormous wall, which seemed at least ninety miles high, and wondered how he should ever get up: but, when he hinted that to the truncheon, it settled the matter in a moment. For it whisked round, and gave him such a shove behind as sent him up to the roof in no time, with his little dog under his arm.

And there he walked along the leads, till he met another truncheon, and told him his errand.

" Very good," it said. " Come along: but it will be of no use." He is the most unremorseful, hard-hearted, foulmouthed fellow I have in charge; and thinks about nothing but beer and pipes, which are not allowed here, of course."

So they walked along over the leads, and very sooty they were, and Tom thought the chimneys must want sweeping very much. But he was surprised to see that the soot did not stick to his feet, or dirty them in the least. Neither did the live coals, which were lying about in plenty, burn him; for, being a water baby, his radical humours were of a moist and cold nature, as you may read at large in Lemnius, Cardon, Van Helmont, and other gentlemen, who knew as much as they could, and no man can know more.

And at last they came to chimney No. 345. Out of the top of it, his head and shoulders just showing, stuck poor Mr. Grimes; so sooty, and bleared, and ugly, that Tom could hardly bear to look at him. And in his mouth was a pipe: but it was not alight, though he was pulling at it with all his might.

"Attention, Mr. Grimes," said the truncheon; "here is a gentleman come to see you."

But Mr. Grimes only said bad words; and kept grumbling, "My pipe won't draw. My pipe won't draw."

"Keep a civil tongue, and attend!" said the truncheon; and popped up just like Punch, hitting Grimes such a crack over the head with itself, that his brains rattled inside like a dried walnut in its shell. He tried to get his hands out, and rub the place: but he could not, for they were stuck fast in the chimney.

Now he was forced to attend.

"Hey!" he said, "why, it's Tom! I suppose you have come here to laugh at me, you spiteful little atomy?"

Tom assured him he had not, but only wanted to help him.

"I don't want anything except beer, and that I can't get; and a light to this bothering pipe, and that I can't get either."

"I'll get you one," said Tom; and he took up a live coal (there were plenty lying about) and put it to Grimes's pipe: but it went out instantly.

"It's no use," said the truncheon, leaning itself up against the chimney, and looking on. "I tell you, it is no use. His heart is so cold that it freezes everything that comes near him. You will see that presently, plain enough."

"Oh, of course, it's my fault. Everything's always my fault," said Grimes. "Now don't go to hit me again" (for the truncheon started upright, and looked very wicked); "you know, if my arms were only free, you daren't hit me then."

The truncheon leant back against the chimney, and took no notice of the personal insult, like a well-trained policeman as it was, though he was ready enough to avenge any transgression against morality or order.

"But can't I help you in any other way? Can't I help you to get out of this chimney?" said Tom.

"No," interposed the truncheon; "he has come to the place where everybody must help themselves; and he will find it out, I hope, before he is done with me."

"Oh, yes," said Grimes, "of course it's me. Did I ask to be brought here into the prison? Did I ask to be set to sweep your foul chimneys? Did I ask to have lighted straw put under me to make me go up? Did I ask to stick fast in the very first chimney of all, because it was so shamefully clogged up with soot? Did I ask to stay here—I don't know how long—a hundred years, I do believe, and never get my pipe, nor my beer, nor nothing fit for a beast, let alone a man."

"No," answered a solemn voice behind. "No more did Tom, when you behaved to him in the very same way."

It was Mrs. Bedonebyasyoudid. And, when the truncheon saw her, it started bolt upright—Attention!—and made such a low bow, that if it had not been full of the spirit of justice, it must have tumbled on its end, and probably hurt its one eye. And Tom made his bow too.

"Oh, ma'am," he said, "don't think about me; that's all past and gone, and good times and bad times and all times pass over. But may not I help poor Mr. Grimes? Mayn't I try and get some of these bricks away, that he may move his arms?"

"You may try, of course," she said.

So Tom pulled and tugged at the bricks: but he could not move one. And then he tried to wipe Mr. Grimes's face: but the soot would not come off.

"Oh, dear!" he said, "I have come all this way, through all these terrible places, to help you, and now I am of no use after all."

"You had best leave me alone," said Grimes; "you

Seau Cruickshanks.

are a good-natured forgiving little chap, and that's truth; but you'd best be off. The hail's coming on soon, and it will beat the eyes out of your little head."

"What hail?"

"Why, hail that falls every evening here; and, till it comes close to me, it's like so much warm rain: but then it turns to hail over my head, and knocks me about like small shot."

"That hail will never come any more," said the strange lady. "I have told you before what it was. It was your mother's tears, those which she shed when she prayed for you by her bedside; but your cold heart froze it into hail. But she is gone to heaven now, and will weep no more for her graceless son."

Then Grimes was silent awhile; and then he looked very sad.

"So my old mother's gone, and I never there to speak to her! Ah! a good woman she was, and might have been a happy one, in her little school there in Vendale, if it hadn't been for me and my bad ways."

"Did she keep the school in Vendale?" asked Tom. And then he told Grimes all the story of his going to her house, and how she could not abide the sight of a chimney-sweep, and then how kind she was, and how he turned into a water baby.

"Ah!" said Grimes, "good reason she had to hate the sight of a chimney-sweep. I ran away from her and took up with the sweeps, and never let her know where I was, nor sent her a penny to help her, and now it's too late— too late!" said Mr. Grimes.

And he began crying and blubbering like a great baby, till his pipe dropped out of his mouth, and broke all to bits.

"Oh dear, if I was but a little chap in Vendale again, to see the clear beck, and the apple-orchard, and the yew-hedge, how different I would go on! But it's too late now. So you go along, you kind little chap, and don't stand to look at a man crying, that's old enough to be your father, and never feared the face of man, nor of worse neither.

But I'm beat now, and beat I must be. I've made my bed, and I must lie on it. Foul I would be, and foul I am, as an Irishwoman said to me once; and little I heeded it. It's all my own fault: but it's too late." And he cried so bitterly that Tom began crying too.

" Never too late," said the fairy, in such a strange soft new voice that Tom looked up at her; and she was so beautiful for the moment, that Tom half fancied she was her sister.

No more was it too late. For, as poor Grimes cried and blubbered on, his own tears did what his mother's could not do, and Tom's could not do, and nobody's on earth could do for him; for they washed the soot off his face and off his clothes; and then they washed the mortar away from between the bricks; and the chimney crumbled down; and Grimes began to get out of it.

Up jumped the truncheon, and was going to hit him on the crown a tremendous thump, and drive him down again like a cork into a bottle. But the strange lady put it aside.

" Will you obey me if I give you a chance? "

" As you please, ma'am. You're stronger than me, that I know too well, and wiser than me, I know too well also. And, as for being my own master, I've fared ill enough with that as yet. So whatever your ladyship pleases to order me; for I'm beat, and that's the truth."

" Be it so then—you may come out. But remember, disobey me again, and into a worse place still you go."

" I beg pardon, ma'am, but I never disobeyed you that I know of. I never had the honour of setting eyes upon you till I came to these ugly quarters."

" Never saw me? Who said to you, Those that will be foul, foul they will be? "

Grimes looked up; and Tom looked up too; for the voice was that of the Irishwoman who met them the day that they went out together to Harthover. " I gave you your warning then: but you gave it yourself a thousand times before and since. Every bad word that you said— every cruel and mean thing that you did—every time that you got tipsy—every day that you went dirty—you were disobeying me, whether you knew it or not."

" If I'd only known, ma'am——"

" You knew well enough that you were disobeying something, though you did not know it was me. But come out and take your chance. Perhaps it may be your last."

So Grimes stept out of the chimney, and, really, if it had not been for the scars on his face, he looked as clean and respectable as a master-sweep need look.

" Take him away," said she to the truncheon, " and give, him his ticket-of-leave."

" And what is he to do, ma'am? "

" Get him to sweep out the crater of Etna; he will find some very steady men working out their time there, who will teach him his business: but mind, if that crater gets choked again, and there is an earthquake in consequence, bring them all to me, and I shall investigate the case very severely."

So the truncheon marched off Mr. Grimes, looking as meek as a drowned worm.

And for aught I know, or do not know, he is sweeping the crater of Etna to this very day.

" And now," said the fairy to Tom, " your work here is done. You may as well go back again."

" I should be glad enough to go," said Tom, " but how am I to get up that great hole again, now the steam has stopped blowing? "

" I will take you up the backstairs: but I must bandage your eyes first; for I never allow anybody to see those backstairs of mine."

" I am sure I shall not tell anybody about them, ma'am, if you bid me not."

" Aha! So you think my little man. But you would soon forget your promise if you got back into the land-world. For, if people only once found out that you had been up my backstairs, you would have all the fine ladies kneeling to you, and the rich men emptying their purses before you, and statesmen offering you place and power;

and young and old, rich and poor, crying to you, ' Only tell us the great backstairs secret, and we will be your slaves; we will make you lord, king, emperor, bishop, archbishop, pope, if you like—only tell us the secret of the backstairs. For thousands of years we have been paying, and petting, and obeying, and worshipping quacks who told us they had the key of the backstairs, and could smuggle us up them; and in spite of all our disappointments, we will honour, and glorify, and adore, and beautify, and translate, and apotheotize you likewise, on the chance of your knowing something about the backstairs, that we may all go on pilgrimage to it; and, even if we cannot get up it, lie at the foot of it, and cry:

" ' Oh backstairs,
precious backstairs,   aristocratic backstairs,
invaluable backstairs,   respectable backstairs,
requisite backstairs,   gentlemanlike backstairs,
necessary backstairs,   ladylike backstairs,
good-natured backstairs,   commercial backstairs,
cosmopolitan backstairs,   economical backstairs,
comprehensive backstairs,   practical backstairs,
accommodating backstairs,   logical backstairs,
well-bred backstairs,   deductive backstairs,
comfortable backstairs,   orthodox backstairs,
humane backstairs,   probable backstairs,
reasonable backstairs,   credible backstairs,
long-sought backstairs,   demonstrable backstairs,
coveted backstairs,   irrefragable backstairs,
                potent backstairs,
        all-but-omnipotent backstairs,
                    etc.

Save us from the consequences of our own actions, and from the cruel fairy, Mrs. Bedonebyasyoudid! ' Do not you think that you would be a little tempted then to tell what you know, laddie? "

Tom thought so certainly. "But why do they want so to know about the backstairs? " asked he, being a little frightened at the long words, and not understanding them the least; as, indeed, he was not meant to do, or you either.

"That I shall not tell you. I never put things into little folks' heads which are but too likely to come there of themselves. So come—now I must bandage your eyes." So she tied the bandage on his eyes with one hand, and with the other she took it off.

"Now," she said, "you are safe up the stairs." Tom opened his eyes very wide, and his mouth too; for he had not, as he thought, moved a single step. But, when he looked round him, there could be no doubt that he was safe up the back stairs, whatsoever they may be, which no man is going to tell you, for the plain reason that no man knows.

The first thing which Tom saw was the black cedars, high and sharp against the rosy dawn; and St. Brandan's Isle reflected double in the still broad silver sea. The wind sang softly in the cedars, and the water sang among the caves; the sea-birds sang as they streamed out into the ocean, and the land-birds as they built among the boughs; and the air was so full of song that it stirred St. Brandan and his hermits, as they slumbered in the shade; and they moved their good old lips, and sang their morning hymn amid their dreams. But among all the songs one came across the water more sweet and clear than all; for it was the song of a young girl's voice.

And what was the song which she sang? Ah, my little man, I am too old to sing that song, and you too young to understand it. But have patience, and keep your eye single, and your hands clean, and you will learn some day to sing it yourself, without needing any man to teach you.

And as Tom neared the island, there sat upon a rock the most graceful creature that ever was seen, looking down, with her chin upon her hand, and paddling with her feet in the water. And when they came to her she looked up, and behold it was Ellie.

"Oh, Miss Ellie," said he, "how you are grown!"

" Oh, Tom," said she, " how you are grown, too! "

And no wonder; they were both quite grown up—he into a tall man, and she into a beautiful woman.

" Perhaps I may be grown," she said. " I have had time enough; for I have been sitting here waiting for you many a hundred years, till I thought you were never coming."

" Many a hundred years? " thought Tom; but he had seen so much in his travels that he had quite given up being astonished; and, indeed, he could think of nothing but Ellie. So he stood and looked at Ellie, and Ellie looked at him; and they liked the employment so much that they stood and looked for seven years more, and neither spoke or stirred.

At last they heard the fairy say, " Attention, children! Are you never going to look at me again? "

" We have been looking at you all this while," they said. And so they thought they had been.

" Then look at me once more," said she.

They looked—and both of them cried out at once, " Oh, who are you, after all? "

" You are our dear Mrs. Doasyouwouldbedoneby."

" No, you are good Mrs. Bedonebyasyoudid; but you are grown quite beautiful now! "

" To you," said the fairy. " But look again."

" You are Mother Carey," said Tom, in a very low, solemn voice; for he had found out something which made him very happy, and yet frightened him more than all that he had ever seen.

" But you are grown quite young again."

" To you," said the fairy. " Look again."

" You are the Irishwoman who met me the day I went to Harthover! "

And when they looked she was neither of them, and yet all of them at once.

" My name is written in my eyes, if you have eyes to see it there."

And they looked into her great, deep, soft eyes, and they changed again and again into every hue, as the light changes in a diamond.

"Now read my name," said she, at last.

And her eyes flashed, for one moment, clear, white, blazing light: but the children could not read her name; for they were dazzled, and hid their faces in their hands.

"Not yet, young things, not yet," said she, smiling; and then she turned to Ellie.

"You may take him home with you now on Sundays, Ellie. He has won his spurs in the great battle, and become fit to go with you, and be a man; because he has done the thing he did not like."

So Tom went home with Ellie on Sundays, and sometimes on week-days, too; and he is now a great man of science, and can plan railroads, and steam-engines, and electric telegraphs, and rifled guns, and so forth; and knows everything about everything, except why a hen's egg don't turn into a crocodile, and two or three other little things which no one will know till the coming of the Cocqcigrues. And all this from what he learnt when he was a water baby, underneath the sea.

"And of course Tom married Ellie?"

My dear child, what a silly notion! Don't you know that no one ever marries in a fairy tale, under the rank of a prince or a princess?

"And Tom's dog?"

Oh, you may see him any clear night in July; for the old dog-star was so worn out by the last three hot summers that there have been no dog-days since; so that they had to take him down and put Tom's dog up in his place. Therefore, as new brooms sweep clean, we may hope for some warm weather this year. And that is the end of my story.

MORAL

And now, my little man, what should we learn from this parable?

We should learn thirty-seven or thirty-nine things, I am not exactly sure which: but one thing, at least, we may learn, and that is this—when we see efts in the ponds, never to throw stones at them, or catch them with crooked pins, or put them into vivariums with sticklebacks, that the sticklebacks may prick them in their poor little stomachs, and make them jump out of the glass into somebody's work-box, and so come to a bad end. For these efts are nothing else but the water babies who are stupid and dirty, and will not learn their lessons and keep themselves clean; and, therefore (as comparative anatomists will tell you fifty years hence, though they are not learned enough to tell you now), their skulls grow flat, their jaws grow out, and their brains grow small, and their tails grow long, and they lose all their ribs (which I am sure you would not like to do), and their skins grow dirty and spotted, and they never get into the clear rivers, much less into the great wide sea, but hang about in dirty ponds, and live in the mud, and eat worms, as they deserve to do.

But that is no reason why you should ill-use them: but only why you should pity them, and be kind to them, and hope that some day they will wake up, and be ashamed of their nasty, dirty, lazy, stupid life, and try to amend, and become something better once more. For, perhaps, if they do so, then after 379,423 years, nine months, thirteen days, two hours, and twenty-one minutes (for aught that appears to the contrary), if they work very hard and wash very hard all that time, their brains may grow bigger, and their jaws grow smaller, and their ribs come back, and their tails wither off, and they will turn into water babies again, and, perhaps, after that into land babies; and after that, perhaps, into grown men.

You know they won't? Very well, I dare say you know best. But, you see, some folks have a great liking for those poor little efts. They never did anybody any harm, or could if they tried; and their only fault is, that they do no good—any more than some thousands of their betters. But what with ducks, and what with pike, and what with sticklebacks, and what with water-beetles, and what with naughty boys, they are "sae sair haddened doun," as the Scotsmen say, that it is a wonder how they live; and some folks can't help hoping, with good Bishop Butler, that they may have another chance, to make things fair and even, somewhere, somewhen, somehow.

Meanwhile, do you learn your lessons, and thank God that you have plenty of cold water to wash in; and wash in it too, like a true Englishman. And then, if my story is not true, something better is; and if I am not quite right, still you will be, as long as you stick to hard work and cold water.

But remember always, as I told you at first, that this is all a fairy tale, and only fun and pretence; and, therefore, you are not to believe a word of it, even if it is true.

POEMS: A SELECTION

CONTENTS

8

CONTENTS

SELECTIONS FROM ANDROMEDA

The Greek story tells how Andromeda, daughter of Cepheus and Cassiopeia, of Ethiopia, was sacrificed to a sea-monster sent, along with a flood, by the god Poseidon, who had been angered by Cassiopeia's boasting of her beauty.

Andromeda is chained to a rock and set at the monster's mercy, this being, according to the Oracle of Ammon, the only way of ridding the country of the monster.

Perseus, fresh from killing the Gorgon, arrives in the nick of time and, slaying the beast, sets free the princess and wins a bride.

I. THE MONSTER

OVER the sea, past Crete, on the Syrian shore to the southward,
Dwells in the well-tilled lowland a dark-haired Aethiop people,
Skilful with needle and loom, and the arts of the dyer and carver,
Skilful, but feeble of heart; for they know not the lords of Olympus,
Lovers of men; neither broad-browed Zeus, nor Pallas Athené,
Teacher of wisdom to heroes, bestower of might in the battle;
Share not the cunning of Hermes, nor list to the songs of Apollo.
Fearing the stars of the sky, and the roll of the blue salt water,
Fearing all things that have life in the womb of the seas and the rivers,
Eating no fish to this day, nor ploughing the main, like the Phoenics,
Manful with black-beaked ships, they abide in a sorrowful region,

227

Vexed with the earthquake, and flame, and the sea-floods,
  scourge of Poseidon.
  Whelming the dwellings of men, and the toils of the
    slow-footed oxen,
Drowning the barley and flax, and the hard-earned gold
  of the harvest,
Up to the hillside vines, and the pastures skirting the
  woodland,
Inland the floods came yearly; and after the waters a
  monster,
Bred of the slime, like the worms which are bred from the
  muds of the Nile-bank,
Shapeless, a terror to see; and by night it swam out to
  the seaward,
Daily returning to feed with the dawn, and devoured of
  the fairest,
Cattle, and children, and maids, till the terrified people
  fled inland.

II. THE CHAINING OF ANDROMEDA

Slowly, the priests, and the queen, and the virgin bound in
  the galley.
Slowly they rowed to the rocks: but Cepheus far in the
  palace
Sate in the midst of the hall, on his throne, like a shepherd
  of people,
Choking his woe, dry-eyed, while the slaves wailed loudly
  around him.
They on the sea-girt rock, which is washed by the surges
  for ever,
Set her in silence, the guiltless, aloft with her face to the
  eastward.
Under a crag of the stone, where a ledge sloped down to
  the water;
There they set Andromeda, most beautiful, shaped like
  a goddess,
Lifting her long white arms wide-spread to the walls of
  the basalt,

Chaining them, ruthless, with brass; and they called on
    the might of the Rulers.
  "Mystical fish of the seas, dread Queen whom Æthiops
    honour,
Whelming the land in thy wrath, unavoidable, sharp as
    the sting-ray,
Thou, and thy brother the Sun, brain-smiting, lord of the
    sheepfold,
Scorching the earth all day, and then resting at night in
    thy bosom,
Take ye this one life for many, appeased by the blood of
    a maiden,
Fairest, and born of the fairest, a queen, most priceless of
    victims."

III. THE COMING OF PERSEUS

. . . In the spray, like a hovering foam-bow,
Hung, more fair than the foam-bow, a boy in the bloom
    of his manhood,
Golden-haired, ivory-limbed, ambrosial; over his shoulder
Hung for a veil of his beauty the gold-fringed folds of the
    goat-skin,
Bearing the brass of his shield, as the sun flashed clear on
    its clearness.
Curved on his thigh lay a falchion; and under the gleam
    of his helmet
Eyes more blue than the main shone awful, around him
    Athené
Shed in her love such grace, such state, and terrible daring.
Hovering over the water he came, upon glittering pinions,
Living, a wonder, outgrown from the tight-laced gold of
    his sandals;
Bounding from billow to billow, and sweeping the crests
    like a sea-gull;
Leaping the gulfs of the surge, as he laughed in the joy
    of his leaping.

IV. The Slaying of the Monster

" Kiss me but once, and I go."

                    Then lifting her neck, like a sea-bird
Peering up over the wave, from the foam-white swells of
    her bosom,
Blushing she kissed him: afar, on the topmost Idalian
    summit
Laughed in the joy of her heart, far-seeing, the queen
    Aphrodité.
  Loosing his arms from her waist he flew upward, awaiting
    the sea-beast.
Onward it came from the southward, as bulky and black
    as a galley,
Lazily coasting along, as the fish fled leaping before it;
Lazily breasting the ripple, and watching by sandbar and
    headland,
Listening for laughter of maidens at bleaching, or song of
    the fisher,
Children at play on the pebbles, or cattle that pawed on
    the sand-hills.
Rolling and dripping it came, where bedded in glistening
    purple
Cold on the cold sea-weeds lay the long white sides of the
    maiden,
Trembling, her face in her hands, and her tresses afloat on
    the water.
  As when an osprey aloft, dark-eyebrowed, royally
    crested,
Flags on by creek and by cove, and in scorn of the anger
    of Nereus
Ranges, the king of the shore; if he see on a glittering
    shallow,
Chasing the bass and the mullet, the fin of a wallowing
    dolphin,
Halting, he wheels round slowly, in doubt at the weight
    of his quarry,
Whether to clutch it alive, or to fall on the wretch like a
    plummet,

Stunning with terrible talon the life of the brain in the
  hindhead:
Then rushes up with a scream, and stooping the wrath of
  his eyebrows
Falls from the sky, like a star, while the wind rattles hoarse
  in his pinions.
Over him closes the foam for a moment; and then from
  the sand-bed
Rolls up the great fish, dead, and his side gleams white in
  the sunshine.
Thus fell the boy on the beast, unveiling the face of the
  Gorgon;
Thus fell the boy on the beast; thus rolled up the beast in
  his horror.
Once, as the dead eyes glared into his; then his sides,
  death-sharpened,
Stiffened and stood, brown rock, in the wash of the wan-
  dering water.
  Beautiful, eager, triumphant, he leapt back again to his
    treasure;
Leapt back again, full blest, toward arms spread wide to
  receive him.
Brimful of honour he clasped her, and brimful of love she
  caressed him,
Answering lip with lip; while above them the queen
  Aphrodité
Poured on their foreheads and limbs, unseen, ambrosial
  odours,
Givers of longing, and rapture, and chaste content in
  espousals.
Happy whom ere they be wedded anoints she, the Queen
  Aphroditè!

THE SANDS OF DEE

" O MARY, go and call the cattle home,
    And call the cattle home,
    And call the cattle home
    Across the sands of Dee;"
The western wind was wild and dank with foam,
    And all alone went she.

The western tide crept up along the sand,
    And o'er and o'er the sand,
    And round and round the sand,
    As far as eye could see.
The rolling mist came down and hid the land:
    And never home came she.

" Oh! is it weed, or fish, or floating hair—
    A tress of golden hair,
    A drowned maiden's hair
    Above the nets at sea?
Was never salmon yet that shone so fair
    Among the stakes on Dee."

They rowed her in across the rolling foam,
    The cruel crawling foam,
    The cruel hungry foam,
    To her grave beside the sea:
But still the boatmen hear her call the cattle home
    Across the sands of Dee.

THE THREE FISHERS

THREE fishers went sailing away to the West,
    Away to the West as the sun went down;
Each thought on the woman who loved him the best,
    And the children stood watching them out of the town;

For men must work, and women must weep,
And there's little to earn, and many to keep,
    Though the harbour bar be moaning.

Three wives sat up in the lighthouse tower,
  And they trimmed the lamps as the sun went down;
They looked at the squall, and they looked at the shower,
  And the night-rack came rolling up ragged and brown.
  But men must work, and women must weep,
  Though storms be sudden, and waters deep,
    And the harbour bar be moaning.

Three corpses lay out on the shining sands
  In the morning gleam as the tide went down,
And the women are weeping and wringing their hands
  For those who will never come home to the town;
  For men must work, and women must weep,
  And the sooner it's over, the sooner to sleep;
    And good-bye to the bar and it's moaning.

LORRAINE, LORRAINE, LOREE

" ARE you ready for your steeple-chase, Lorraine, Lorraine,
    Loree?
  You're booked to ride your capping race to-day at
    Coulterlee,
You're booked to ride Vindictive, for all the world to see,
To keep him straight, and keep him first, and win the run
    for me."

She clasped her new-born baby, poor Lorraine, Lorraine,
    Loree.
  " I cannot ride Vindictive, as any man might see,
And I will not ride Vindictive, with this baby on my knee;
He's killed a boy, he's killed a man, and why must he
    kill me?"

" Unless you ride Vindictive, Lorraine, Lorraine, Lorree,
  Unless you ride Vindictive to-day at Coulterlee,
And land him safe across the brook, and win the blank for
      me,
It's you may keep your baby, for you'll get no keep from
      me."

" That husbands could be cruel," said Lorraine, Lorraine,
      Lorree,
    " That husbands could be cruel, I have known for
      seasons three;
But oh! to ride Vindictive while a baby cries for me,
And be killed across a fence at last for all the world to see! "

She mastered young Vindictive—Oh! the gallant lass was
      she,
    And kept him straight and won the race as near as near
      could be;
But he killed her at the brook against a pollard willow tree,
Oh! he killed her at the brook, the brute, for all the world
      to see,
But no one but the baby cried for poor Lorraine, Lorree.

AIRLY BEACON

AIRLY Beacon, Airly Beacon;
    Oh the pleasant sight to see
Shires and towns from Airly Beacon
    While my love climbed up to me!

Airly Beacon, Airly Beacon;
    Oh the happy hours we lay
Deep in fern on Airly Beacon,
    Courting through the summer's day!

Airly Beacon, Airly Beacon;
    Oh the weary haunt for me,
All alone on Airly Beacon,
    With his baby on my knee!

POEMS

A FAREWELL

My fairest child, I have no song to give you;
  No lark could pipe to skies so dull and grey:
Yet, ere we part, one lesson I can leave you
            For every day.

Be good, sweet maid, and let who will be clever;
  Do noble things, not dream them, all day long:
And so make life, death, and that vast for-ever
            One grand, sweet song.

ELEGIACS

Wearily stretches the sand to the surge, and the surge to
      the cloudland;
Wearily onward I ride, watching the water alone.
Not as of old, like Homeric Achilles, κυδεϊ γαιων,
Joyous knight-errant of God, thirsting for labour and
      strife;
No more on magical steed borne free through the regions
      of ether,
But, like the hack which I ride, selling my sinew for gold.
Fruit-bearing autumn is gone; let the sad quiet winter
      hang o'er me—
What were the spring to a soul laden with sorrow and
      shame?
Blossoms would fret me with beauty; my heart has no time
      to bepraise them;
Grey rock, bough, surge, cloud, waken no yearning within.
Sing not, thou sky-lark above! even angels pass hushed by
      the weeper.
Scream on, ye sea-fowl! my heart echoes your desolate
      cry.
Sweep the dry sand on, thou wild wind, to drift o'er the
      shell and the sea-weed;
Sea-weed and shell, like my dreams, swept down the
      pitiless tide.

Just is the wave which uptore us; 'tis nature's own law
    which condemns us;
Woe to the weak who, in pride, build on the faith of the
    sand!
Joy to the oak of the mountain: he trusts to the might of
    the rock-clefts;
Deeply he mines, and in peace feeds on the wealth of the
    stone.

*   *   *   *   *   *

DARTSIDE. 1849

I CANNOT tell what you say, green leaves,
  I cannot tell what you say:
But I know that there is a spirit in you,
  And a word in you this day.

I cannot tell what you say, rosy rocks,
  I cannot tell what you say:
But I know that there is a spirit in you,
  And a word in you this day.

I cannot tell what you say, brown streams,
  I cannot tell what you say:
But I know that in you too a spirit doth live,
  And a word doth speak this day.

" Oh green is the colour of faith and truth,
And rose the colour of love and youth,
  And brown of the fruitful clay.
Sweet Earth is faithful, and fruitful, and young,
And her bridal day shall come ere long,
And you shall know what the rocks and the streams
  And the whispering woodlands say."

A LAMENT

THE merry merry lark was up and singing,
   And the hare was out and feeding on the lea;
And the merry merry bells below were ringing,
   When my child's laugh rang through me.

Now the hare is snared and dead beside the snowyard,
   And the lark beside the dreary winter sea;
And the baby in his cradle in the churchyard
   Sleeps sound till the bell brings me.

THE UGLY PRINCESS

My parents bow, and lead them forth,
   For all the crowd to see—
Ah well! the people might not care
   To cheer a dwarf like me.

They little know how I could love,
   How I could plan and toil,
To swell those drudges' scanty gains,
   Their mites of rye and oil.

They little know what dreams have been
   My playmates, night and day;
Of equal kindness, helpful care,
   A mother's perfect sway.

Now earth to earth in convent walls,
   To earth in churchyard sod:
I was not good enough for man,
   And so am given to God.

ABSENCE

THE baby sings not on its mother's breast;
Nor nightingales who nestle side by side:
Nor I by thine: but let us only part,
Then lips which should but kiss, and so be still.
As having uttered all, must speak again—
Oh stunted thoughts! Oh chill and fettered rhyme!
Yet my great bliss, though still entirely blest,
Losing its proper home, can find no rest:
  So, like a child who whiles away the time
With dance and carol till the eventide,
Watching its mother homeward through the glen;
Or nightingale, who, sitting far apart,
Tells to his listening mate within the nest
The wonder of his star-entranced heart
Till all the wakened woodlands laugh and thrill—
  Forth all my being bubbles into song;
  And rings aloft, not smooth, yet clear and strong.

THE LONGBEARDS' SAGA. A.D. 400

OVER the camp-fires
Drank I with heroes,
Under the Donau bank,
Warm in the snow trench:
Saga heard I there,
Men of the Longbeards,
Cunning and ancient,
Honey-sweet-voiced.
Scaring the wolf cub,
Scaring the horn-owl,
Shaking the snow-wreaths
Down from the pine-boughs,
Up to the star roof
Rang out their song.
Singing how Winil men,
Over the ice-floes

Sledging from Scanland
Came unto Scoring;
Singing of Gambara,
Freya's belovèd,
Mother of Ayo,
Mother of Ibor.
Singing of Wendel men,
Ambri and Assi;
How to the Winilfolk
Went they with war-words
" Few are ye, strangers,
And many are we:
Pay us now toll and fee,
Cloth-yarn, and rings, and beeves;
Else at the raven's meal
Bide the sharp bill's doom."
Clutching the dwarf's work then,
Clutching the bullock's shell,
Girding grey iron on,
Forth fared the Winils all,
Fared the Alruna's sons;
Ayo and Ibor.
Mad at heart stalked they:
Loud wept the women all,
Loud the Alruna wife;
Sore was their need.

Out of the morning land,
Over the snow-drifts,
Beautiful Freya came,
Tripping to Scoring.
White were the moorlands
And frozen before her:
Green were the moorlands,
And blooming behind her.
Out of her gold locks
Shaking the spring flowers,
Out of her garments
Shaking the south wind,

Around in the birches
Awakening the throstles.
And making chaste housewives all
Long for their heroes home,
Loving and love-giving,
Came she to Scoring.
Came unto Gambara,
Wisest of Valas,—
" Vala, why weepest thou?
Far in the wide-blue,
High up in the Elfin-home,
Heard I thy weeping."

" Stop not my weeping,
Till one can fight seven.
Sons have I, heroes tall,
First in the sword-play;
This day at the Wendels' hands
Eagles must tear them.
Their mothers, thrall-weary,
Must grind for the Wendels."
Wept the Alruna wife;
Kissed her fair Freya:—
" Far off in the morning land,
High in Valhalla,
A window stands open;
Its sill is the snow-peaks,
Its posts are the water-spouts,
Storm-rack its lintel;
Gold cloud-flakes above it
Are piled for the roofing,
Far up to the Elfin-home,
High in the wide-blue.
Smiles out each morning thence
Odin Allfather;
From under the cloud-eaves
Smiles out on the heroes,
Smiles on chaste housewives all,
Smiles on the brood-mares,

Smiles on the smith's work:
And theirs is the sword-luck,
With them is the glory,—
So Odin hath sworn it,—
Who first in the morning
Shall meet him and greet him."
Still the Alruna wept:—
" Who then shall greet him?
Women alone are here:
Far on the moorlands
Behind the war-lindens,
In vain for the bill's doom
Watch Winil heroes all,
One against seven."
Sweetly the Queen laughed:—
" Hear thou my counsel now;
Take to thee cunning,
Belovèd of Freya.
Take thou thy women-folk,
Maidens and wives:
Over your ankles
Lace on the white war-hose;
Over your bosoms
Link up the hard mail-nets;
Over your lips
Plait long tresses with cunning;—
So war-beasts full-bearded
King Odin shall deem you,
When off the grey sea-beach
At sunrise ye greet him."

Night's son was driving
His golden-haired horses up;
Over the eastern firths
High flashed their manes.
Smiled from the cloud-eaves out
Allfather Odin,
Waiting the battle-sport:
Freya stood by him.

" Who are these heroes tall,—
Lusty-limbed Longbeards?
Over the swans' bath
Why cry they to me?
Bones should be crashing fast,
Wolves should be full-fed,
Where'er such, mad-hearted,
Swing hands in the sword-play."

Sweetly laughed Freya:—
" A name thou hast given them,
Shames neither thee nor them,
Well can they wear it.
Give them the victory,
First have they greeted thee;
Give them the victory.
Yokefellow mine!
Maidens and wives are these,—
Wives of the Winils;
Few are the heroes
And afar on the war-road,
So over the swans' bath
They cry unto thee."

Royally laughed he then;
Dear was that craft to him,
Odin Allfather,
Shaking the clouds.
" Cunning are women all,
Bold and importunate!
Longbeards their name shall be,
Ravens shall thank them:
Where women are heroes,
What must the men be?
Theirs is the victory;
No need of me! "

THE SWAN-NECK

EVIL sped the battle play
On the Pope Calixtus' day;
Mighty war-smiths, thanes and lords,
In Senlac slept the sleep of swords.
Harold Earl, shot over shield,
Lay along the autumn weald;
Slaughter such was never none
Since the Ethelings England won.

Thither Lady Githa came,
Weeping sore for grief and shame,
How may she her first-born tell?
Frenchmen stript him where he fell,
Gashed and marred his comely face;
Who can know him in his place?

Up and spake two brethren wise,
" Youngest hearts have keenest eyes;
Bird which leaves its mother's nest,
Moults its pinions, moults its crest.
Let us call the Swan-neck here,
She that was his leman dear,
She shall know him in this stound;
Foot of wolf, and scent of hound,
Eye of hawk, and wing of dove
Carry woman to her love."

Up and spake the Swan-neck high.
" Go! to all your thanes let cry
How I loved him best of all,
I whom men his leman call;
Better knew his body fair
Than the mother which him bare.
When ye lived in wealth and glee
Then ye scorned to look on me;
God hath brought the proud ones low
After me afoot to go."

Rousing erne and sallow glede,
Rousing grey wolf off his feed,

Over franklin, earl, and thane,
Heaps of mother-naked slain,
Round the red field tracing slow,
Stooped that Swan-neck white as snow;
Never blushed nor turned away,
Till she found him where he lay;
Clipt him in her armés fair,
Wrapt him in her yellow hair,
Bore him from the battle-stead,
Saw him laid in pall of lead,
Took her to a minster high,
For Earl Harold's soul to cry.

Thus fell Harold, bracelet-giver:
Jesu rest his soul for ever;
Angels all from pain deliver;
    Miserere Domine.

IT WAS EARL HALDAN'S DAUGHTER

It was Earl Haldan's daughter,
 She looked across the sea;
She looked across the water,
 And long and loud laughed she:
" The locks of six princesses
 Must be my marriage fee,
So hey bonny boat, and ho bonny boat!
 Who comes a wooing me? "

It was Earl Haldan's daughter,
 She walked along the sand;
When she was aware of a knight so fair,
 Came sailing to the land.
His sails were all of velvet,
 His mast of beaten gold,
And " Hey bonny boat, and ho bonny boat!
 Who saileth here so bold? "

"The locks of five princesses
I won beyond the sea;
I clipt their golden tresses,
To fringe a cloak for thee.
One handful yet is wanting,
But one of all the tale;
So hey bonny boat, and ho bonny boat!
Furl up thy velvet sail!"

He leapt into the water,
That rover young and bold;
He gript Earl Haldan's daughter,
He clipt her locks of gold;
"Go weep, go weep, proud maiden,
The tale is full to-day.
Now hey bonny boat, and ho bonny boat!
Sail Westward ho away!"

THE LAST BUCCANIER

OH England is a pleasant place for them that's rich and
high,
But England is a cruel place for such poor folks as I;
And such a port for mariners I ne'er shall see again
As the pleasant Isle of Avès, beside the Spanish main.

There were forty craft in Avès that were both swift and
stout,
All furnished well with small arms and cannons round
about;
And a thousand men in Avès made laws so fair and free
To choose their valiant captains and obey them loyally.

Then we sailed against the Spaniard with his hoards of
plate and gold,
Which he wrung with cruel tortures from Indian folk of
old;

Likewise the merchant captains, with hearts as hard as
    stone,
Who flog men and keel-haul them, and starve them to the
    bone.

Oh the palms grew high in Avès, and fruits that shone like
    gold,
And the colibris and parrots they were gorgeous to behold;
And the negro maids to Avès from bondage fast did flee,
To welcome gallant sailors, a-sweeping in from sea.

Oh sweet it was in Avès to hear the landward breeze
A-swing with good tobacco in a net between the trees,
With a negro lass to fan you, while you listened to the roar
Of the breakers on the reef outside, that never touched the
    shore.

But Scripture saith, an ending to all fine things must be;
So the King's ships sailed on Avès, and quite put down
    were we.
All day we fought like bulldogs, but they burst the booms
    at night;
And I fled in a piragua, sore wounded, from the fight.

Nine days I floated starving, and a negro lass beside,
Till for all I tried to cheer her, the poor young thing she
    died;
But as I lay a gasping, a Bristol sail came by,
And brought me home to England here, to beg until I die.
And now I'm old and going—I'm sure I can't tell where;
One comfort is, this world's so hard, I can't be worse off
    there:
If I might but be a sea-dove, I'd fly across the main,
To the pleasant Isle of Avès, to look at it once again.

ODE TO THE NORTH-EAST WIND

WELCOME, wild North-easter!
　　Shame it is to see
Odes to every zephyr;
　　Ne'er a verse to thee.
Welcome, black North-easter;
　　O'er the German foam;
O'er the Danish moorlands,
　　From thy frozen home.
Tired we are of summer,
　　Tired of gaudy glare,
Showers soft and steaming,
　　Hot and breathless air.
Tired of listless dreaming,
　　Through the lazy day:
Jovial wind of winter
　　Turn us out to play!
Sweep the golden reed-beds;
　　Crisp the lazy dyke;
Hunger into madness
　　Every plunging pike.
Fill the lake with wild fowl;
　　Fill the marsh with snipe;
While on dreary moorlands
　　Lonely curlew pipe.
Through the black fir-forest
　　Thunder harsh and dry,
Shattering down the snow flakes
　　Off the curdled sky.
Hark! The brave North-easter!
　　Breast-high lies the scent,
On by holt and headland,
　　Over heath and bent.
Chime, ye dappled darlings,
　　Through the sleet and snow.
Who can over-ride you?
　　Let the horses go!

Chime, ye dappled darlings,
  Down the roaring blast;
You shall see a fox die
  Ere an hour be past.
Go! and rest to-morrow,
  Hunting in your dreams,
While our skates are ringing
  O'er the frozen streams.
Let the luscious South-wind
  Breathe in lovers' sighs,
While the lazy gallants
  Bask in ladies' eyes.
What does he but soften
  Heart alike and pen?
'Tis the hard grey weather
  Breeds hard English men.
What's the soft South-wester?
  'Tis the ladies' breeze,
Bringing home their trueloves
  Out of all the seas:
But the black North-easter,
  Through the snow-storm hurled,
Drives our English hearts of oak
  Seaward round the world.
Come, as came our fathers,
  Heralded by thee,
Conquering from the eastward,
  Lords by land and sea.
Come; and strong within us
  Stir the Vikings' blood;
Bracing brain and sinew;
  Blow, thou wind of God!

TO G***

A HASTY jest I once let fall—
  As jests are wont to be, untrue—
  As if the sum of joy to you
Were hunt and picnic, rout and ball.

Your eyes met mine: I did not blame;
  You saw it: but I touched too near
  Some noble nerve; a silent tear
Spoke soft reproach, and lofty shame.

I do not wish those words unsaid.
  Unspoilt by praise and pleasure, you
  In that one look to woman grew,
While with a child, I thought, I played.

Next to mine own beloved so long!
  I have not spent my heart in vain.
  I watched the blade; I see the grain;
A woman's soul, most soft, yet strong.

THE NIGHT BIRD

A FLOATING, a floating
Across the sleeping sea,
All night I heard a singing bird
Upon the topmast tree.

" Oh came you off the isles of Greece,
Or off the banks of Seine;
Or off some tree in forests free,
Which fringe the western main? "

" I came not off the old world
Nor yet from off the new—
But I am one of the birds of God
Which sing the whole night through."

" Oh sing, and wake the dawning—
Oh whistle for the wind;
The night is long, the current strong,
My boat it lags behind."

" The current sweeps the old world,
The current sweeps the new;
The wind will blow, the dawn will glow
Ere thou has sailed them through."

THE WORLD'S AGE

WHO will say the world is dying?
    Who will say our prime is past?
Sparks from Heaven, within us lying,
    Flash, and will flash, till the last.
Fools! who fancy Christ mistaken;
    Man a tool to buy and sell;
Earth a failure, God-forsaken,
    Anteroom of Hell.

Still the race of Hero-spirits
    Pass the lamp from hand to hand;
Age from age the Words inherits—
    " Wife, and Child, and Fatherland."
Still the youthful hunter gathers
    Fiery joy from wold and wood;
He will dare as dared his fathers
    Give him cause as good.

While a slave bewails his fetters;
    While an orphan pleads in vain;
While an infant lisps his letters,
    Heir of all the ages' gain;
While a lip grows ripe for kissing;
    While a moan from man is wrung;
Know, by every want and blessing,
    That the world is young.

A CHRISTMAS CAROL

It chanced upon the merry merry Christmas eve,
  I went sighing past the church across the moorland
    dreary—
    " Oh! never sin and want and woe this earth will leave,
  And the bells but mock the wailing round, they sing so
    cheery.
How long, O Lord! how long before Thou come again?
  Still in cellar, and in garret, and on moorland dreary
The orphans moan, and widows weep, and poor men toil
    in vain,
  Till earth is sick of hope deferred, though Christmas
    bells be cheery."

Then arose a joyous clamour from the wild-fowl on the
    mere,
  Beneath the stars, across the snow, like clear bells
    ringing,
And a voice within cried—" Listen!—Christmas carols
    even here!
  Though thou be dumb, yet o'er their work the stars and
    snows are singing.
Blind! I live, I love, I reign; and all the nations through
  With the thunder of my judgments even now are
    ringing;
Do thou fulfil thy work but as yon wild-fowl do,
  Thou wilt heed no less the wailing, yet hear through it
    angels singing."

A PARABLE FROM LIEBIG

The church bells were ringing, the devil sat singing
  On the stump of a rotting old tree;
" Oh faith it grows cold, and the creeds they grow old,
  And the world is nigh ready for me."

The bells went on ringing, a spirit came singing,
    And smiled as he crumbled the tree;
    Yon wood does but perish new seedlings to cherish,
    And the world is too live yet for thee."

MY HUNTING SONG

FORWARD! Hark forward's the cry!
One more fence and we're out on the open,
So to us at once, if you want to live near us!
Hark to them, ride to them, beauties! as on they go.
Leaping and sweeping away in the vale below!
Cowards and bunglers, whose heart or whose eye is slow,
    Find themselves staring alone.

So the great cause flashes by;
Nearer and clearer its purposes open,
While louder and prouder the world-echoes cheer us:
Gentlemen sportsmen, you ought to live up to us,
Lead us, and lift us, and hallo our game to us—
We cannot call the hounds off, and no shame to us—
Don't be left staring alone!

ALTON LOCKE'S SONG. 1848

WEEP, weep, weep and weep.
    For pauper, dolt, and slave!
Hark! from wasted moor and fen,
Feverous alley, stifling den,
Swells the wail of Saxon men—
    Work! or the grave!

Down, down, down and down
    With idler, knave, and tyrant!
Why for sluggards cark and moil
He that will not live by toil
Has no right on English soil!
    God's word's our warrant!

Up, up, up and up!
  Face your game and play it!
The night is past, behold the sun!
The idols fall, the lie is done!
The Judge is set, the doom begun!
  Who shall stay it?

THE BAD SQUIRE

THE merry brown hares came leaping
  Over the crest of the hill,
Where the clover and corn lay sleeping
  Under the moonlight still.

Leaping late and early,
  Till under their bite and their tread
The swedes and the wheat and the barley
  Lay cankered and trampled and dead.

A poacher's widow sat sighing
  On the side of the white chalk bank,
Where under the gloomy fir-woods
  One spot in the ley throve rank.

She watched a long tuft of clover,
  Where rabbit or hare never ran;
For its black sour haulm covered over
  The blood of a murdered man.

She thought of the dark plantation,
  And the hares, and her husband's blood,
And the voice of her indignation
  Rose up to the throne of God.

" I'm long past wailing and whining—
  I have wept too much in my life:
I've had twenty years of pining

As an English labourer's wife.
" A labourer in Christian England,
   Where they cant of a Saviour's name,
And yet waste men's lives like the vermin's
   For a few more brace of game.

" There's blood on your new foreign shrubs,
     squire,
   There's blood on your pointer's feet;
There's blood on the game you sell, squire,
   And there's blood on the game you eat.

" You have sold the labouring-man, squire,
   Body and soul to shame,
To pay for your seat in the House, squire,
   And to pay for the feed of your game.

" You made him a poacher yourself, squire,
   When you'd give neither work nor meat,
And your barley-fed hares robbed the garden
   At our starving children's feet;

" When, packed in one reeking chamber,
   Man, maid, mother, and little ones lay;
While the rain pattered in on the rotting bride
     bed,
   And the walls let in the day.

" When we lay in the burning fever
   On the mud of the cold clay floor,
Till you parted us all for three months, squire,
   At the dreary workhouse-door.

" We quarrelled like brutes, and who wonders?
   What self-respect could we keep,
Worse housed than your hacks and your pointers,
   Worse fed than your hogs and your sheep.

" Can your lady patch hearts that are breaking
  With handfuls of coals and rice,
Or by dealing out flannel and sheeting
  A little below cost price?

" You may tire of the jail and the workhouse,
  And take to allotments and schools,
But you've run up a debt that will never
  Be paid us by penny-club rules.

" In the season of shame and sadness,
  In the dark and dreary day,
When scrofula, gout, and madness
  Are eating your race away;

" When your youngest, the mealy-mouthed
      rector,
  Lets your soul rot asleep to the grave,
You will find in your God the protector
  Of the freeman you fancied your slave."

She looked at the tuft of clover,
  And wept till her heart grew light;
And at last, when her passion was over,
  Went wandering into the night.

But the merry brown hares came leaping
  Over the uplands still,
Where the clover and corn lay sleeping
  On the side of the white chalk hill.

A THOUGHT FROM THE RHINE

I HEARD an eagle crying all alone
Above the vineyards through the summer night,
Among the skeletons of robber towers;
Because the ancient eyrie of his race
Was trenched and walled by busy-handed men,

And all his forest-chace and woodland wild,
Wherefrom he fed his young with hare and roe,
Were trim with grapes which swelled from hour to hour,
And tossed their golden tendrils to the sun
For joy at their own riches:—So, I thought,
The great devourers of the earth shall sit,
Idle and impotent, they know not why,
Down-staring from their barren height of state
On nations grown too wise to slay and slave,
The puppets of the few, while peaceful lore
And fellow-help make glad the heart of earth,
With wonders which they fear and hate, as he,
The Eagle, hates the vineyard slopes below.

THE DAY OF THE LORD

The Day of the Lord is at hand, at hand!
  It storms roll up the sky:
The nations sleep starving on heaps of gold;
  All dreamers toss and sigh;
The night is darkest before the morn;
When the pain is sorest the child is born,
    And the Day of the Lord at hand.

Gather you, gather you, angels of God—
  Freedom, and Mercy, and Truth;
Come! for the Earth is grown coward and old;
  Come down, and renew us her youth.
Wisdom, Self-Sacrifice, Daring, and Love,
Haste to the battle-field, stoop from above
    To the Day of the Lord at hand.

Gather you, gather you, hounds of hell—
  Famine, and Plague, and War;
Idleness, Bigotry, Cant, and Misrule,
  Gather, and fall in the snare!
Hireling and Mammonite, Bigot and Knave,
Crawl to the battle-field, sneak to your grave,
    In the Day of the Lord at hand.

Who would sit down and sigh for a lost age of gold,
　　While the Lord of all ages is here?
True hearts will leap up at the trumpet of God,
　　And those who can suffer, can dare.
Each old age of gold was an iron age too,
And the meekest of saints may find stern work
　　to do,
　　　　In the Day of the Lord at hand.

IN AN ILLUMINATED MISSAL

I WOULD have loved: there are no mates in heaven;
I would be great: there is no pride in heaven;
I would have sung, as doth the nightingale
The summer's night aneath the mooné pale:
But saintés hymns alone in heaven prevail.
My love, my song, my skill, my high intent,
Have I within this seely book y-pent:
And all that beauty which from every part
I treasured still alway within mine heart,
Whether of form or face angelical,
Or herb or flower, or lofty cáthedral,
Upon these sheets below doth lie y-spred,
In quaint devices deftly blazonèd.
　　Lord, in this tome to thee I sanctify
　　The sinful fruits of worldly fantasy.

THE WEIRD LADY

THE swevens came up round Harold the Earl,
　　Like motes in the sunnés beam;
And over him stood the Weird Lady,
In her charmèd castle over the sea,
　　Sang " Lie thou still and dream."

" Thy steed is dead in his stall, Earl Harold,
  Since thou has bid with me;
The rust has eaten thy harness bright,
And the rats have eaten thy greyhound light,
  That was so fair and free."

Mary Mother she stooped from heaven;
She wakened Earl Harold out of his sweven,
  To don his harness on;
And over the land and over the sea
He wended abroad to his own countrie.
  A weary way to gon.

O but his beard was white with eld,
  O but his hair was grey;
He stumbled on by stock and stone,
And as he journeyed he made his moan
  Along that weary way.

Earl Harold came to his castle wall;
  The gate was burnt with fire;
Roof and rafter were fallen down,
The folk were strangers all in the town,
  And strangers all in the shire.

Earl Harold came to a house of nuns,
  And he heard the dead-bell toll;
He saw the sexton stand by a grave;
" Now Christ have mercy, who did us save,
  Upon yon fair nun's soul."

The nuns they came from the convent gate
  By one, by two, by three;
They sang for the soul of a lady bright
Who died for the love of a traitor knight:
  It was his own lady.

He stayed the corpse beside the grave;
  "A sign, a sign!" quod he.
"Mary Mother who rulest heaven
Send me a sign if I be forgiven
  By the woman who so loved me."

A white dove out of the coffin flew;
  Earl Harold's mouth is kist;
He fell on his face, wherever he stood;
And the white dove carried his soul to God
  Or ever the bearers wist.

PALINODIA. 1841

YE mountains, on whose torrent-furrowed slopes;
And bare and silent brows uplift to heaven,
I envied oft the soul which fills your wastes
Of pure and stern sublime, and still expanse
Unbroken by the petty incidents
Of noisy life: Oh hear me once again!

Winds, upon whose racked eddies, far aloft,
Above the murmur of the uneasy world,
My thoughts in exultation held their way:
Whose tremulous whispers through the rustling glade
Were once to me unearthly tones of love,
Joy without object, wordless music, stealing
Through all my soul, until my pulse beat fast
With aimless hope, and unexpressed desire—
Thou sea, who wast to me a prophet deep
Through all thy restless waves, and wasting shores,
Of silent labour, and eternal change;
First teacher of the dense immensity
Of ever-stirring life, in thy strange forms
Of fish, and shell, and worm, and oozy weed
To me alike thy frenzy and thy sleep
Have been a deep and breathless joy: Oh hear!

Mountains, and winds, and waves, take back your child!
Upon thy balmy bosom, Mother Nature,
Where my young spirit dreamt its years away,
Give me once more to nestle: I have strayed
Far through another world, which is not thine.
Through sunless cities, and the weary haunts
Of smoke-grimed labour, and foul revelry
My flagging wing has swept. A mateless bird's
My pilgrimage has been; through sin and doubt
And darkness, seeking love. Oh hear me, Nature!
Receive me once again: but not alone;
No more alone, Great Mother! I have brought
One who has wandered, yet not sinned, like me.
Upon thy lap, twin children, let us lie;
And in the light of thine immortal eyes
Let our souls mingle, till the Father calls
  To some eternal home the charge He gives thee.

A HOPE

Twin stars, aloft in ether clear,
  Around each other roll away,
Within one common atmosphere
  Of their own mutual light and day.

And myriad happy eyes are bent
  Upon their changeless love alway;
As, strengthened by their one intent,
  They pour the flood of life and day.

So we through this world's waning night
  May, hand in hand, pursue our way;
Shed round us order, love, and light,
  And shine unto the perfect day.

A NEW FOREST BALLAD

OH she tripped over Ocknell plain,
  And down by Bradley Water;
And the fairest maid of the forest side
  Was Jane, the keeper's daughter.

She went and went through the broad grey lawns
  As down the red sun sank,
And chill as the scent of a new-made grave
  The mist smelt cold and dank.

" A token, a token! " that fair maid cried,
  " A token that bodes me sorrow;
For they that smell the grave by night
  Will see the corpse to-morrow.

" My own true love in Burley Walk
  Does hunt to-night, I fear;
And if he meet my father stern,
  His game may cost him dear.

" Ah, here's a curse on hare and grouse,
  A curse on hart and hind;
And a health to the squire in all England,
  Leaves never a head behind."

Her true love shot a mighty har
  Among the standing rye,
When on him leapt that keeper old
  From the fern where he did lie.

The forest laws were sharp and stern,
  The forest blood was keen;
They lashed together for life and death
  Beneath the hollies green.

261

The metal good and the walnut wood
   Did soon in flinders flee;
They tost the orts to south and north,
   And grappled knee to knee.

They wrestled up, they wrestled down,
   They wrestled still and sore;
Beneath their feet the myrtle sweet
   Was stamped to mud and gore.

Ah cold pale moon, thou cruel pale moon,
   That starest with never a frown
On all the grim and the ghastly things
   That are wrought in thorpe and town;

And yet cold pale moon, thou cruel pale moon
   That night hadst never the grace
To lighten two dying Christian men
   To see one another's face.

They wrestled up, they wrestled down,
   They wrestled sore and still:
The fiend who blinds the eyes of men
   That night he had his will.

Like stags full spent, among the bent
   They dropped a while to rest;
When the young man drove his saying knife
   Deep in the old man's breast.

The old man drove his gunstock down
   Upon the young man's head;
And side by side, by the water brown,
   Those yeomen twain lay dead.

They dug three graves in Lyndhurst yard;
   They dug them side by side;
Two yeomen lie there, and a maiden fair,
   A widow and never a bride.

THE RED KING

THE King was drinking in Malwood Hall,
There came in a monk before them all;
He thrust by squire, he thrust by knight,
Stood over against the dais aright;
And, " The world of the Lord, thou cruel Red King,
The word of the Lord to thee I bring.
A grimly sweven I dreamt yestreen;
I saw thee lie under the hollins green,
And thorough thine heart an arrow keen;
And out of thy body a smoke did rise,
Which smirched the sunshine out of the skies;
So if thou God's anointed be
I rede thee unto thy soul thou see.
For mitre and pall thou hast y-sold,
False knight to Christ, for gain and gold;
And for this thy forest were digged down all,
Steading and hamlet and churches tall;
And Christés poor were ousten forth,
To beg their bread from south to north.
So tarry at home, and fast and pray,
Lest fiends hunt thee in the judgement-day."

The monk he vanished where he stood;
King William sterte up wroth and wod;
Quod he, " Fools' wits will jump together;
The Hampshire ale and the thunder weather
Have turned the brains for us both, I think;
And monks are curst when they fall to drink.
A lothly sweven I dreamt last night,
How there hoved anigh me a griesly knight,
Did smite me down to the pit of hell;
I shrieked and woke, so fast I fell.
There's Tyrrel as sour as I, perdie,
So he of you all shall hunt with me;
A grimly brace for a hart to see."

The Red King down from Malwood came;
His heart with wine was all a-flame,

His eyne were shotten, red as blood,
He rated and swore, wherever he rode.

    They roused a hart, that grimly brace,
A hart of ten, a hart of grease,
Fled over against the kingés place.
The sun it blinded the kingés ee,
A fathom behind his hocks shot he:
  "Shoot thou," quod he, "in the fiendés name,
To lose such a quarry were seven years' shame,"
And he hove up his hand to mark the game.
Tyrrel he shot full light, God wot;
For whether the saints they swerved the shot,
Or whether by treason, men knowen not,
But under the arm, in a secret part,
The iron fled through the kingés heart.
The turf it squelched where the Red King fell;
And the fiends they carried his soul to hell,
Quod "His master's name it hath sped him well."
Tyrrel he smited full grim that day,
Quod "Shooting of kings is no bairns play;"
And he smote in the spurs, and fled fast away.
As he pricked along by Fritham plain,
The green tufts flew behind like rain;
The waters were out, and over the sward:
He swam his horse like a stalwart lord;
Men clepen that water Tyrrel's ford.
By Rhinefield and by Osmondsleigh,
Through glade and furze brake fast drove he,
Until he heard the roaring sea;
Quod he, "Those gay waves they call me."
By Mary's grace a seely boat
On Christchurch bar did lie afloat;
He gave the shipmen mark and groat,
To ferry him over to Normandie,
And there he fell to sanctuarie;
God send his soul all bliss to see.

And fend our princes every one,
From foul mishap and trahison;
But kings that harrow Christen men,
Shall England never bide again.

THE OUTLAW

OH, I wadna be a yeoman, mither, to follow my father's
trade,
To bow my back in miry banks, at pleugh and hoe and
spade.
Stinting wife, and bairns, and kye, to fat some courtier
lord,—
Let them die o' rent wha like, mither, and I'll die by sword.

Nor I wadna be a clerk, mither, to bide aye ben,
Scrabbling ower the sheets o' parchment with a weary,
weary pen;
Looking through the lang stane windows at a narrow strip
o' sky,
Like a laverock in a withy cage, until I pine away and die.

Nor I wadna be a merchant, mither, in his lang furred
gown,
Trailing strings o' footsore horses through the noisy dusty
town;
Louting low to knights and ladies, fumbling o'er his wares,
Telling lies, and scraping siller, heaping cares on cares.

Nor I wadna be a soldier, mither, to dice wi' ruffian bands,
Pining weary months in castles, looking over wasted lands,
Smoking byres, and shrieking women, and the grewsome
sights o' war—
There's blood on my hand eneugh, mither; it's ill to make
it mair.

If I had married a wife, mither, I might ha' been douce
    and still,
And sat at hame by the ingle side to crack and laugh my
    fill;
Sat at hame wi' the woman I looed, and wi' bairnies at my
    knee:
But death is bauld, and age is cauld, and luve's no for me.

For when first I stirred in your side, mither, ye ken full
    well
How you lay all night up among the deer out on the open
    fell;
And so it was that I won the heart to wander far and near,
Caring neither for land nor lassie, but the bonny dun deer.

Yet I am not a lose and idle, mither, nor a thief that steals;
I do but hunt God's cattle, upon God's ain hills;
For no man buys and sells the deer, and the bonnie fells
    are free
To a belted knight with hawk on hand, and a gangrel loon
    like me.

So I'm aff and away to the muirs, mither, to hunt the dun
    deer,
Ranging far frae frowning faces, and the douce folk here;
Crawling up through burn and bracken, louping down the
    screes,
Looking out frae craig and headland, drinking up the
    simmer breeze.

Oh, the wafts o' heather honey, and the music o' the brae,
As I watch the great harts feeding, nearer, nearer a' the
    day.
Oh, to hark the eagle screaming, sweeping, ringing round
    the sky!—
That's a bonnier life than stumbling ower the muck to colt
    and kye.

And when I'm taen and hangit, mither, a brittling o' my
    deer,
Ye'll no leave your bairn to the corbie craws, to dangle in
    the air;
But ye'll send up my two douce brethren, and ye'll steal
    me frae the tree,
And bury me up on the brown brown muirs, where I aye
    looed to be.

Ye'll bury me 'twixt the brae and the burn, in a glen far
    away,
Where I may hear the heathcock craw, and the great harts
    bray;
And gin my ghaist can walk, mither, I'll go glowering at
    the sky,
The livelong night on the black hill sides where the dun
    deer lie.

SING HEIGH-HO!

    THERE sits a bird on every tree,
        Sing heigh-ho!
    There sits a bird on every tree,
    And courts his love, as I do thee;
        Sing heigh-ho, and heigh-ho!
    Young maids must marry.

    There grows a flower on every bough,
        Sing heigh-ho!
    There grows a flower on every bough,
    It's petals kiss—I'll show you how:
        Sing heigh-ho, and heigh-ho!
    Young maids must marry.

    From sea to stream the salmon roam;
        Sing heigh-ho
    From sea to stream the salmon roam;
    Each finds a mate, and leads her home;

Sing heigh-ho, and heigh-ho!
Young maids must marry.

The sun's a bridegroom, earth a bride;
Sing heigh-ho!
They court from morn till eventide:
The earth shall pass, but love abide.
Sing heigh-ho, and heigh-ho!
Young maids must marry.

OLD AND NEW

A PARABLE

SEE how the autumn leaves float by, decaying,
Down the wild whirls of yon rain-swollen stream;
So fleet the works of men, back to their earth again;
Ancient and holy things fade like a dream.

Nay! see the spring-blossoms steal forth a-maying,
Clothing with tender hues orchard and glen;
So, though old *forms* go by, ne'er their *spirit* die,
Look! England's bare boughs show green leaf again!

THE KNIGHT'S LEAP AT ALTENAHR

" So the foeman has fired the gate, men of mine,
And the water is spent and done;
Then bring me a cup of the red Ahr-wine;
I never shall drink but this one.

" And fetch me my harness, and saddle my horse,
And lead him me round to the door;
He must take such a leap to-night perforce
As horse never took before.

" I have lived by the saddle for years a score,
  And if I must die on tree,
The old saddle tree, which has borne me of yore,
  Is the properest timber for me.

" I have lived my life, I have fought my fight,
  I have drunk my share of wine;
From Trier to Cöln there was never a knight
  Lived a merrier life than mine.

" So now to show bishop, and burgher, and priest
  How the Altenahr hawk can die.
If they smoke the old falcon out of his nest,
  He must take to his wings and fly."

He harnest himself by the clear moonshine,
  And he mounted his horse at the door,
And he took such a pull at the red Ahr-wine
  As ever man took before.

He spurred the old horse, and he held him tight,
  And he leapt him out over the wall;
Out over the cliff, out into the night,
  Three hundred feet of fall.

They found him next morning below in the glen,
  And never a bone in him whole:
But heaven may yet have more mercy than men
  On such a bold rider's soul.

THE SONG OF THE LITTLE BALTUNG

A.D. 395

A HARPER came over the Danube so wide,
  And he came into Alaric's hall,
And he sang the song of the little Baltung
  To him and his heroes all.

"The old old Balt and the young young Balt
   Rode out of Caucaland,
With the royal elephant's trunk on helm
   And the royal lance in hand.

Thuringer heroes, counts and knights,
   Pricked proud in their meinie;
For they are away to the great Kaiser,
   In Byzant beside the sea.

And when they came to the Danube so wide
   They shouted from off the shore,
'Come over, come over, ye Roman knaves,
   And ferry your masters o'er.'

And when they came to Adrian's burgh,
   With its towers so smooth and high
'Come out, come out, ye Roman knaves,
   And see your lords ride by.'

But when they came to the long long walls
   That stretch from sea to sea,
That old old Balt let down his chin,
   And a thoughtful man grew he.

'Oh, oft have I scoffed at brave Fridigern,
   But never will I scoff more,
If these be the walls which kept him out
   From the Micklegard there on the shore.'

Then out there came the great Kaiser,
   With twice ten thousand men;
But never a Thuring was coward enough
   To wish himself home again.

'Bow down thou rebel, old Athanarich,
   And beg thy life this day;
The Kaiser is lord of all the world,
   And who dare say him nay?'

' I never came out of Caucaland
    To beg for less nor more;
But to see the pride of the great Kaiser
    In his Micklegard here by the shore.

' I never came out of Caucaland
    To bow to mortal wight,
But to shake the hand of the great Kaiser,
    And God defend my right.'

He shook his hand, that cunning Kaiser,
    And he kissed him courteouslie,
And he has ridden with Athanarich
    That wonder-town to see.

He showed him his walls of marble white—
    A mile o'erhead they shone;
Quoth the Balt, ' Who would leap into that garden,
    King Siegfried's boots must own.'

He showed him his engines of arsmetrick
    And his wells of quenchless flame,
And his flying rocks, that guarded his walls
    From all that against him came.

He showed him his temples and pillared halls,
    And his streets of houses high;
And his watch-towers tall, where his star-gazers
    Sit reading the signs of the sky.

He showed him his ships with their hundred oars,
    And their sides like a castle wall,
That fetch home the plunder of all the world,
    At the Kaiser's beck and call.

He showed him all nations of every tongue
    That are bred beneath the sun,
How they flowed together in Micklegard street
    As the brooks flow all into one.

He showed him the shops of the china ware,
  And of silk and sendal also,
And he showed him the baths and the waterpipes
  On arches aloft that go.

He showed him ostrich and unicorn,
  Ape, lion, and tiger keen;
And elephants wise roared 'Hail Kaiser!'
  As though they had Christians been.

He showed him the hoards of the dragons and trolls,
  Rare jewels and heaps of gold——
'Hast thou seen, in all thy hundred years,
  Such as these, thou king so old?'

Now that cunning Kaiser was a scholar wise,
  And could of gramarye,
And he cast a spell on that old old Balt,
  Till lowly and meek spake he.

'Oh oft have I heard of the Micklegard,
  What I held for chapmen's lies;
But now do I know of the Micklegard,
  By the sight of mine own eyes.

'Woden in Valhalla,
  But thou on earth art God;
And he that dare withstand thee, Kaiser,
  On his own head lies his blood.'

Then out and spake that little Baltung,
  Rode at the king's right knee,
Quoth 'Fridigern slew false Kaiser Valens,
  And he died like you or me.'

'And who art thou, thou pretty bold boy,
  Rides at the king's right knee?'
'Oh I am the Baltung, boy Alaric,
  And as good a man as thee.'

'As good as me, thou pretty bold boy,
   With down upon thy chin?'
'Oh a spae-wife laid a doom on me,
   The best of thy realm to win.'

'If thou be so fierce, thou little wolf cub,
   Or ever thy teeth be grown;
Then I must guard my two young sons
   Lest they should lose their own.'

'Oh, it's I will guard your two lither lads
   In their burgh beside the sea,
And it's I will prove true man to them
   If they will prove true to me.

But it's you must warn your two lither lads,
   And warn them bitterly,
That if I shall find them two false Kaisers,
   High hanged they both shall be.'

Now they are gone into the Kaiser's palace
   To eat the peacock fine,
And they are gone into the Kaiser's palace
   To drink the good Greek wine.

The Kaiser alone, and the old old Balt,
   They sat at the cedar board;
And round them served on the bended knee
   Full many a Roman lord.

'What ails thee, what ails thee, friend Athanarich,
   What makes thee look so pale?'
'I fear I am poisoned, thou cunning Kaiser,
   For I feel my heart-strings fail.

'Oh would I had kept that great great oath
   I swore by the horse's head,
I would never set foot on Roman ground
   Till the day that I lay dead.

273

'Oh would I were home in Caucaland,
    To hear my harpers play,
And to drink my last of the nut-brown ale,
    While I gave the gold rings away.

'Oh would I were home in Caucaland,
    To hear the Gothmen's horn,
And watch the wagons, and brown brood mares
    And the tents where I was born.

'But now I must die between four stone walls
    In Byzant beside the sea:
And as thou shalt deal with my little Baltung,
    So God shall deal with thee.'

The Kaiser he purged himself with oaths,
    And he buried him royally,
And he set on his barrow an idol of gold,
    Where all Romans must bow the knee.

And now the Goths are the Kaiser's men,
    And guard him with lance and sword,
And the little Baltung is his sworn son-at-arms,
    And eats at the Kaiser's board.

And the Kaiser's two sons are two false white lads
    That a clerk may beat with cane.
The clerk that should beat that little Baltung
    Would never sing mass again.

Oh the gates of Rome they are steel without
    And beaten gold within;
But they shall fly wide to the little Baltung
    With the down upon his chin.

Oh the fairest flower in the Kaiser's garden
    Is Rome and Italian land,
But it all shall fall to the little Baltung
    When he shall take lance in hand.

And when he is parting the plunder of Rome,
  He shall pay for this song of mine,
Neither maiden nor land, neither jewel nor gold,
  But one cup of Italian wine."

THE KNIGHT'S RETURN

HARK, hark, hark,
The lark sings high in the dark,
The were wolves mutter, the night hawks moan,
The raven croaks from the raven-stone:
What, what care I for his boding groan!
Riding the moorland to come to mine own.
Hark, hark, hark,
The lark sings high in the dark.

Hark, hark, hark,
The lark sings high in the dark.
Long have I wander'd by land and by sea,
Long have I ridden by moorland and lea;
Yonder she sits, with my babe on her knee,
Sits at the window and watches for me.
Hark, hark, hark,
The lark sings high in the dark.

CHRISTMAS-DAY

How will it dawn, the coming Christmas-day?
A northern Christmas, such as painters love,
And kinsfolk, shaking hands but once a year,
And dames who tell old legends by the fire?
Red sun, blue sky, white snow, and pearled ice,
Keen ringing air, which sets the blood on fire,
And makes the old man merry with the young,
Through the short sunshine, through the longer night?
  Or southern Christmas, dark and dank with mist,
And heavy with the scent of steaming leaves,

And rose-buds mouldering on the dripping porch;
One twilight, without rise or set of sun,
Till beetles drone along the hollow lane,
And round the leafless hawthorns, flitting bats,
Hawk the pale moths of winter? Welcome then,
At best, the flying gleam, the flying shower,
The rain-pools glittering on the long white roads,
And shadows sweeping on from down to down
Before the salt Atlantic gale: yet come
In whatsoever garb, or gay, or sad,
Come fair, come foul, 'twill still be Christmas-day.
　　How will it dawn, the coming Christmas-day?
To sailors lounging on the lonely deck
Beneath the rushing trade-wind? Or to him,
Who by some noisome harbour of the East,
Watches swart arms roll down the precious bales,
Spoils of the tropic forests; year by year
Amid the din of heathen voices, groaning
Himself half heathen? How to those—brave hearts!
Who toil with laden loins and sinking stride
Beside the bitter wells of treeless sands
Towards the peaks which flood the ancient Nile,
To free a tyrant's captives? How to those—
New patriarchs of the new-found underworld—
Who stand, like Jacob, on the virgin lawns,
And count their flocks' increase? To them that day
Shall dawn in glory, and solstitial blaze
Of full midsummer sun: to them that morn
Gay flowers beneath their feet, gay birds aloft
Shall tell of nought but summer: but to them
Ere yet, unwarned by carol or by chime,
They spring into the saddle, thrills may come
From that great heart of Christendom which beats
Round all the worlds; and gracious thoughts of youth;
Of steadfast folk, who worship God at home;
Of wise words, learnt beside their mothers' knee;
Of innocent faces, upturned once again
In awe and joy to listen to the tale
Of God made man, and in a manger laid:

May soften, purify, and raise the soul
From selfish cares, and growing lust of gain,
And phantoms of this dream, which some call life,
Toward the eternal facts; for here or there,
Summer or winter, 'twill be Christmas-day.

Blest day, which aye reminds us, year by year,
What 'tis to be a man: to curb and spurn
The tyrant in us: that ignobler self
Which boasts, not loathes, its likeness to the brute,
And owns no good save ease, no ill save pain,
No purpose, save its share in that wild war
In which, through countless ages, living things
Compete in internecine greed.—Ah God!
Are we as creeping things, which have no Lord?
That we are brutes, great God, we know too well:
Apes daintier-featured; silly birds, who flaunt
Their plumes, unheeding of the fowler's step;
Spiders, who catch with paper, not with webs;
Tigers, who slay with cannon and sharp steel,
Instead of teeth and claws;—all these we are.
Are we no more than these, save in degree?
No more than these; and born but to compete—
To envy and devour, like beast or herb;
Mere fools of nature; puppets of strong lusts,
Taking the sword, to perish with the sword
Upon the universal battle-field,
Even as the things upon the moor outside?
The heath eats up green grass and delicate flowers,
The pine eats up the heath, the grub the pine,
The finch the grub, the hawk the silly finch;
And man, the mightiest of all beasts of prey,
Eats what he lists:—the strong eat up the weak,
The many eat the few; great nations, small;
And he who cometh in the name of all
Shall, greediest, triumph by the greed of all;
And, armed by his own victims, eat up all;
While ever out of the eternal heavens
Looks patient down the great magnanimous God,

Who, Maker of all worlds, did sacrifice
All to himself. Nay, but himself to one;
Who taught mankind on that first Christmas-day,
What 'twas to be a man; to give, not take;
To serve, not rule; to nourish, not devour;
To help, not crush; if need, to die, not live.
  Oh, blessed day, which givest the eternal lie
To self, and sense, and all the brute within;
Oh, come to us, amid this war of life;
To hall and hovel, come; to all who toil
In senate, shop, or study; and to those
Who, sundered by the wastes of half a world,
Ill-warned, and sorely tempted, ever face
Nature's brute powers and men unmanned to brutes.
Come to them, blest and blessing, Christmas-day.
Tell them once more the tale of Bethlehem;
The kneeling shepherds, and the Babe Divine;
And keep them men indeed, fair Christmas-day.

EASTER WEEK

SEE the land, her Easter keeping,
    Rises as her Maker rose.
Seeds, so long in darkness sleeping,
    Burst at last from winter snows.
Earth with heaven above rejoices;
    Fields and gardens hail the spring;
Shaughs and woodlands ring with voices,
    While the wild birds build and sing.
You, to whom your Maker granted
    Powers to those sweet birds unknown,
Use the craft by God implanted;
    Use the reason not your own.
Here, while heaven and earth rejoices,
    Each his Easter tribute bring—
Work of fingers, chant of voices,
    Like the birds who build and sing.

TO MARY RUSSELL MITFORD

AUTHORESS OF " OUR VILLAGE "

THE single eye; the daughter of the light,
   Well pleased to recognise in lowliest shade
   Some glimmer of its parent ray, and made,
By daily draughts of brightness, inly bright;
The style severe, yet graceful, trained aright
   To classic depths of clearness and repaid
   By thanks and honour from the wise and staid;
By pleasant skill to blame and yet delight,
   And hold communion with the eloquent throng
   Of those who shaped and toned our speech and
      song;
All these are yours.　The same examples lure,
You in rich woodland, me on breezy moor,
   With kindred aims the same sweet paths along,
To knit in loving knowledge rich and poor.

VERSES FROM " THE SAINT'S TRAGEDY "

I

BABY Jesus, who dost lie
Far above that stormy sky,
In Thy mother's pure caress,
Stoop and save the motherless.

Happy birds! whom Jesus leaves
Underneath His sheltering eaves;
There they go to play and sleep,
May not I go in to weep?

All without is mean and small,
All within is vast and tall;
All without is harsh and shrill,
All within is hushed and still.

Jesus, let me enter in,
Wrap me safe from noise and sin;
Let me list the angels' songs,
See the picture of Thy wrongs;

Let me kiss Thy wounded feet,
Drink Thine incense, faint and sweet,
While the clear bells call Thee down
From Thine everlasting throne.

At Thy door-step low I bend,
Who have neither kin nor friend;
Let me here a shelter find,
Shield the shorn lamb from the wind.
Jesu, Lord, my heart will break,
Save me for Thy great love's sake!

II

Far among the lonely hills,
As I lay beside my sheep,
Rest came down upon my soul,
From the everlasting deep.

Changeless march the stars above,
Changeless morn succeeds to even;
And the everlasting hills,
Changeless watch the changeless heaven.

See the rivers how they run,
Changeless to a changeless sea;
All round is forethought sure,
Fixed will and stern decree.

Can the sailor move the main?
Will the potter heed the clay?
Mortal! where the spirit drives,
Thither must the wheels obey.

Neither ask, nor fret, nor strive:
Where thy path is, thou shalt go.
He who made the stream of time
Wafts thee down to weal or woe.

III

Oh! that we two were Maying
Down the stream of the soft spring breeze;
Like children with violets playing
In the shade of the whispering trees.

Oh! that we two sat dreaming
On the sward of some sheep-trimmed down,
Watching the white mist steaming
Over river and mead and town.

Oh! that we two lay sleeping
In our nest in the churchyard sod,
With our limbs at rest on the quiet earth's breast,
And our souls at home with God!

IV

CRUSADER CHORUS

(Men-at-Arms pass singing.)

The tomb of God before us,
Our fatherland behind,
Our ships shall leap o'er billows steep,
Before a charmed wind.

Above our van great angels
Shall fight along the sky;
While martyrs pure and crowned saints,
To God for rescue cry.

281

The red-cross knights and yeomen
Throughout the holy town,
In faith and might, on left and right,
Shall tread the paynim down.

Till on the Mount Moriah
The Pope of Rome shall stand;
The Kaiser and the King of France
Shall guard him on each hand.

There shall he rule all nations,
With crozier and with sword;
And pour on all the heathen,
The wrath of Christ the Lord.

(*Women—bystanders.*)

Christ is a rock in the bare salt land,
To shelter our knights from the sun and sand;
Christ the Lord is a summer sun,
To ripen the grain while they are gone.

Then you who fight in the bare salt land,
And you who work at home,
Fight and work for Christ the Lord,
Until His kingdom come.

(*Old Knights pass.*)

Our stormy sun is sinking;
Our sands are running low;
In one fair fight, before the night,
Our hard-worn hearts shall glow.

We cannot pine in cloister;
We cannot fast and pray;
The sword which built our load of guilt,
Must wipe that guilt away.

We know the doom before us;
The dangers of the road;
Have mercy, mercy, Jesu blest,
When we lie low in blood.

When we lie gashed and gory,
The holy walls within,
Sweet Jesu, think upon our end,
And wipe away our sin.

(*Boy Crusaders pass.*)

The Christ-child sits on high—
He looks through the merry blue sky—
He holds in His hand a bright lily-band,
For the boys who for Him die.

On holy Mary's arm,
Wrapt safe from terror and harm,
Lulled by the breeze in the paradise trees,
Their souls sleep soft and warm.

Knight David, young and true,
The giant Saldan slew,
And our arms so light, for the Christ-child's right,
Like noble deeds can do.

(*Young Knights pass.*)

The rich East blooms fragrant before us;
All Fairyland beckons us forth;
We must follow the crane in her flight o'er the main,
From the posts and the moors of the North.

Our sires in the youth of the nations
Swept westward through plunder and blood,
But a holier quest calls us back to the East,
We fight for the kingdom of God.

Then shrink not, and sigh not, fair ladies,
The red cross which flames on each arm and each
      shield,
Through philtre and spell, and the black charms of
      hell,
Shall shelter our true love in camp and in field.

      (Old Monk looking after them.)

Jerusalem, Jerusalem!
The burying place of God!
Why gay and bold, in steel and gold,
O'er the paths where Christ hath trod?
     [*The Scene closes.*

INDEX TO FIRST LINES OF POEMS

BIBLIOGRAPHY

Novels and Tales:

1850   *Alton Locke: Tailor & Poet.*
1851   *Yeast: A Problem.*
1853   *Hypatia, or New Foes with an Old Face.*
1855   *Westward Ho!*
1856   *The Heroes.*
1857   *Two Years Ago.*
1863   *The Water Babies.*
1866   *Hereward the Wake.*
1868–78 *The Hermits.*
1873   *Prose, Idylls, New and Old.*
1916   *The Tutor's Story* (From an unfinished MS. revised and completed by his daughter Mary under the pseudonym " Lucas Malet ").

Poems:

1848   *The Saint's Tragedy.*
1858   *Andromeda and Other Poems.*
1870–2 *Poems* (Collected edition).
        Also numerous sermons, lectures, essays and pamphlets, published singly, and later in his collected works.

Collected works:

The Works of Charles Kingsley (28 vols.) 1880–5 and 1888–9.
The Life and Works of Charles Kingsley (19 vols.) 1900–3.

The following contain information on his life and works:
Letters and Memories of His Life edited by his Wife (2 vols. 1876).
Prefatory Memoir to Alton Locke by Tom Hughes (1876).
Life of Charles Kingsley by J. Ellis (1890).
Charles Kingsley: Christian Socialist & Social Reformer by M. Kaufmann (1892).

Charles Kingsley's Place in Literature by F. Harrison (1895).
Charles Kingsley & the Christian Social Movement by C. M. Stubbs (1899).
Short Life of Kingsley for Boys & Girls by M. F. Brown (1904).
A Day with Charles Kingsley by Maurice Clare (1911).
The Political & Social Novel by Sir A. W. Ward (1916) (Vol. 13 of the *Cambridge History of English Literature*).
The Work and Influence of Parson Lot by W. H. Brown (1924).
Biography of Kingsley by M. F. Thorp (1937).
Charles Kingsley and His Ideas by Guy Kendall (1947).
Canon Charles Kingsley by Una Pope Hennessey (1948).

Also essays on Kingsley by the following:

Henry James	(1876).
Sir Leslie Stephen	(1879).
W. E. Henley	(1880).
A. Lang	(1891).
Sir J. A. R. Marriott	(1892).
A. C. Benson	(1911).